IN HIS KISS

"Erica," Jake whispered, closing the last few inches between them and kissing her.

It was astonishing how this man, whose face was all hard planes and sharp angles, could have a mouth that was as soft as silk and as smooth as satin. And he knew how to use it, Erica realized, as his lips played over hers, coaxing, inciting, demanding….

Midnight SATIN

LAURIE GRANT

LEISURE BOOKS NEW YORK CITY

To Tom—I'm so glad you've come into my life!
And to Helene Maroscher, in grateful appreciation for
being my "Mutti" and for correcting my German in this book.

A LEISURE BOOK®

November 2004

Published by

Dorchester Publishing Co., Inc.
200 Madison Avenue
New York, NY 10016

ISBN 0-8439-5457-4

The name "Leisure Books" and the stylized "L" with design are trademarks of Dorchester Publishing Co., Inc.

Printed in the United States of America.

Visit us on the web at www.dorchesterpub.com.

Midnight
SATIN

Chapter One

Taylor Hall, Brazos County, Texas

"Papa, you've got to see reason," Jake Taylor said for perhaps the dozenth time since he'd begun the after-supper discussion. To fortify himself against his father's stubbornness, he took another sip of the brandy his father had hoarded through most of the War Between the States just for his homecoming. "The North has broken the back of our cotton economy. What we used to do isn't going to work anymore, now that we no longer have free labor—not that I believe it was ever right to make our fortunes on the backs of other people," he added frankly, referring to the fact that Taylor Hall's cotton had once been grown and picked by their slaves. "I really think you ought to consider raising horses and maybe cattle too, rather than cotton."

"A fine homecoming celebration this is!" snapped Frank Taylor, grinding out the cigar he knew he shouldn't be smoking because of his heart. "I looked forward to your return, son, all through this cursed war, and kept your inheritance as secure as I could against the damned bluebellies . . . and now you've hardly brushed the travel dust off yourself before you're tryin' t'tell me how to run the plantation! Damnation, boy, cotton raising's the only life I know."

"Papa, I know it'd be a big change for you, but change has already come," Jake said. "The North won the war, and because of that, you have to pay the folks who'd hoe and pick your cotton now—*and* provide them with housing. I just don't think we can make a go of it under those conditions, not with the Reconstruction government charging so much in taxes."

"Nonsense," his father scoffed. "Sharecropping, that's the way. You don't pay out cash money in wages, you pay out a share of the crop. The share-croppers can live in the same cabins our people have always lived in. Or did you propose to send folks like Mose and Vespasia out on the road to earn their own bread when they've never done so and don't have a clue how to go about it?"

"Of course not," Jake said patiently. "Mose and Vespasia will continue taking care of the barn and the house as they always have." He couldn't imagine Taylor Hall without the presence of the old couple. "And if any other of our people drift back, they could be offered jobs taking care of livestock. But the fact is, there are precious few of those left, and you know it."

His father nodded in acknowledgment. While

only a few of their slaves had run off during the war, most of the rest had been tempted away after the war by the extravagant promises of the carpetbaggers from the North—promises largely unfulfilled.

"If you sharecrop the land, you lose profits by having to give the sharecroppers a portion," Jake went on. "And you need a lot of laborers. You need fewer people for livestock. There's money to be made selling remounts to the cavalry, as well as beef to the North."

"Bah! As if I'd let any horseflesh of mine be sold to a Yankee!" his father said with a disgusted snort. "I'm surprised at you, a captain in the Confederate army, talking that way."

Jake sighed. He was bone-weary, having ridden all the way from the Texas-Louisiana line on a bony nag that certainly wasn't the equal of a Taylor plantation mount. He was lucky to be riding at all, though, he knew too well. Many of his comrades were journeying home on foot, and in some cases, barefoot at that. But he'd won the old horse in a chance game of poker and he'd seized the opportunity to make his way home faster than he could walk.

"Papa, I'm a *former* captain in an army that no longer exists," Jake reminded his father. "I'm just being realistic. The biggest market for horses these days is the United States Cavalry. That's not to say it would be our only market."

"Hmmpf," Frank Taylor said. "What you need is to marry and settle down. Then you wouldn't be talking such nonsense. You ought t'go call on Lilybelle Harris," he added with a return of enthusiasm to his voice. "Why, I saw her in town last week and

3

she couldn't stop asking about your return."

Jake searched his memory, coming up with only a vague image of the lady. "Papa, I hardly knew Lily-belle Harris. She never had any use for me, either—seems I recollect she was after that Billy Wayne Moorehead. Didn't she end up marrying him?"

Frank Taylor nodded, his face assuming a mournful expression. "Yes, and he died at First Manassas right after their wedding. She's had plenty of time to mourn and be ready to start anew. Or you could go after her younger sister, if you aren't interested in a field that's already been plowed."

Jake stifled a frown at his father's crude expression. He was never going to change the old man's ways, but he wasn't particularly interested in following Frank Taylor's suggestion. Oh, he planned to marry someday, of course, but he'd do his own selecting.

"Papa, about my idea of raising horses and cattle instead of cotton—" he began carefully.

"Damnation, boy!" Frank Taylor shouted, pounding the table as his face got as red as the field of the Stars and Bars flag. "We're raising cotton, and that's final! You can just wait till I'm dead and gone before you go changin' what this plantation was founded on!" Then he suddenly stilled, his fist against his chest.

As if she'd been listening at the door between the kitchen and the dining room, Vespasia entered, moving with surprising speed and grace for such a big woman. "Mist' Taylor, you know better'n to shout and git excited like dat, with yo' heart. Here, take one o' these," she said, handing him the pill that usually eased his chest pain in short order, and

4

pouring a glass of water from the pitcher on the sideboard so he could wash it down. "And you know better than this, too," she said, snatching the second cigar lying by the stub of the old one before he could stop her. She glided out, leaving the old man sputtering in her wake.

"Damn bossy woman," Taylor muttered.

Jake relaxed when he saw that the old man's color had returned to normal and his fist was no longer pressed against his chest. But as much as he was tempted to argue his case one more time in an effort to convince his father, he knew better than to try it. Frank Taylor had always been stubborn and he wasn't going to be convinced until he saw the truth of it for himself.

"Cotton's mostly planted for this year anyway," his father said, as if reading his mind. "Or didn't you notice as you rode in?"

"I saw it." Jake forebore to add that he noticed only about a third of the fields had been planted. Vespasia had already taken him aside to fuss about how her Mose had nearly killed himself taking part in the planting, since there were so few hands to do the job—and those who had planted wouldn't be back till picking time. A man Mose's age shouldn't have to be doing such strenuous labor, she'd said, and Jake knew she was right.

"Don't look so sad, son," his father said, grinning now as he pulled another cigar out of its hiding place in his waistcoat. "I won't live forever. You can always do whatever you want with the place when I go to my reward."

If there's anything left of Taylor Hall, Jake wanted to

say, but instead he murmured, "I hope that's a long time from now."

His father brightened. "So what're your plans, boy, now we've got that decided? You gonna settle down and be a planter? You gonna go court that Lilybelle? You could do a lot worse, you know. About time you had a son and heir yourself. If it hadn't been for the war, you'd probably have married and had a passel of kids by now."

Jake sighed. His father seemed obsessed with inheritance and marriage tonight.

"What about Maria and Bowie?" he said, referring to his sister and the man she had married, Bowie Beckett, who had been one of the teamsters transporting their cotton to Mexico during the war to avoid the blockade in the Gulf. "Didn't you tell me they've given you a grandson already and have another baby on the way?"

Frank Taylor's brow lost its furrow and he smiled. "Sure, and a handsome little boy Jefferson Lamar Beckett is, too—takes after his mama." It was no secret that Frank hadn't thought Bowie Beckett good enough for his daughter. "But they're ranching down in San Marcos and I reckon young Jeff will take over there some day. You're my son, and I want to make sure Taylor Hall's in good hands before I pass on."

"What do you hear from Mama? Or Kate?" Jake asked, as much to prevent having to answer the question just yet as because he wanted to know. His mother had returned to England with his younger sister at the beginning of the war, ostensibly to take their youngest child away from the possibility of danger, but everyone knew Frank and Constance Taylor hadn't gotten along for years, and Constance would not likely return from across the sea.

The old man suddenly looked his sixty-five years and more. "Your mama never was much for correspondence," he said with a heavy sigh. "Kate, she writes occasionally . . . but it's like hearing from a stranger, like she hardly remembers being a little girl here on the plantation."

"She must be quite the grown-up young lady now," Jake murmured.

"Yes, the proper English miss. Constance will convince her she has to marry some earl or duke and we'll be lucky to ever see her again." Frank Taylor looked away then, rubbing his eyes and muttering something about the cigar smoke, and Jake guessed he was trying to hide a tear.

"Perhaps Mama will let her visit now that the war is over," Jake said in an encouraging voice. He planned to write his mother and urge her to do so, for pride would prevent his father from sending such a letter.

"Yes, well, I won't hold my breath," his father said. "Hey, there's a church social in town Saturday night. Could be you'd see Lilybelle Harris there if you were to go."

Lord, but his father could be persistent.

Jake took a deep breath. "Maybe next time. I . . . uh, think before I get settled in here I'll ride down to San Marcos and see Maria and Bowie, since my sister's too *enceinte* to come up and visit me. Get a look at their horse ranching operation."

"Well, that's fine—I'm sure Maria'd welcome a

visit, but don't get any ideas," his father growled. "I'm not going to change my mind about how Taylor Hall is run. We've always grown cotton, and we'll keep on growing cotton."

"Yessir," Jake said, only half listening. While he was so close, perhaps he'd go on to San Antonio and pay a visit to his friend and comrade-in-arms during the war, Dr. John Ransom. He'd always respected John's opinion. Perhaps the physician would have an idea of how to convince Frank Taylor to change his mind, or if the old man remained adamant, how to best get along with the Reconstruction officials so that they wouldn't be cheated out of what little profit they could make on the crop.

Anything sounded better than going into town to attend a social event where at least one man-hungry war widow was on the prowl. Jake Taylor wasn't averse to a little feminine companionship, but he had just lived through a hellish war and he was in no hurry to settle down to matrimony, not after the example of marital misery his parents had set.

Chapter Two

New Braunfels, Texas

Erica Mueller straightened from the row of black-eyed peas she had been hoeing and reached under her sunbonnet to push a strand of blond hair away from her sweaty forehead. The rows she'd weeded this morning would have to do for now. The sun was getting too high in the sky to continue without risking sunstroke.

This wasn't her first Texas summer. The family had emigrated from Germany two years before, when she was sixteen. Nothing in the cool forests of Bavaria had prepared her for the fierceness of the sun in the state of Texas, and it still sometimes caught her by surprise when she was most determined to get something done, such as weeding the vegetable garden before the noon meal.

"Erica! Come into the house immediately. I must speak to you!" called her mother from under the overhanging roof of the back porch. She spoke in German; Hilda Mueller refused to admit she knew a word of English and certainly wouldn't speak it at home.

"Yes, Mutti," Erica called back, wondering what she had done now to merit her mother's sharp tone. She had swept the floor and dusted the house and mended the ripped seam in her younger brother Guenther's trousers—the garden had been a task her mother hadn't even assigned her. But it seemed it didn't take much these days to make her mother cross at her.

"Erica, you will be brown as one of those savage Indians if you work outside in the heat of the day," her mother criticized as Erica came closer. "How will we find you a husband then? It will already be difficult enough, and now you ruin your complexion," Hilda Mueller fretted.

"I was wearing my sunbonnet," Erica pointed out, keeping her tone mild as she knew she must when Mutti was in one of her disapproving moods— which seemed to be all the time lately, now that Erica had become eighteen. *It will already be difficult enough.* Her mother referred to Erica's past shame, the Mueller family's most closely guarded secret.

"Nevertheless," her mother said, "you should not be out here hoeing like a peasant in the hot sun. You must take care of your skin, daughter. Hans and Guenther should be doing the weeding." Her tone said, *You have precious few other assets, now that you have been disgraced.*

Erica smothered the urge to protest that she had not invited Siegfried's attentions, and had not realized until it was too late that the handsome young Bavarian nobleman had had no intention of honorable marriage, only seduction.

"Hans told me he and Guenther were going fishing this morning," Erica reminded the older woman. "I have not seen them return yet."

Hilda Mueller clucked again. "Yes, I know," she said, her lips thinning. "I will see that Hans does not shirk his duty in the future, dawdling with a fishing pole."

"He might bring us a string of fish to make a good dinner," Erica said. She wouldn't have minded some fried perch cooked with Mutti's special herbs.

"I'm sure he will, if fish are flopping on the Widow Wagner's back porch," her mother retorted tartly. "He sends Guenther off to play with her son while he courts that . . . that *seductress*," her mother hissed.

Erica hid a smile. Greta Wagner, with her serene prettiness and quiet manner, hardly seemed to merit such a description. "Hans wants to marry," she said. "Perhaps Vati and you should be discussing his marriage before mine."

Hilda Mueller sputtered, but before she could reply to Erica's suggestion, Erica distracted her by adding, "Did you want something, Mutti? It sounded as if you did when you called me out of the garden."

"Oh! Yes I did, daughter," Hilda said. "Your papa needs to go to San Antonio to see Vetter Dietrich tomorrow, and you must go with him."

"Why?" Erica asked, immediately on her guard. Her father's cousin had a son named Rudolph who had made it very clear in the past that he found Erica attractive. Erica smelled matchmaking, and while Rudolph was a nice enough youth, she didn't want to be his wife. He wore too much hair pomade and he always smelled of pickles.

"Your father . . . ah . . . wants to talk to Dietrich about . . . the loan of some money," her mother said, looking at her hands.

It was news to Erica that they needed money. Her father did very well in his shop in town, where he made and repaired clocks, while their small farm raised enough food to feed them with some left over to sell.

"But why must *I* go?" she persisted. "Why not one of the boys?"

Her mother was suddenly very absorbed with a smudge of dust on her apron. "Why . . . to help him with his English along the way, of course, if he should need to communicate with one of these *Texans*." Hilda said the word as if "Texan" were synonymous with vermin.

Erica blinked. Her father's English wasn't as fluent as hers, but he could certainly hold his own in a conversation with an American. Now she was sure her theory had been right. She wasn't to accompany him merely because her brothers weren't available. The trip was for the purpose of showing her to a prospective bridegroom.

She took a few steps away from her mother. "Mutti, I will not marry Rudolph Schoenbrunn, so if that was why you wanted me to go, I won't," she announced.

Her mother's dark eyes sparked with anger. "Undutiful child! You could do a lot worse than young Rudolph, my girl!"

"Perhaps. But I wish to pick my own husband because I love him, Mother, not to be collateral for a loan of money!"

"The money would have nothing to do with any marriage agreement," Hilda insisted. "But picking a husband for love, bah! Another of the harmful ideas you have picked up from the devil Texans," Hilda snapped, despite the fact that the family had little contact with any non-Germans. "If we were back in the Old Country you would not be defying your parents when they try to do what is good for you!"

A chill ran down Erica's spine. In this German enclave within Texas, most of the Old Country customs were observed, sometimes including arranged marriages. If her parents tried to pressure her into wedlock, there was very little Erica could do short of running away from home.

But Vati would never force me to wed a man unwillingly. She took a deep breath, knowing he would be her ally if it came to that.

Her mother evidently knew it, too, for her tone softened and became coaxing. "Just go with your father, Erica, *liebchen*, for a visit to Vetter Dietrich's nice house, so he will not be alone. I would go, naturally, but who would take care of Hans and Guenther?"

I would, Erica wanted to argue.

"Just think, all that Vetter Dietrich has will be Rudolph's someday. You have not seen the young man for at least a year—maybe you will like him better this time, *ja*? Why, the house he lives in is a veritable mansion compared to this one!" she added, gesturing to the sturdy fieldstone house behind her. "I don't know why your father couldn't have gone into banking with his cousin—we'd be living in a grand house too, not in this tiny one on a few rocky acres," she fretted.

It was an old refrain for Hilda Mueller, one she sang whenever she was displeased with her life.

"Vati loves working with clocks, not money," Erica said. "And we have a very comfortable house. I would like to have one just like it when I am a wife someday." *And I do not want to be a wife to dull Rudolph Schoenbrunn who smells of pickles and pomade.*

Her mother threw up her hands. "You are an ungrateful child! I am only trying to better your life! *Ach*, my head!" she said, rubbing her forehead. "I must go inside—I am getting one of my headaches. You will have to put dinner on for your father."

Whenever her mother's migraines arrived, they resulted in hours of misery. Hilda had to lie in a darkened room with a cool cloth to her head while the rest of the family tiptoed past her door.

Erica took a deep breath. "I'll see that Vati gets dinner," she said. "And I'll go to San Antonio with him tomorrow. But only to keep him company. That must be understood before we leave, *ja?*"

Her mother brightened. "Very well, though I'm certain once you arrive and you see the kind of life you could have, *liebchen*, you will change your mind. I will tell your father you have agreed to go," she added, and whirled, her headache apparently forgotten.

* * *

Jake Taylor let his mount ease back to a walk as they reached a bend on the hilly, dusty road. He'd gotten a late start leaving his sister and brother-in-law's ranch outside of San Marcos because of the huge breakfast Maria had insisted on fixing for him. He had hoped to make it halfway to San Antonio, where he'd visit with his friend Dr. John Ransom, but he wasn't going to meet that goal before dark.

Now he was going to have to camp out for the night. It was dusk and it was too far to the next settlement. He probably should have stopped in New Braunfels, but the little town was full of German immigrants who had backed the Yankees in the war. Jake was not one to hold a grudge; he meant to get on with his life and not worry about who had favored whom in the past struggle. But the Texas militia had punished the German settlers for their disloyalty, even murdering some thirty-four of their men who'd fled rather than wear rebel gray. So Jake didn't figure he would be too welcome among the Germans with his Southern drawl.

He'd find a likely spot soon and make camp there. Jake didn't mind the prospect of a night spent under the stars, since the sultry June breeze held no hint of rain. He had become used to sleeping in the open during his days serving with Hood.

He had been enjoying the smooth paces of the bay gelding his father had urged him to try out as his own mount. The bay, foaled at the beginning of the war, was one of the few saddle horses Frank Taylor had managed to keep despite the demands of the Confederate cavalry agents requisitioning remounts.

Another day's ride, maybe a day and a half,

would bring him to San Antonio if all went well. There was no hurry; John didn't even know he was coming. Jake began to whistle "The Girl I Left Behind Me."

As the bay rounded the bend in the road, he saw that things were not going to go well. The tune died in his throat.

A party of young braves—Comanches, he judged, half a dozen of them—were sitting on their horses, clearly waiting for him. One of their number was holding the reins of a pair of saddled horses. Comanches rarely used saddles, so obviously these mounts had been stolen. He hoped the unfortunate owners had not been on their horses when the thefts occurred—if they were, they were probably lying dead somewhere, perhaps scalped.

But Jake couldn't spare the time right now to worry about the fate of a pair of unknown white men. He had to make sure he didn't become the third victim.

One of the Comanches grinned and pointed. Another raised a rifle—surely stolen as well.

What he wouldn't have given at that moment to be holding his own Winchester carbine. All he had with him was a six-shot Colt, and there were six Indians. He dared not assume each one of his bullets would hit its target before the Comanche with the rifle could hit him.

No, he'd do better to try and outrun them. Thank God he was riding a Taylor Hall horse. He'd have stood no chance at all on the bony nag that had brought him home—but then, these Indians probably would have scorned such a horse except as a meal. If only he weren't so far past New Braun-fels . . .

As he watched, another raised a bow and reached behind him to a leather quiver for an arrow.

"Time to show what you're made of, boy!" He wrenched the bay's head around to the right and touched his spur to the gelding's left flank, turning him, then drummed his heels into the bay's sides.

"*Hyaaaaah!*" Jake shrieked into the beast's ears, and the startled bay bunched its muscles and took off like a bullet, eating up the ground with powerful strides.

The pounding of several sets of hooves and the ex-cited whoops of the Comanches told him they were giving chase; a glance over his shoulder confirmed they were too close for comfort. Their mounts were smaller, almost ponies, really, but despite their smaller size the horses moved quickly, their lack of saddles giving them an advantage.

He was going to have to shoot at them. He doubted he'd hit anything firing over his shoulder, but maybe he could persuade them they didn't re-ally want his horse.

Reaching down to the holster with his right hand while he kept the other hand on the loose reins, Jake yanked out his Colt, cocked it and fired. His first shot went wide, splintering a mesquite branch, but his second hit the lead Comanche's shoulder and knocked him off his horse.

That's more like it, Jake thought grimly, and looked over his shoulder again, aiming for a stocky Indian on a blaze-faced paint. Ignoring the shot that zinged uncomfortably close to his left ear, Jake dropped the stocky man too, and was just aiming for the next in line when he felt the bay's shoulder suddenly fall beneath him as the horse's foreleg dropped into a hole.

He heard the snap of bone as the horse cartwheeled, throwing Jake over his head. The last sound Jake heard was the screaming of the horse as it collapsed on top of him, and then everything went black.

Chapter Three

Erica spotted the buzzards first, their big black wings spread as they circled over some dead creature in the valley below. A pair of cedar brakes and a clump of scrubby mesquite trees hid what it was the buzzards orbited over from Erica and Mr. Mueller's sight.

She pointed. "Look, Vati."

"Something is dead, or dying," her father murmured. "A jackrabbit, maybe, or a coyote. Ah, daughter," he said with a sigh, covering her hands with one of his, "that troubles you. You have such a tender heart. Death is a part of life for animals—for all of us."

She smiled, grateful for his understanding. Her brothers teased her about her sensitivity. They erupted into gales of laughter when she would bribe one of them to wring the neck of a hen when Mama sent her to the barnyard to select a hen for their Sunday chicken dinner.

"A fine morning," her father was saying bracingly, obviously trying to distract her. "Whenever you are hungry, say the word and we will eat the picnic lunch your mother packed. We will stop at Tante Helene's for the night since it is halfway. Then tomorrow we will arrive in San Antonio in time for dinner with my cousin Dietrich, *ja?*"

"*Ja*, Vati," she answered him, but her mind had not been on what her father was saying. They had descended the hill and were drawing nearer to where the buzzards were circling.

"But Vati, what if it . . . what if whatever it is isn't dead? What if it's merely wounded, and we can help it?"

Her father's brow furrowed. "Erica, we can hardly show up at my cousin's mansion carrying a wounded rabbit or a sick coyote. . . ."

Through the fringy leaves of a mesquite she caught a glimpse of something lying on the ground, something much bigger than a rabbit or even a deer.

"Vati, I think . . . I think it's a *horse.* . . ." She caught a whiff of a pungent, coppery odor now, and instinctively she covered her nose. *Blood.* It was the same smell that drove her inside when it was time for her father to butcher a hog in the fall.

Her father peered in the direction she had pointed. "It's wearing a saddle," he said. "We had better stop and check. Someone may be lying injured next to the poor beast. Whoa, Bruno," he called to their horse, pulling back on the reins. Bruno tossed his head and snorted, catching the scent of death, but he halted obediently.

The horse's throat had been slit. A blackened pool

of congealed blood, crusted with flies, lay beneath his neck and shoulders and streamed out across the dusty ground. A huge chunk of his shoulder had been hacked away, leaving a gaping, bloody crater. One foreleg lay bent at an unnatural angle.

Then Erica spotted the man lying partially under the horse. Only the backs of his arms, his shoulders and his head, covered with dark, blood-matted hair, showed under the dead beast. She screamed.

"Erica, stay on the wagon! Cover your eyes!" her father shouted, setting the brake and handing her the reins before he scrambled off to check on the man.

Erica ignored the command. Looping one of the reins around her wrist because she knew even their steady Bruno would find the sight and smell disturbing, she jumped down too. She was beside her father in an instant, kneeling next to him while he reached with a trembling hand to the man's neck. She held her breath until her father murmured, "He lives."

"Thank God."

And then the man uttered a groan.

"Sir! Wake up! We are here to help you!" her father said, leaning down and shouting directly into the man's ear.

The man only groaned again and muttered something unintelligible.

"We have to find a way to get him out from under there," Gustav Mueller muttered.

They couldn't lift the horse, and her father was not able to pull the unconscious man free with the horse's head and neck lying across most of his back and legs.

Erica's father stood back, frustrated at his failure, sweating and breathing heavily from his exertion.

"Perhaps if I held the horse's head up while you pulled . . ."

Her father looked stricken at the prospect of Erica touching the bloodied carcass, but apparently realizing there was no other way, he finally nodded his consent.

Erica first tied Bruno's reins to a nearby live oak trunk, then walked back, trying not to look at the dead beast's gaping throat wound as she approached. She took a deep breath, facing away from the horse, then bent over. She threaded her fingers through the horse's black mane and forelock, clenched her eyes shut and, breathing shallowly through her open mouth, lifted.

Her father, kneeling, reached under the man's arms and pulled. The man screamed as he was pulled free and cried out something that sounded suspiciously like a curse.

As soon as the man was free, Erica let go of the horse's head, trying to ignore the obscene thump as it fell back to the ground. She dashed over to where her father was gently turning the man onto his back.

"Erica, help me pull him into the shade!" her father called over the other man's groans. "We will have to examine him to see if we can tell where his injuries might lie."

The angel bending over him, laying a wonderfully cool, wet cloth over his forehead, was a beautiful blond, blue-eyed female. He wondered if all the angels were colored so, or if Heaven had angels with black, brown, and red hair too, the same as people had on earth.

Jake turned his head to look, only to have the angel frown and lay a hand aside his cheek, saying in an urgent, heavily accented voice, "No, you mustn't move, sir! You may be hurt!"

Shock waves of pain erupted down his spine and across his ribs from his motion. He heard someone groan and realized it was himself. *No 'may be' about it,* he retorted in his mind. *When half a ton of horse falls on you, being hurt is a certainty.*

But he'd thought there wasn't any pain in Heaven. Did that mean he was in Hell? "Not 'sposed to hurt . . . in Heaven . . ." He knew it sounded like an accusation of bad service, but there were some things a person just counted on, and a pain-free afterlife had been one of them.

The blond angel looked puzzled. "I'm sure that you must be in pain, sir. But you are in Texas, not Heaven."

So the fall hadn't killed him, after all. That explained the pain. Then Jake remembered what had led to the bay collapsing, trapping him underneath— their flight from the Comanche raiders, cut short by the damned hole some critter had made. He jerked his head around again, searching wildly for the savages that had brought him to this sorry pass.

"*Was ist los?* Vat's de matter?" the angel demanded, putting a restraining hand on his shoulder when he tried to raise up.

"C-Comanches! Take cover!" Jake cried. If this wasn't Heaven, then the lovely blond girl ministering to him was no angel and the Indians would certainly prize her golden hair.

The girl appeared anxious for a moment, looking around herself, but then she turned back to him, her features smoothing back into a reassuring smile. *"Nein,* there are no Indians around. You are safe, though unfortunately your horse is dead. Where do you hurt?"

"Everywhere." Jake remembered the bay collapsing, then managing to clamber upright on three legs next to Jake as Jake lay on his stomach, stunned. The horse had whinnied in pain as the Comanche raiders had thundered up to them. Jake hoped the savages would shoot both of them before they took his scalp.

Jake had closed his eyes and steeled himself not to move as they dismounted and walked over to him and the horse. He held his breath and prayed they would think he was already dead.

Only by a supreme act of will had he managed not to cry out when one of them poked him in the ribs with a moccasined foot. He heard the Indian step away from him, back to his injured horse. The savage grunted a command to his fellows and then Jake heard the bay whinnying in fright and renewed pain—a cry that was eerily cut off in the middle as a spray of blood drenched the back of Jake's head— blood that had come from the animal's throat when the Comanches had ended the beast's misery. A few heartbeats later, the beast collapsed across him. Jake passed out as the animal thrashed in his death throes.

"You are safe," the golden-haired woman repeated again. "We will help you. What hurts the most?"

He saw an older man leaning into his field of vision and wondered who he was to this young woman. He looked too old to be her husband, but you never knew. "My ribs. I think a couple of them are broken. And my right shoulder."

"You say Indians attack you?" the older man asked. His speech was also thickly accented.

Germans, Jake decided. He nodded, trying to ignore the renewed jolt of pain into his head from the movement. "Comanches. Half a dozen of them. They were after my horse. . . ." He glanced at the horse's carcass as he spoke. The poor beast, dying with his life's blood draining out over the dirt. The damned savages wouldn't even spare his horse a bullet—but maybe they'd been out of ammunition after chasing him. He supposed death would have come nearly as quickly that way, anyway. He hadn't even given the gelding a name yet, and now he was dead—and the Indians had obviously taken horsemeat for their dinner. He hoped they choked on it.

The German looked nervously around him. "I am Gustav Mueller," he informed Jake. "And this is Erica, my daughter."

She was his daughter. He couldn't imagine why that should dull the pain a bit. "Jake Taylor, sir, ma'am. I . . . thank you both for stopping to help me."

The young woman smiled shyly at him. Maybe he was in Heaven after all.

"Erica, we must take Herr Taylor back to our home," Mueller said, then turned back to Jake. "Can you stand if we help you, do you think? We will have to assist you into the wagon."

"I . . . I think so."

He made it into the wagon bed simply because he didn't want to faint in front of the pretty young woman. He felt the blackness closing in on him as soon as he lay down, though, and he let it flood his brain.

Jake came to again just as the wagon pulled to a stop. He heard a woman—older, he guessed by the timbre of her voice—calling out to the wagon in a guttural tongue which he guessed was German. She sounded surprised.

The older man replied in the same guttural language, and then the girl spoke too. The woman's reply sounded decidedly displeased now, Jake thought. She probably didn't cotton to the idea of having a stranger to nurse. Then she shouted out two names, and he heard the sound of running footsteps. The next thing he knew, Erica Mueller was gently shaking him "awake" and a tow-headed youth and a younger boy were helping him to his feet. He flinched as the boy unwittingly moved his right arm and agony shot through his shoulder. The boy quickly moved to support him against his side, but his broken ribs protested that, too. The boy looked uncertain as to what to do.

"It's okay—you didn't know this is the side that hurts the most," Jake murmured, hoping the child understood English.

"*Mein frau*—that is to say, my wife Hilda," Gustav

Mueller introduced the pinch-faced, frowning woman standing by the wagon and staring at him.

The elder of the two boys jumped down and extended a hand to Jake. Jake took it with his left hand, biting his lip so he wouldn't cry out as he descended. The pain made him downright queasy.

"I'm right pleased to make your acquaintance, Miz Mueller, ma'am," Jake said in his politest voice, but the gray-haired dragon didn't thaw in the least. If anything, she looked frostier as his voice confirmed that he was not German. "I appreciate your husband and daughter stopping to help me. I'm not sure I could have walked to get help, all stove up as I am."

The woman looked flustered by his words and aimed some more rapid-fire German at her husband. Jake saw that Erica looked distressed at what the woman said.

Mueller spoke back in German, and his tone was firm. From the way the woman's face hardened, Jake guessed she hadn't liked her husband's response.

"Forgive me for speaking in German, but my wife does not speak much English," Mueller said. "I have told her of the attack which befell you and that you have injuries, that you will require a bed and some care for a few days."

"Oh, that's not necessary," Jake said, guessing the woman had expressed more than a little displeasure at the idea of Jake crossing her threshold. "If you could just help me reach the local hotel, maybe help me get ahold of some whiskey as a painkiller . . ."

"Of course you must not consider any such course,"

Mueller told him. "You are much too injured to rest among strangers. *Gott in Himmel*, you lay unconscious the entire journey back to town. We will"—it came out *ve vill*—"take care of you until you are well enough to ride on. It is our duty as Christians."

"Thank you," Jake said, bowing to the inevitable. He truly didn't feel well enough to go a step farther.

"These are my sons, Hans and Guenther," Mueller said, indicating with a nod the fair-haired youth and boy holding Jake up. "They will show you to the spare room."

"Much . . . obliged," Jake muttered, fighting a wave of pain and weakness that threatened to bring the black fog down over his head again.

Chapter Four

"Very well, the devil Texan now lies insensible in Hans's bed. Today is a total loss, of course," sniffed Hilda Mueller, "but I suppose you can make an early start tomorrow, Gustav. Erica, come help me with preparations for supper."

"Oh, I don't think we will be attempting to go see Cousin Dietrich until Herr Taylor is back on his feet again," Gustav Mueller said.

Erica's mother's jaw dropped and her sallow complexion paled. "This unfortunate . . . ah, rescue must not cause you to postpone your journey!"

One of Gustav's eyebrows rose. "Oh? And what is the need for haste? Neither Helene nor Dietrich knew we were coming, so a few days one way or the other will not matter, yes?"

Suddenly he looked closely at Erica, his eyes troubled. "Wife, you are not saying there is some . . . ahem! . . . urgent need for our daughter to marry soon?"

Even Erica knew what his question meant. "No, Vati, of course there is no such need," she said quickly, hurt that he could even think such a thing. "I have not done anything to make you ashamed of me since we came to America. Mutti merely cannot wait to see me married off and gone from the house." She could not help the bitter tinge that crept into her tone. Her mother's constant harping on getting her married stung.

"Erica, I think no such thing," her mother protested. "It's merely that I don't wish you to lose such an opportunity." She turned back to her husband. "What will our neighbors think when they discover we are harboring a devil Texan in the home where we have a vulnerable daughter of marriageable age? The gossip will be horrible!"

"You don't think they would gossip if I left for San Antonio with Erica, leaving my wife alone here with him?" her father pointed out. "You're not exactly an old crone, my dear!"

His implied compliment sent a flush of color into Hilda's cheeks, but she sputtered, "Nonsense. The boys will be here."

"And would nosy old Mrs. Von Hesselberg consider them adequate chaperones? I think not, especially if she comes calling when they are out fishing. No, my mind is made up, wife, we will wait until Herr Taylor is back on his feet and well enough to leave before we do," her father repeated, cutting off his wife in mid-protest.

"Very well, husband." Hilda's jaw tightened and she turned on her heel, calling, "Erica, come peel the potatoes," over her shoulder.

"Yes, Mutti."

Erica's father caught at her wrist before she could follow her mother into the kitchen. "Erica, I'm sorry, *liebchen*, I didn't mean . . ." His voice trailed off, for of course he *had* meant to ask if his daughter had somehow strayed off the narrow path of virtue and gotten herself into the family way. "That is to say—I didn't intend to hurt your feelings. Your mother and I . . . we just want you to be happy and safe," he finished with a shrug.

Erica felt a pang of regret as she looked into her father's worried eyes. He—and, she supposed if she were to be fair, her mother also—only wanted what was best for her.

"I know, Vati. Don't worry. As soon as Herr Taylor is well enough to leave, we'll go to San Antonio." But I still won't marry Cousin Rudolph, she vowed inwardly.

At first Jake thought the sound was the buzzing of flies, but gradually the sound separated itself into two distinct voices: a younger, boyish treble, and an older one, both speaking in a language he couldn't understand. He thought for a moment, and it all came back to him—the attack, and the horse falling on him, the subsequent pain and fear, followed by oblivion—until the German man and his daughter had found him and brought him to their home. Then oblivion again.

He could feel a sling anchoring his arm over his chest, and tight cloth wrapped beneath and above that, binding the arm close to his side. Someone had strapped his broken ribs and fixed his dislocated shoulder, Jake realized. Lord, he hoped whoever had relocated the shoulder had known what they were doing—he'd seen a hapless corporal's shoulder badly fixed by a drunken army sawbones, and the arm had been useless afterward. Jake figured he was going to need his right arm.

He kept his eyes shut, listening, but if the bright light seeping under his eyelids from the window facing him meant what it usually did, he had slept through the night and into the morning.

He raised one eyelid—the one closest to the door—the smallest amount, but even before he could focus in the direction of the voices, his action caused a boyish squeak and the sound of running away.

He raised the eyelid some more, and saw that while the younger boy had fled, the older one—was his name Hans?—remained and was staring at him with some concern.

When he realized Jake was looking at him, Hans bowed and said in his accented but correct English, "I am sorry ve disturbed you, Herr Taylor. My brother was vorried because you slept so long—I had to show him you had not died in your sleep."

Jake smiled to show the boy he wasn't angry. "That's okay," he said. "I had to wake up sometime, and by the looks of the sun out there, I slept pretty late as it is." He nodded toward the sunlight streaming in through the lace-edged curtains—a big mistake, he realized, as even that slight motion sent pain screaming through his body. He tightened his jaw in order to squelch the groan that tried to escape.

The boy was sharp-eyed, though, and had evidently seen Jake's expression change, for he paled and his eyes widened. "Herr Taylor, are you in pain? I vill go and get my mother!"

Yes, he hurt like hell, but that glaring harpy was the last person he needed to see. She begrudged him the air that he breathed and the bed space he took up. She'd only be glad he hurt.

"No, wait!" he called, but evidently the boy was too far away to hear him, because he didn't come back. Jake shut his eyes again. Perhaps if he feigned unconsciousness, the harpy would leave well enough alone.

"Herr Taylor, Hans says you are hurting," said a voice. "Herr Taylor?"

It didn't sound like the harpy. The voice was too light, too pleasant. Could it be . . . ? He looked through the screen of his eyelashes. Yes! It was the blond angel! He'd open his eyes for her, all right!

"Good mornin', Miss Mueller," he said, smiling at her with all the charm he could muster. "Yes, I'm a mite achy, but I reckon that's only to be expected. It'll pass—don't you worry none."

He saw her brow furrow as she attempted to follow the drawl he'd exaggerated until it resembled molasses in January. Damnation, but she was cuter than a bug's ear even when she was confused.

" 'A mite achy'? Does this mean much pain?" she asked, her blue eyes clouded with concern, taking a step closer. "We have laudanum, if you have need of it."

"No, honey, it means I'm just hurtin' a little," Jake said, enjoying the sight of her as she bent over him, her golden braids falling forward to let him glimpse the breasts that filled out the bodice of her dark blue everyday dress just the right amount. He couldn't help but imagine cupping those breasts—naked, of course, in his imagination—in his hands, and all at once he was suffering in a whole different area of his anatomy. He had to keep her looking at his face, or she'd notice, and then she'd run shrieking away from him—and her fright, unlike her brothers', would not be feigned.

"I'm sure the pain will get better soon," he assured her quickly. "Do you . . . do you think my color's better today?" he asked, gesturing towards his face despite the pain the movement caused, hoping to keep her attention from wandering down his body.

She studied his face for a long moment, as if the secret of life were hidden there. "I think you are still a little . . . ah, pale, Herr Taylor, though it is difficult to tell, of course, because you are so . . . so brown from the sun, *ja?*"

"*Ja,*" he found himself answering. "That is, I suppose I am."

"You need to eat. I vill bring you *leichtes Mittagessen.*"

"Uh . . . what kind of food is that?" he asked, a little dubiously.

She looked upward, obviously searching her mind for the English equivalent. "The noonday meal. Dinner, *ja?*"

He thought the way she made the word into two distinct syllables was enchanting. "Yeah, dinner." All at once he realized how long it had been since he had eaten, and his stomach growled as if to echo the thought.

Erica giggled at the sound.

"Yes, please, I reckon something to eat would be right nice." He hoped it would be something substantial, and that the knowledge that he was awake wouldn't bring her gorgon of a mother up there to glare at him.

"I vill return soon," she promised, straightening and departing the room with a graceful economy of movement.

She was as good as her word, and came back in just a few minutes, without the gorgon and flanked by the two boys. Hans was carrying a cloth-covered tray and Guenther bore a fluffy pillow.

"Ve vill help you to sit up," she said. She gestured for Hans to set the tray on the bedside stand and assist her in raising Jake—who stifled a moan at the wave of pain the movement caused—so that the younger boy could tuck the big pillow between Jake's back and the headboard. Then she settled the tray over his knees and whisked off the cloth, revealing a stew of beef and vegetables and a big slab of brown bread thickly slathered with butter. There was also a tall, thick mug of some liquid; the yeasty smell that reached his nose proclaimed it beer. Well, it wasn't a steak dinner, but it would certainly do until he could get one. Rising steam wafted the savory aroma of the stew just as his stomach rumbled again.

This time it was the boys who laughed.

"Do you think you will be able to eat with your left hand, Herr Taylor?" Erica asked. "I brought things that would not need to be cut up," she added, studying him a bit anxiously.

He'd been rather enchanted by the notion of her

feeding him, but he said, "Oh, sure, I can manage." But when he suited action to his words, the mere motion of moving his left arm and bending forward slightly, so that his left-handed awkwardness would not land the stew in his lap, sent pain screaming through him and beading his forehead with sweat. He could feel the blood draining from his face at the effort it took to keep from crying out.

I'm acting like some feeble invalid, he thought with disgust. "I reckon I'm going to need some help after all, Miss Erica," he murmured. "If it wouldn't be too much trouble . . ."

"You are in pain, *ja*? It hurts you to move even so little!" Erica said in a worried voice. "Vy didn't you say so?" She turned to Hans and Guenther, who were eyeing him with concern from the other side of the bed, and aimed some rapid-fire German at them. The boys dashed from the room as if there were a prairie fire right behind them, and Jake could hear the thud of their sturdy boots echoing down the hall.

"I have sent them to fetch some laudanum and a spoon," she said. "It is not necessary to lie here in pain." It sounded like a reproof.

"I don't need laudanum," he protested, even though his shoulder was arguing to the contrary.

"Nonsense," she responded. "Vy do you lie about something so *selbstverstandlich*—so clear to the eye? There is no need to be so . . . how do you say it? Falsely heroic?"

He didn't like the notion that she thought he was being false about anything. "No, it's just that I don't want to sleep the rest of the day away," he insisted. "I can take a little pain."

"Tomorrow you may take the pain if you wish," she countered as her brothers returned with the requested items. "Today you need to eat something, then rest more. Your body has been badly injured." Not waiting for agreement, she poured a generous spoonful of the dark liquid from the amber bottle, cupping a hand under the spoon as she raised it to his mouth.

"Good," she murmured as Jake obediently opened his mouth and sipped the bitter-tasting concoction, then raised the tankard of beer to his lips so he could wash it down.

He felt the pain ease as she began to spoon mouthfuls of the delicious, hearty stew into his mouth, interspersing them with bite-sized squares of the buttered bread and sips of the dark beer. Soon his stomach stopped growling and laudanum-induced drowsiness stole over him even as he fought to smother the yawns so he could remain awake to enjoy her company. But he soon lost the battle and almost fell asleep while he was chewing a piece of bread.

"You need to sleep now," he heard her murmur, and he struggled to raise his heavy lids and argue the matter.

"No, stay awhile and talk to me, Miss Erica. I . . . I can sleep later," he managed to say before a yawn escaped him.

Erica Mueller laughed, the sound as sweet as the church bell in the distance that was even now chiming the hour—which hour, he couldn't tell, and he was too drowsy to count the chimes.

"I think"—it came out *tink*—"you are lying again,

Herr Taylor. I think you will sleep now, and I will wake you for *Abendbrot.*"

Jake wasn't sure what that was, but he supposed he could wait to find out.

Chapter Five

He was barely awake the next morning when a knock sounded at his bedroom door. Before he could even frame the words, "Come in," the gorgon swept in, followed by Hans, who was carrying Jake's breakfast tray.

She stopped stock-still at the foot of his bed, as if some unseen general had barked a command to halt, and studied him.

Jake tried a tentative, "Good morning."

The gorgon said something in German that sounded more like an accusation than a greeting.

Hans stepped around his mother. "Good morning, Herr Taylor," he said. "My mother does not speak much English. She says that you slept through supper last night."

His growling stomach had already informed him of that fact. "I-I'm sorry," Jake said, since the announcement seemed to call for an apology. "I'm sure

I missed a delicious meal. I expect it was the laudanum that made me sleep so long." He aimed his most devastatingly charming smile at Mrs. Mueller.

Hilda Mueller sniffed after Hans had translated, then fired another speech at him.

Hans looked sympathetic as he reframed his mother's words into his accented English. "She says you should not expect to be allowed to lie around in a—I'm sorry, Herr Taylor—in a stupor today. As soon as you have breakfasted, I am to help you with your bath. And then you will come and sit on the porch, where the fresh air will help you recover your strength."

Jake could feel the boy's embarrassment at having to repeat the harsh words. He nodded to show Hans he understood that the sentiments were not the boy's, then aimed his sunniest smile in the gorgon's direction. "Tell your mother, please, that nothing would please me more than to do whatever will help me get better as soon as possible and be on my way. I appreciate what y'all've been doing for me, but I don't want to be a burden to your family." He wanted to ask Hans where his beautiful sister was, and if there was any chance she could join him on the porch to keep him company, but he was afraid the gorgon understood more English than she spoke. Better to wait until she had gone.

Hilda Mueller looked partially placated after Hans had reworded Jake's answer in German. She nodded stiffly, and after a last muttered command to her son, turned on her heel and left the room.

Jake had been hoping for bacon and eggs, but he

managed to keep a poker face when Hans lifted the cloth over the tray to reveal a bowl containing some kind of thick gruel. Did the gorgon think such a breakfast was going to inspire his recovery? He'd get better if only to escape such a meal!

Hans placed the tray on Jake's lap. "I am sorry Mutti—that is, my mother—seems so . . . what is the word?—*not welcoming*," he said, fresh color rising in his rosy cheeks.

"Your mama runs a tight ship, that's all," Jake said. "Nothing wrong with that." He saw Hans blink in confusion at the phrase, and he quickly added, "A tight ship—that means she keeps a good eye on her household, and she doesn't need useless mouths to feed, like mine."

Hans looked reassured that Jake had taken no offense. He pulled up a chair by the bed and sat down. "I am sure you are not useless normally, Herr Taylor, when you are well. Is it really true that you held off a whole passel of Comanches before they finally killed your horse?"

Jake smiled, wondering where a German boy had come by the word "passel."

"Well, I can't say as I really tried to hold them off. There were about six of them and only one of me, so I was hoping we could outrun 'em. We might've done so, too, if my horse hadn't put his leg in a hole."

Hans's eyes were wide as saucers. "You are lucky to still have your scalp, Herr Taylor."

"I am, and that's a fact," Jake agreed, flattered in spite of himself by the boy's rapt admiration. "If my horse hadn't fallen on me, those redskins would have seen I wasn't dead."

"Herr Taylor, you were a soldier in the war, *ja?*"

Jake nodded.

Hans said, "Will you tell me stories about being a soldier?"

"Sure, Hans, but maybe you'd better fetch that bathwater while I'm eating this—this whatever-it-is. We wouldn't want your mama to think I'm being a lazy layabout, would we?" He didn't really care too much about what Mama Mueller thought of him, but he sure didn't want to smell like a day-old goat carcass when he next saw Erica.

"You are right. I will get your bathwater, and that is *Hafergrutze,*" Hans said over his shoulder as he left the room.

The explanation left Jake still mystified, but when he managed to get a spoonful of the gruel to his mouth with his left hand, he discovered it was oatmeal, sweetened with honey—and tastier than it looked. It would fill him up, and he was relieved not to have an audience while he perfected the art of eating with his left hand.

There was a staccato knock at the door just then, however, which startled him so much that he dropped a spoonful of oatmeal right in his lap.

"Ah! Herr Taylor! You look much better today!" proclaimed Gustav Mueller as he strode into the room, swiping a handkerchief over his sweaty forehead. Mueller's shirt was damp with perspiration and dust coated his trousers.

"I reckon I am, sir, thank you," Jake replied, wondering what sort of strenuous work the older man had been doing. He looked on the verge of sunstroke. "Please tell Miz Mueller not to fret—I plan to be out of your hair as quick as possible." Jake saw the German man's puzzled expression and added, "That is, I don't want to inconvenience y'all with my presence any longer than necessary."

Comprehension flashed across Gustav Mueller's face, but his eyes looked troubled. "I'm sorry. My good wife can be . . . abrupt, shall we say? I fear she has spoken in an inhospitable way, Herr Taylor. But as the head of the family, I tell you you are welcome to stay as long as you need to."

The man was obviously sincere, so Jake smiled back at him. "Much obliged, Mr. Mueller. I just wish I was able to help you at whatever you've been doing," he said, gesturing toward the handkerchief Mueller was now swiping over the back of his neck.

"*Ach,* I was just trying to hoe the weeds in the garden, but it is already too warm. I drank almost a bucketful of *wasser*—that is, water—from the well, but I think I will have to make an earlier start tomorrow."

"Yes, our Texas sun can be a killer if you're not careful," Jake agreed. "You ought to rest a spell, sir."

"Perhaps I will, since my wife has gone to the store in town," Mueller said ruefully, as if that were the only reason he dared take a rest.

Hans returned then. A towel was draped around his shoulders and he bore a basin of water. He set the water down and dug a bar of soap and a razor out of his pocket.

"I see my son has brought everything you will need for your bath. As soon as I wash, I had best get to my shop. I am a clockmaker, you see. I will see you later, Herr Taylor, and please, you have only to let us know if you require anything for your comfort," Mueller said, bowing.

Warmed by the German's Old World hospitality, Jake thought about asking him where his lovely daughter was, since her company would make him about as comfortable as a man could hope to be this side of Heaven, but he thought he'd better not push his luck. Even Old World hospitality probably had its limits when it came to daughters.

Erica's first thought, when she approached the house from the vegetable garden and spotted the wounded Texan sitting in the shade of the back porch with Hans and Guenther, was how alive and vital Jake Taylor looked—despite the fact that his right arm was cradled in a sling—compared to the pale, weak man to whom she had ministered in the bedroom upstairs only yesterday. Much of his color had returned, and he had shaved—or perhaps Hans had shaven him—and the strong angle of his jawbone was once again visible. His head was bent towards the boys, who were sitting on the top step at his feet, and he was speaking to them. He hadn't yet seen her.

"And so we men of Hood's Texas Brigade pushed Hooker's men back across that cornfield," Jake was saying. Erica could tell from Hans and Guenther's stillness and upturned heads that they were giving Jake their undivided attention as he spoke of two of their favorite subjects: soldiers and war. After each sentence or two he would pause and give Hans time to translate, since Guenther's English was not as good as his elder brother's. Erica hoped Jake wouldn't mind too much that he had just gained two shadows for the duration of his stay.

She saw Guenther whisper something into Hans's ear, and then Hans said, "My brother wants to know if you miss the army. He thinks being a soldier is a very fine life, having a uniform and a horse and rifle, and having brave comrades."

Even in profile, she could see Jake's face become pensive. He suddenly looked older. Erica remained motionless in the shade of the live oak tree, wanting to hear what he would say. She guessed it would reveal much about the character of the man sitting there, and she was not disappointed.

"I thought it was a fine life too when I first left home to join up," Jake Taylor said. "I thought I looked very dashing in my gray uniform. But you see, it wasn't long before that uniform was patched and stained—and even had a bullet hole in it—from a minor wound, fortunately—and I lost too many of those brave comrades in battle. I reckon it's necessary to have soldiers to protect the peace and all, but it's not all glory and honor."

Erica saw Guenther's face become doubtful as Hans began to translate what the Texan had said. Clearly, at his age, the boy couldn't picture the grim reality of war. She waited to see if Jake would say more, but just then he looked away from the boys and caught sight of her, and immediately his face brightened.

"Why, Miss Erica, you're lookin' pretty as a field of bluebonnets this mornin'! Can you come join us and sit a spell?" He patted the place on the step next to him and smiled invitingly.

Erica felt the force of his charm like the rays of the sun. She knew his compliment had to be pure flattery: she was aware that wisps of her hair had escaped her braid and she felt the perspiration-damp patches of cloth under her arms. But at the moment she also felt beautiful, and she couldn't help but smile back.

"Good morning, Herr Taylor. You look much improved today," she murmured. "I hope the pain is better too?"

"It's tolerable," he said. "As long as I remember not to laugh very hard, or sneeze, that is. But if you'd just sit down here by me, I'm sure I couldn't feel anything but wonderful."

She hesitated, knowing she shouldn't. Hadn't her disgrace at the hands of Siegfried Von Schiller back in Regensberg begun with just such blandishments as these?

"Please, Miss Erica? You look like you could use some time out of the sun."

"Yes, sit down, Erica! Herr Jake tells the best stories!" pleaded Guenther.

"I'm sure I should start getting the noon meal together, since Mutti is not yet back," she murmured, unaware that in her confusion she spoke in German, not moving.

She saw Jake wince as he laboriously got to his feet.

"What—what are you doing?" she asked, taking a step or two forward.

46

"Miss Erica, as a gentleman, if you won't sit, I'm kinda compelled to stand," he said gently.

Was it only her embarrassed imagination, or had his color faded somewhat with his effort? Quickly, fearing he might faint at any moment, she sat, and was rewarded with a grin from their injured houseguest.

"Herr Taylor, you were telling us about the war," Hans reminded him eagerly.

Jake glanced at Erica, then said, "Oh, I don't know, fellas, I think we might oughta talk about somethin' more cheerful around your sister. . . ."

"Nonsense, Herr Taylor—"

He interrupted her. "I reckon when you call me 'Herr Taylor,' it's the same as 'Mr. Taylor,' and when someone does that I start lookin' 'round for my father. Do you suppose you could just call me Jake?" he asked, his Texas drawl wrapping itself around her heart and making her feel even warmer than she had before.

"Jake," she said, forming the hard *j* with some difficulty because in German *j* was said as a *y*.

"That's right," he said with an encouraging smile to reward her. "See, doesn't that sound better?"

"I suppose it's all right for me since we are both adults," she said, "but my parents would probably object if they heard the boys doing so."

"Mr. Jake or Herr Jake for them, then," Jake said.

The boys parroted him delightedly: "Herr Jake! Herr Jake!"

"Now, where were we?" Jake asked.

"You were saying that perhaps you should not

47

discuss being a soldier in front of me," she reminded him. "I had been about to tell you that I am not a stranger to soldiers and war. Indeed, we left Germany partly because of political unrest that threatened to become war." *And partly because I had disgraced the family.*

"All right, then . . ." He began talking again, but Erica noted that his tales had more to do with amusing things that happened around a camp full of soldiers, or word portraits of the men with whom he had served, rather than conflict between the two sides. She soon lost track of time as she listened, rapt as her brothers.

". . . And General Hood, after he'd danced with all the belles at the ball—"

"God in heaven, Erica, what do you think you are doing?"

Chapter Six

Erica jumped to her feet as her mother opened the gate with her free hand—the other was laden with brown paper-wrapped parcels—and stalked up the path that led to the house. Fury was written all over her face at the sight of "the devil Texan" sitting on her front porch.

Beside Erica, Jake rose respectfully, and only she heard the slight intake of breath that evidenced the pain he suffered from such a quick movement.

"M-Mutti," Erica began, "I did not expect you back so soon! I . . . I guess I lost track of the time. I—"

"*That* is all too obvious," Hilda Mueller snapped in German, glaring at Jake and Erica in turn. "I come home expecting to find the noon meal ready to serve, and instead I find you loitering like a trollop with this . . . this Texan! Quick, there is no time to lose!" She darted a panicked glance over her shoulder, almost as if she were being pursued. "He must take himself off to the guest room and stay there! Where's your father?"

"I—I—" Erica began helplessly. "He went to his shop some time ago," she said, nodding to the small outbuilding at the side of their property. "He said it had gotten too hot to work in the garden. He said he'd be back in time for the meal. . . ."

"Mutti, what is wrong?" Hans asked innocently.

Hilda ignored her son, acting as if Erica had asked the question. "You foolish girl! The mayor's wife invited herself for *leichtes Mittagessen* and I asked her to give me a few minutes to come home and see that all was in readiness and to set an extra place at the table! Instead I find that the food is nowhere near ready to serve! *Ach*, this is a disaster! She must not find *him* here—" she declared, glaring again at Jake, "or you will never find a husband—nor will the boys find decent *frauleins* to marry!"

Her mother was out of breath and red in the face when she finished this speech, but she was already making shooing motions with her hands.

"What is she saying?" Jake asked Erica in a low undertone.

Erica turned to him and quickly explained, though she tried to be more tactful than her mother had been. "I'm sorry," she finished, "but you must go upstairs, as quickly as you can—"

"*Ach!* It is already too late! She will already have seen you! *Gott in Himmel*," Hilda Mueller moaned, as the landau carrying Frau Von Hesselberg rounded the bend in the road, its pair of matched dapple-grays carrying the mayor's wife towards them at a spanking trot.

Erica said as soothingly as she could, "Mutti, we will just have to make the best of it. It won't be so bad, you'll see. She will only think what a good man Vati is to have helped Herr Taylor."

"You are naïve, daughter. This will ruin us," was Hilda Mueller's dark prediction. She cast a last blaming glare at Jake and then stiffened her back-bone like a general preparing to sound the charge. "Hans, as soon as the carriage stops, you go out and show her driver back to the barn where he can un-hitch and water the team. Guenther, you will make a bow, then run and get your father. Explain that the Frau Von Hesselberg is to be our guest for luncheon. Erica, once introductions have been made, you will hasten to the kitchen to do what you should have been doing an hour ago, and get the meal ready to serve. Herr Taylor, you will go upstairs and not leave your room unless you are told to do so."

As Hilda Mueller had spoken in German, Jake once again had to whisper a request for Erica to translate, even as her mother was forcing her fea-tures into a welcoming smile.

The older woman, as plump as Hilda Mueller was bony, was helped from the carriage by her driver, a blond young man in a livery coat of spotless navy blue with stiff gold braid and shiny brass buttons. As she waddled up the walk, Frau Von Hesselberg stared through a lorgnette at Jake Taylor with undis-guised and gleeful curiosity.

Jake, Erica saw out of the corner of her eye, smiled politely as the old woman approached.

"Ah, you did not tell me you had a houseguest, Frau Mueller," the mayor's wife said archly. "Aren't you the one for surprises? And who is he? He looks American, is it not so? You must tell me how he comes to be here," she added in a imperative voice. "Fraulein Mueller, hello," she added in belated acknowledgment of Erica's presence.

Erica fought the urge to shout at the woman. Couldn't she see that Jake's arm was in a sling, and that his face was bruised and scraped? Couldn't the gossipy old cow tell that he'd been injured, and guess that the Muellers were helping him, instead of sounding so suspicious? Instead, Erica curtsied politely and waited for her mother to explain.

"Frau Von Hesselberg, I have the . . . honor to present Herr Jacob Taylor." Then, in her difficult English, she added, "Herr Taylor, Frau Von Hesselberg, the wife of our good mayor."

"I'm pleased to make your acquaintance, ma'am," Jake said, making his very best bow as Erica translated his words.

Frau Von Hesselberg nodded in acknowledgment as his words were translated, her small eyes darting speculatively between him and Erica and back again.

Erica's mother said quickly, "My husband rescued Herr Taylor after he had been set upon by savages, who barely left him with his life, as you can see. Then he brought him here."

"Indeed, the demands of decency dictate no less," the mayor's wife murmured piously. "Still, I am surprised that he would not realize the risk of introducing one of these brash Americans into the sanctity of your home with an innocent daughter in residence. . . ." Her arched brows implied a wealth of possibilities, none of them good.

Erica was thankful that Jake understood no German, and she flushed in anger at the woman's innuendo. It was fortunate, she fumed, that her mother was present, for otherwise she would have been tempted to tell Frau Von Hesselberg what she thought of her rudeness. But she knew her mother held the mayor's wife as the arbiter of behavior in New Braunfels, and felt the whole family's social position depended on Frau Von Hesselberg's goodwill.

With a last glance at Jake, whose relaxed features made her hope he had not guessed what was being said in front of him, Erica cleared her throat and spoke. "Excuse me, Frau Von Hesselberg, I will go and get the meal ready." She curtsied again and whirled on her heel, reaching the door as her father, still buttoning his waistcoat, came from the direction of his shop.

One glance at his still, set face confirmed that Gustav Mueller had overheard Frau Von Hesselberg's words.

"Frau Von Hesselberg," he said, his tone cordial but firm as he took Erica's place on the porch, "how honored we are that you will take luncheon with us. I see you have already been introduced to our guest, Herr Taylor. I think I should tell you that Herr Taylor comes of a good family whose plantation on the Brazos River is well known."

Erica felt her heart swell with love for her father as she hurried to the kitchen. He had just made it clear that as head of the household, he had given Jake his seal of approval.

"It was nice meeting you, ma'am," Jake said, and started towards the stairs to go to the guest room, trying his best to ignore Guenther's barely muffled cry of disappointment, but Gustav Mueller put a restraining hand on Jake's shoulder.

"But of course you will take the noon meal with us, Herr Taylor—if you are not too tired or in too much pain, of course." He gestured towards the dining room.

Jake was aware of Hilda Mueller's dismayed face and the mayor's wife's scandalized expression, and tried gracefully to decline. He didn't want to make trouble for the kindly man—or his daughter, Jake thought, catching a glimpse through the doorway of Erica hastily tying an apron around her slender waist in the kitchen. He could lie that his wounds were hurting him more than they actually were, of course, but tarnation, he wanted to remain, if only to be in Erica's presence a little longer. And upsetting the pompous mayor's wife by remaining would be frosting on the cake.

Jake couldn't understand German, of course, but he had taken Frau Von Hesselberg's measure before she had even opened her mouth. He knew the woman's type. It seemed as if there were some old biddy like her in every small town, one who felt she'd been divinely appointed to push other folks around and who used her approval and disapproval like weapons.

He didn't let the woman's obvious disapprobation

bother him much. He reckoned she might be surprised to know that same kind of stigma could be attached to a Texan household if they'd been discovered harboring a German immigrant. Anti-German feelings still ran high among the Texans who had supported the Confederacy, since the German newcomers had been such avid Unionists.

"Thank you, sir, I'd be much obliged," he said.

"The Wiener schnitzel was very good, though I must say the venison sausage was a bit spicy for my taste," Frau Von Hesselberg commented after she had helped herself to seconds on everything including the peach pie. "I see that your Erica will be adequate to assume the task of running a household of her own. Perhaps I should send my daughter Gunilla down to teach her how to make some of my specialties."

"Why, thank you, Frau Von Hesselberg," Hilda responded, as if the woman had praised Erica to the skies. "And that would be very good of you. Gunilla has always been such a model of everything good in a German girl. Erica has always found her delightful company."

Erica stifled an unladylike snort. She couldn't stand Gunilla Von Hesselberg, a vain, self-satisfied young copy of her mother. And she had thought it unfortunate that the conversation was being conducted in a language their Texan guest did not comprehend, and so had been translating it into English for Jake during the meal—or at least as much of it as she could without repeating any of Frau Von Hessel-

berg's pointed comments about Jake himself. She
had just duly repeated what had been said and felt
the flush rise in her cheeks because she was speaking of herself.

"I thought the food was much more than 'adequate,' Miss Erica—I'd say it was downright delicious. And I happen to like spicy things," Jake
responded with an encouraging smile, causing her
blush to deepen.

The byplay had not been missed by Frau Von Hesselberg, of course.

"*Ach*, did you encourage your daughter to become
so fluent in that barbaric tongue?" the mayor's wife
asked Frau Mueller, and smirked in satisfaction
when her jab made the woman look embarrassed all
over again.

Gustav Mueller saw his daughter blink in astonishment at Frau Hesselberg's rudeness and came to
her rescue. "Our daughter is just being polite,
madame," Gustav Mueller responded. "Our guest,
you see, does not understand German."

The mayor's wife sniffed. Her face said, *Of course
he doesn't.* "Perhaps you are considering looking for
an American husband for her?" she asked with a sly
glance toward Jake, who was sitting down the long
rectangular oak table from her and across from Erica.

Hilda said quickly, "Oh, no, be assured we would
never do such a thing! We would only select a German youth of impeccable family for our Erica!"

"My primary concern would be that any such
prospective groom make my daughter happy, Frau

Von Hesselberg," Gustav Mueller insisted. "Erica, *liebchen*, Herr Taylor's glass is empty. Perhaps he would care for some more of your elderberry wine? And some more for you too, Frau Von Hesselberg?"

Erica shot her father a grateful look as she endeavored not to let her hands shake as she poured the wine from the red cut glass decanter they had brought all the way from Bavaria.

After consuming a generous slice of the peach pie Jake arose and thanked his hostesses for the tasty meal and once again professed himself delighted to have made the mayor's wife's acquaintance.

Frau Von Hesselberg patently doubted the compliment, to judge by the way she narrowed her already tiny eyes, but Jake was past caring about the slight. By this time his shoulder and ribs really were aching, and he wished he had a big dose of laudanum to ease the pain. He was damned if he'd ask for it in front of that woman, though.

But Erica must have guessed somehow, because he was just trying to get comfortable in the bed when Hans appeared.

"Erica says you need this," the boy said, holding out the same small amber bottle Erica had brought up yesterday, a spoon, and a fresh glass of water.

"Thanks, amigo," Jake said gratefully, adding, "That means 'friend,'" when the boy looked confused.

Hans grinned. "Ah, *freund!* Maybe you will tell more stories about soldiers after you rest, *ja?*"

"*Ja*, maybe," Jake said, and his use of a German word made the boy giggle. He ruffled the boy's head, thinking of how he might have had a child himself by now if the damned war hadn't gotten in the way.

He went to sleep to the sound of someone playing the piano down in the parlor for their important guest, and Erica singing along in a high clear soprano.

Chapter Seven

The laudanum, of course, caused him to sleep through supper, and he awoke in the middle of the night, achingly aware that he had dreamed of Erica Mueller.

In his dream he was making love to her, her golden hair spread out on the pillow beneath her as she cried out in ecstasy, arching to meet his thrust. . . .

Damn! He felt himself getting hard all over again and strode to the window, throwing it open with the hope of cooling his heated blood. The sound caused a sleepy bird perching in the live oak tree next to the window to chirp confusedly and take flight into the darkness.

The trouble was that he'd been without a woman too long. That's all it was. Once he was well enough to leave the Muellers and be on his way to his friend John Ransom's house in San Antonio, he'd stop by some saloon along the way and spend an hour or two in the arms of some soiled dove who'd relieve him of this annoying randiness.

Maybe he should ask his sister Maria, next time he visited her, to introduce him to some young lady she thought suitable as a wife for him. But while the idea of settling down and raising a passel of kids was appealing to him as long as it didn't mean wedding any of the overeager ladies of Bryan, what did he really have to offer a wife? He was not going to stay at the Taylor Hall plantation if his father remained adamant about sharecropping, and if Jake had to strike out on his own, it might be quite a while before he was able to support a family.

Jake sighed heavily. He heard the hoot of an owl, and from somewhere in the back of the property, the croaks of a couple of bullfrogs. The faint breeze brought the scent of roses wafting towards his nose from the garden to the left of the tree.

Then a movement in the moon-dappled yard below caught his eye, and looking between the branches, Jake spotted a slim figure in a light-colored nightgown. Erica, he realized, seeing the gleam of a golden braid reaching down her back nearly to her waist. What was she doing out there? Was she waiting for someone?

The thought that she might have a lover sent a pang of jealous fury arrowing through his heart.

Get ahold of yourself, Taylor. Erica Mueller is nothing to you but the girl who'd helped her father play Good Samaritan. Sure, she was downright beautiful, and she'd been kind to him, but she'd have done the same for any injured man, probably even a Comanche. He had no reason, beyond a blush or two, to think she was attracted to him. And even if she was, Erica belonged to a close-knit people who didn't mingle with their Anglo neighbors, but stuck with their own kind.

He knew he'd remember her forever, but he'd be able to put her golden loveliness and sweetness into perspective once he'd found some pretty Texas girl to call his own and was raising younguns to carry on the Taylor name. At least he hoped so.

As he watched, she turned to gaze up at the full moon, her features in profile to him. Even from here the expression on her face appeared to be one of longing.

Who—or what—was she yearning for? Did she merely miss her native land? Or had she left some sweetheart across the ocean?

Then Erica astonished him by turning and looking up in the direction of his window. He was so startled he nearly ducked out of sight, not wanting her to know he'd been staring at her as she wandered alone in the moonlit yard. The leaves, and the lack of a lit lamp in the room, probably kept her from seeing clearly into his window; but he remained still, not wanting to chance it.

Perhaps she was just looking back towards the house to check if her mother and father had noticed her absence. By now he knew that her parents' bedroom was next to his. Or maybe she'd spotted a shooting star over the roofline? He hardly dared to breathe as he continued to kneel there at the window, watching her and wondering what she was thinking.

All at once he saw her cock her head ever so

slightly to the side, almost as if she'd asked him a question and was waiting for his answer.

Had she sensed he was there, and was she inviting him to join her? Had his dream about making love to her been prophetic? Was she perhaps not the innocent miss she'd seemed to be? Even if she was, surely she didn't expect him to take her to his bed in the room adjacent to her parents' bedroom, or in the shadows of one of the cottonwood trees, where anyone with an open window could hear their cries of passion?

Even as he finished the thought, though, he was ashamed of his speculation about her. In the glow of moonlight, her beauty was ethereal, almost otherworldly. Surely this German girl had never known a man intimately.

Perhaps she just wanted to speak to him away from the prying eyes and listening ears of her mama and papa? That possibility had the compelling force of a siren song.

Going down to join her would mean taking a tremendous chance, he knew. If they were discovered together by her parents, even if they were only talking, he knew Papa Mueller would suddenly yank up the welcome mat he'd laid out for Jake. It wouldn't matter that it was the middle of the night.

He wouldn't regret that consequence for himself, but he didn't want to leave Erica behind to bear her parents' anger.

Then he remembered the last few words she'd translated from the conversation from the midday meal. Maybe Erica wanted to tell him how she felt about being discussed by the mayor's wife and her

parents almost as if she weren't there, and knowing
that her parents would select her future husband?

That thought made his decision. He wanted Erica
to know that this was America, not the Old Country,
and that she shouldn't have to marry anyone she
didn't want to. He felt chivalrous now, like a knight
of old on a mission to rescue a damsel in distress.
Come to think of it, that old biddy Mrs. Von Hesselberg had been rather akin to a dragon.

Jake shifted his weight to prepare to rise from his
kneeling position, and the stab of pain from his broken ribs mocked his fantasy of a few minutes earlier.
What a fool he was to even imagine for a second that
he was capable of becoming her lover tonight, with
one arm in a sling and a couple of broken ribs to jab
him with every deep breath, every movement!

Once he'd managed to get his pants on—an awkward job with only one hand he could use—he
stepped back to the window to see if she was still
looking up at the window. She was—and was there a
smile playing about her mouth? Had she seen a flash
of movement when he'd stood up and knew he was
coming to her? He wondered what she would have
to say to him in her charming, heavily accented English. He prayed the floorboards in this sturdy German house didn't creak. . . .

And then, just as he started to turn away from the
window and head for the bedroom door, he heard
the front door beneath his window open and saw
her whirl to meet whoever was coming through it.
He heard a male voice—her father's—saying something to her in German as he came out from under
the roof and strode to her side. His tone was gently

chiding as he handed Erica a robe and helped her to put it on. She shrugged, replying in the same tongue, her voice light and unconcerned, as if she explained her presence by saying she couldn't sleep.

Jake moved to the side of the window where he could still watch what was going on, but where he could not be seen if the leaves didn't conceal him as much as he thought.

He saw Erica's father put his arm around her as if urging her towards the house; she nodded and allowed him to propel her in that direction. Just before she passed out of his sight Jake thought Erica looked up towards his window, but he could not be certain.

He smothered a groan and went back to bed, knowing he would lie awake until he heard the family stirring. Now he would probably never know for sure if Erica had wanted him to come down to her—and what would have happened if he had.

It would have interested him to know that Erica didn't sleep the rest of the night, either.

She had not been certain that she had seen Jake at the window, or what she had wanted to happen if he *had* sneaked down to join her in the shadows. All she knew was that when her mother and the mayor's wife had been discussing the match that would eventually be made for her, she had suddenly felt like a small bird beating its wings against the bars of an ever-shrinking cage. If she didn't manage to escape it, she would be crushed.

Somehow this Texan, Jake Taylor, made her think he just might have the key to her cage. The depths of his clear blue eyes held freedom. However, there were other experiences lying in those depths too— experiences not to be found in her cage, qualities dangerous to the safe, virtuous existence she had led since the family had left Germany.

But they didn't frighten her nearly as much as the thought of being made to marry some "German youth of impeccable family," like Rudolph Schoenbrunn with his round, red-cheeked face and sober ways.

Something about the way Jake Taylor looked at her—no, *caressed* was surely the better word—made her feel beautiful and daring and desirable. She could not imagine Rudolph Schoenbrunn, the banker's son, ever making her feel that way.

But probably Jake looked at all young women in that fashion, she told herself as she poured some cool water from the ewer into the basin and tried to wash the sleepiness from her eyes. After all, he was a *Jungsselle*—a bachelor—who had recently been through the hell of war. Looking at a woman was merely an enjoyment, one that meant nothing. No doubt he would marry someday, and his wife would be some vivacious young lady of the wealthy, ornamental type that southern Americans called *belles*. Perhaps he had already selected such a young miss and was eager to return to her, to squire her to barbecues and church socials and the like.

Yet he hadn't seemed anxious about sending word home after his injury. He had hardly mentioned home, in fact, or his destination, after responding to her father's questions. But she found it difficult to believe that a man with such a ruggedly handsome face, with such dazzling blue eyes under that thatch of midnight-black hair, would lack a sweetheart.

The thought made her feel more hopeless than she had before.

She descended to the kitchen to help Mutti get breakfast on the table and found her mother already hard at work, frying sausage and beating eggs. A pot of coffee on the stove spread its savory aroma about the room.

"Mutti, you should have called me earlier," she said to her mother's back, seeing that there was little left to do but set the table.

"No, your father said to let you sleep if you would, for you had been restless last night—not that I could sleep either, once he got up to see about you!" her mother added, a trifle sharply.

"I'm sorry. It was so hot. . . . I thought if I went outside and walked around a bit, I would cool off," Erica said, watching Hilda carefully as if her mother might have read her mind and known that Erica had hoped to meet Jake in the yard last night. But her mother, never cheerful in the morning, looked no crosser than usual.

"Well, you might think of someone besides your-self once in a while!"

"Sorry—" Erica began again, only to be inter-rupted by the sound of someone outside on the back porch, whistling.

It had to be Jake. Her father never whistled like that, and her mother didn't feel it was seemly for the boys to do so, either, at least so early in the morning around the house.

66

Well, she must have been wrong about seeing his face in the window last night, or he would not sound so energetic!

"Here, take this coffee out to that man so he'll have something else to do with his mouth," her mother said sourly as she poured a big mugful and handed it to Erica.

Erica stepped through the door and saw Jake, his back to her, still whistling and taking the last, left-handed swipe at his face with a razor as he peered into a mirror held by Guenther. Her little brother stared worshipfully up at the tall Texan as if he knew for a fact that Jake Taylor had hung the moon.

While she stood there holding the steaming crockery mug, Jake laid the razor down on the porch rail and grabbed for the towel perched on Guenther's shoulder. He made an elaborate show of scrubbing the remainders of the shaving soap off with a towel while making noises and motions like a horse snorting and shaking off a fly.

Guenther laughed delightedly. There was no language barrier, obviously, with clowning.

Something—perhaps the aroma of freshly brewed coffee—made Jake aware that he and Guenther were no longer alone. He turned, smiling broadly when he spotted Erica.

"Good morning, Herr Jake. Some coffee?" she said, trying not to notice how devastatingly good-looking he was, freshly shaved, with beads of water still clinging to his cheek. "Obviously you slept well?" Was she wrong, or did the question startle Jake a little?

"Guenther," she added in German, "perhaps you should find Hans and tell him breakfast is almost ready."

"Yes, Erica." With one last adoring look at the Texan, Guenther scampered off in the direction of the barn.

The interruption had given Jake time to regain his poise.

"Yes, ma'am, I slept just fine until I couldn't sleep any more," he said enigmatically. "I'm sorry I slept through supper again. Reckon I'd better stop taking that laudanum."

"No apologies are necessary, Herr Jake," she said. "We wouldn't want you to be in pain."

"Aw, the pain isn't that bad now, just an ache. Time to stop babyin' myself so I can get my strength back. Your brother said he'd take me down to the river today so I could take a proper bath."

An instant image of Jake's naked body emerging from the Comal River, water dripping off his lean hips, sent the color flooding across her cheekbones and she turned around in confusion, intending to go back inside.

"That will be nice for you, Herr—"

"Uh-uh, just Jake, remember?" he said, coming up behind her quickly—too quickly. A sparkle in his eyes told her that he had seen her blush and guessed the reason.

"Jake," she echoed with deliberate austerity, as if the color of her face weren't red as an apple. "And now perhaps you should bring your coffee inside. Breakfast is nearly ready."

Chapter Eight

Jake had gone off with Erica's brothers right after breakfast for the promised bath and swim in the river.

It must be nice, Erica thought enviously as she shoved the plunger into the churn once again, feeling the butter thickening beneath her paddle. How blissful to be immersed in the cool, clear, spring-fed waters of the Comal instead of churning butter on the back porch, with perspiration dripping from her forehead and the constant litany of her mother's chatter droning in her ears!

She had swum in the Comal earlier that spring, when the Lutheran church's Young Ladies' Society had held a special swimming party. The older matrons like her mother had stood guard lest any young men catch a glimpse of the *frauleins* frolicking in the water with their long, dark gowns plastered wetly to their forms. But swimming parties for young ladies were few and far between, despite the heat, while the boys and young men could go anytime. The male sex had such freedom!

"I don't know why your father had to select such an infernally hot place for us. Why, we could have gone anywhere! There are places in America—north of here, of course—with the same temperate climate we knew at home," her mother grumbled as she snapped peas. "Pennsylvania, Michigan . . ."

"Vati said the land was less expensive here. And there were many other Germans, such as his cousin, already living in this part of Texas," Erica said, knowing her mother knew these facts as well as she did and they did not appease her.

"Bah! You get what you pay for, and what we paid for is a land hot as hell itself! And as for living with other Germans, there are enclaves of Germans in many of the big northern cities, but no, your father had to come to the place Cousin Dietrich said was best! At the very least, we could be living in San Antonio near him! Ah, what I wouldn't give to be able to stroll in the Black Forest again, listening to the birds sing and the breeze rustle the pine boughs so far above our heads," Hilda Mueller murmured, her face wistful now. "I remember when your father and I were courting, we would take a picnic there. I would pack a schnitzel and good black bread, and of course a good Rhine wine. . . ."

Erica paused in her churning and caught the dreamy expression in her mother's eyes, and realized with a start that her mother had once been young and carefree and in love.

As she herself had been, Erica thought, recalling

with bitterness the time when she had stolen off into the forest with Siegfried for a delightful picnic—which had transformed itself as if by magic into a passionate coupling amidst the flowers and grasses of a meadow surrounded by the whispering pines. . . .

She had thought them both so much in love, like lovers of the old legends, until she understood later that her lover had hidden witnesses in the surrounding thickets—spies who had reported back to other cronies how quickly Siegfried managed to persuade her to spread her legs for him, so he could collect on a wager made with one of the other dissolute young nobles.

And because of that, her family had uprooted itself and come halfway across the world so that she could have a fresh start, and not be stigmatized forevermore as Siegfried Von Schiller's whore.

She felt the tears stinging her eyes as they always did when she thought of how shamed she had been. The whispering began whenever she walked with her mother in the *Marktplatz* or followed her parents into their family pew in their church in Regensberg—the same church in which she had foolishly hoped to be married to her lover, "her" Siegfried.

Her Siegfried! What a joke! Siegfried belonged to no one but himself. And she had only been his for a time, until he tired of her body. He had begun seducing a younger *fraulein* the following week.

Erica closed her eyes, surreptitiously wiping away a tear, and deliberately forced her mind back to what her mother had been saying.

"But Texas is beautiful too, Mutti," she said, trying

to cheer her mother if she could not cheer herself. "Remember in the spring how glorious those fields full of those little blue and white flowers—what are they called? Oh yes, bluebonnets—appear? It is only March when they begin to bloom, but the fields are full of them and it's warm and sunny. Just think, back in Bavaria it would still be cold and rainy! And then in May the bluebonnets are gone and all those yellow-gold flowers spring up—it's like a carpet of gold in Heaven!"

"But the spring is so soon over, and then we have this beastly, unmerciful heat," her mother groused, swiping a work-reddened hand across her sweaty brow.

"Why don't you go inside?" suggested Erica. She wanted to be alone with her thoughts.

"*Ach*, then there would not even be the chance of a breeze. And no one to talk to, since your father is in his shop and will not wish to be disturbed."

Erica stifled a groan of exasperation at her mother's constant complaining.

"I'm sure he wouldn't consider it a disturbance if it was you, Mutti. Why not take him a cup of tea and some of your delicious *Kuchen*?"

"It would spoil his lunch. He stays cooped up in there all day, with only his clocks and watches for company."

Erica knew there was a good chance her father had only fled to the shop to daydream—or escape his wife's constant carping. It was an odd pairing, this malcontent, sour woman and the methodical, quiet man. But her parents must have been young and passionately in love once. Erica still caught glimpses of that love when she saw the gentle, tender way her father looked at his wife when she was not aware. And the way her mother fussed over her father, making sure he got enough rest and proper meals, wasn't that love?

But may she never become such a complainer as her mother! She knew her mother's grumbling wore upon her father, and she guessed a lesser man might have found a way of leaving. Erica wanted to be considered a pleasure to be around, so that the love between her and the man she married remained ever green.

The butter was done—she could feel that it had solidified in the churn. The afternoon stretched out endlessly before her. There was nothing to look forward to except more chores, for she was very sure her mother would keep her too busy to sit and chat with their Texan houseguest, once he returned.

"Mutti," she began carefully, "the butter is done. As soon as I put it away in the springhouse, do you think I might go visit the Wilhelms? It seems like forever since I've seen Minna!"

Minna was her best friend in New Braunfels, the eldest daughter of a schoolteacher, whose sturdy fieldstone house was right in town rather than outside it as the Muellers' was.

"Oh, sure, go off and leave me with all the extra work caused by that Texan your father allowed to stay here!" her mother cried.

What work? Erica wanted to ask. It was surely no harder to cook for six than it was for five, and she herself had done the laundry yesterday, including the sheets from Herr Jake's bed. But she knew it would not help her cause to argue with her mother, and resigned herself to another boring, hot afternoon.

"I think it might be very good for Erica to go and visit Fraulein Wilhelm," said her father, and both women jumped, not having heard the door from the kitchen open behind them.

Hilda's face assumed a mutinous, mulish look.

Her father seemed to ignore it. "Erica, go and change your clothes and get ready. Churning butter is hard work and you deserve a treat. I'll put it in the springhouse while you change."

"Oh, thank you, Vati!" Erica cried, springing up and kissing his whiskery cheek, not daring to look again at her mother's resentful face. She fairly flew upstairs, planning to wear her blue-sprigged muslin dress that her friend said brought out the blue in her eyes.

She was just pulling her milk-splashed work dress over her head, however, when she heard voices from below. Her parents had evidently forgotten that her bedroom was right over the back porch, and when her window was open, she could hear anything that was said.

"You spoil her, Gustav. It is not good for her. Only attending to her duty will undo the damage that—"

"She does everything you ask and more every day, Hilda. You have watched her with the eyes of a hawk since *Herr* Taylor came, as if you feared if you took your eyes away for a moment, you would find them misbehaving together!"

"That's not true, husband, I—"

"She deserves some innocent fun with a girl-friend. All hard work and no play is not good for any young person, girls as well as boys! It only breeds rebellion. It will be soon enough that she assumes the responsibilities of being a wife. And if you're concerned about the presence in this house of a charming, handsome man, I would think you would be delighted to have her away from the house, even for a few hours!"

"In that case, why not see if Erica would like to stay there until the damned Texan departs?" snapped his wife. "I'm sure if you explained it, the Wilhelms would be delighted to comply!"

"You don't mean that, *liebchen*," he chided her. "I know I would miss her, and you would, too. Come now, admit it."

Erica heard her mother give a gusty sigh. "Very well, I admit it. I just could not bear it if she ruined her life over some good-for-nothing charmer as she almost did at home. As I—"

"Ssssh, sssh, now, none of that," Erica's father soothed.

"We just cannot pack up and run again, Gustav. And that Texan has the devil dancing in his eyes—I can see it!"

"Hilda, Hilda, I think you are imagining things. Certainly I would assume that Herr Jacob Taylor has noticed how pretty our Erica is—yes, I will always say *our* Erica, for she is, Hilda—but every handsome young man is not of Siegfried Von Schiller's ilk!"

What was the meaning of her father's emphasis on "our Erica"? She only had a moment to wonder about that before her mother went on, "You judge no one harshly, husband. You did not see what Von Schiller was up to until it was too late."

Now it was her father's turn to sigh. "No, I didn't. To my eternal regret."

"Besides, how do we know she will really go and see Minna? Perhaps she has already arranged a meeting with that Texan and—"

"If it would set your mind at ease, Hilda," Gustav interrupted, "I will escort Erica to the Wilhelms' house. It's too far for her to walk in the heat of the day, anyway. Besides, Herr Wilhelm borrowed a book of mine months ago and I need to see if he is done with it."

"Very well."

Minutes later, Erica, still puzzling over what she had overheard, was about to climb up into the passenger seat of the family buckboard for the short journey into New Braunfels when she spotted Jake and her brothers coming down the road from the same direction.

"Where are you going, Erica?" demanded Guenther in German.

"In English, Guenther," she reproved her brother gently. "Our guest does not know our language, remember." And she wanted Jake to know where she was going.

"Maybe you could give me lessons in German during my stay, to help pass the time," Jake said, his drawl sweet as honey to her ears. "I know a little Spanish lingo. . . . It'd be nice to know yours, too."

She felt herself coloring at the thought of a teacher-pupil relationship with Jake, and knew she could not let her father see how ·delicious that sounded.

"*Ach*, but I'm sure you will not be here long enough to master the intricacies of the German tongue, Herr Jake," she said coolly.

"Ah, but I'm a quick learner, when I set my mind to it," he said, a challenging light in his eyes as he met her gaze squarely.

She lifted her chin, determined to quash the tension humming in the air before her father became aware of it. "Perhaps the short time you will be with us would be better spent in helping my brother improve his English," she said. "Or perhaps I could help you write a letter so your father won't worry about your absence."

"Oh, I wasn't planning on going straight home anyway," he said easily. "I have a friend in San Antonio to visit."

Was this friend female? she wondered. She turned back to her father. "Vati, perhaps we had better go now, or we will never get to the Wilhelms' house."

Chapter Nine

Minna had been delighted to see Erica.

"Oh, Herr Mueller, might Erica not stay the night? An afternoon is too short a time to catch up on all the news since the last time I saw her!"

Erica's father rubbed his chin thoughtfully. "I suppose that would be all right, if you would agree to be back in time to help your mother cook the midday meal, Erica."

Minna gave a squeal of delight, and as soon as Erica had bidden her father good-bye, whisked her out to the kitchen where they made a pitcher of lemonade and went out to drink it in the shade of the grape arbor. The air was thick with heat and the smell of ripening grapes.

"So, Erica, New Braunfels is abuzz with talk of this Texan staying at your house," Minna gushed.

Erica gave a rueful groan. She should have known the mayor's wife would have spread the gossip all over town in less than a day. And she was piqued that she would not be the first to tell her friend about Jake Taylor.

"And does Frau von Hesselberg say he has horns and a tail and carries a pitchfork, since he is a Texan?"

Minna giggled. "And smells of sulphur? No, but she said she does *not* approve since 'the Muellers have a maiden daughter living under the same roof—what can they be thinking?'" Her imitation of the mayor's wife in a high falsetto sent both young women into gales of laughter.

"But *has* he tried to make passionate love to you yet?" Minna persisted, while Erica was hoping that the rest of the town would not be influenced by the mayor's busybody wife.

Thinking of the night she had wandered sleepless in the garden, and how she thought she had seen him looking out at her from the window, Erica felt a flush rise up her neck.

"Ah, he has!" Minna crowed triumphantly. "Erica, tell! Tell!"

"No, he most certainly hasn't," Erica said in what she hoped was a quelling tone. "Herr Taylor has been the soul of propriety." If one didn't look deep into his eyes, she added to herself, remembering the way he had met her gaze just before she had come here.

"But you'd like him to," Minna guessed shrewdly. "Tell me, is he rakishly handsome?"

"Is that what the mayor's wife said?" Somehow Erica couldn't picture the woman being so charitable.

"She said he looked like a *Lüstling*," Minna said with a giggle.

"A libertine? Oh, Minna, I'm sure he is no such thing!" Erica cried. But did she really have any way of knowing? "He has black hair and blue eyes, and yes, I suppose you could say he is well favored." She attempted to sound as if the Texan's looks affected her not in the least.

"Hmmmm! And what sort of blue are his eyes? There are all kinds of blue, you know," Minna said. "Pale, watery blue, like Pastor Emsch's?"

"Oh, no," Erica said. "As blue as bluebonnets, those little flowers that bloom here in spring."

"Ah, comparing his eyes to the color of a flower! Erica, you are smitten, admit it!"

This time Erica could not explain away her blush. "He is very handsome. And he seems nice. But we know nothing about him other than what he says about himself, do we? And he is only staying until he recovers from his injuries, and then he will be riding away, so it all means nothing."

"But wouldn't you like to be wed to someone like that, Erica? Why, your eyes sparkle when you speak of him, even when you are trying to make it sound as if you are unmoved!"

Erica sighed. Minna could always see right through her. She only hoped Jake couldn't also. "You know my parents would never allow me to wed someone like him—he is not a 'good young German,'" she said. "If they have their way, I will end up with Rudolph Schoenbrunn, that banker's son in San Antonio that I told you about. That's where we were on the way to when we found Herr Taylor, you know, my father's cousin Dietrich Schoenbrunn's house in San Antonio. My mother was hoping I'd come back betrothed, and now the trip has been postponed and she is so upset!"

"I can think of worse things than to be married to a banker, Erica," Minna said, ever the pragmatist. "Perhaps I will arrange to meet this Rudolph if you are not interested in him!"

"You're welcome to take him, Minna. He always smells of pickles. But what about Heinrich Emsch?" she said, mentioning Pastor Emsch's son, now away at seminary training to be a minister himself. "You know very well he wants you to be his wife when he is through with seminary," Erica reminded her friend.

Minna rolled her eyes. "Erica, I don't know if I could be a pastor's wife and always be held up as an example. I can't sew a perfect seam and my tortes are always lopsided. I can't carry a tune, so I couldn't sing the solos during the church services. I think I would rather marry a wicked, dashing Texan! Of course, I would not dream of taking yours, dear friend!"

"Minna, you are assuming Herr Taylor is even remotely interested in me, which of course he is not."

"And why would he not be? You're a beautiful girl, Erica, and you have a lovely figure," Minna, ever her stout defender, asserted. "I only wish I had a waist as tiny as yours!" she added, her face wistful. Minna was overly fond of her mother's linzer torte.

"Minna, you're very pretty, and you know it. You never lack for partners at the dances."

"Still, I should love to get a look at this handsome Texan of yours. How about if I walk you home tomorrow? Perhaps I will get a glimpse of him," she said, laying a hand dramatically over her breast.

"Very well, but you must promise not to embarrass me," Erica pleaded. "Nothing can come of it, so you must swear you will not betray by so much as a whisper . . ." Her voice trailed off, for Erica was uncertain what to say.

"That you are already half in love with him?" Minna asked, and held up a hand when Erica would have protested again. "Don't worry, I will be the soul of discretion. Your secret is safe with me. Just name your firstborn daughter after me."

"Honestly, Minna, you haven't listened to a word I've said!" Erica retorted. "All right, you will walk me home, but then who will walk you home?"

"Perhaps I shall ask your devilish Texan," teased Minna. "After all, with an arm in a sling and broken ribs, he can't possibly be any threat to my virtue, can he? And all the way home I will flirt with him and convince him he and I should run away together!" She laughed when Erica involuntarily frowned. "See? You're jealous, which means you *are* interested in your handsome houseguest! Ah, I cannot wait to cast my eyes on him. But never fear, Erica, I'm sure your brother Hans will walk me home. I think he has a crush on me anyway."

Erica chuckled. Hans was at that stage where he was in love with anything in a skirt. "Perhaps I had better send Guenther along as a chaperone."

Her friend pelted her with an unripe grape.

When Erica and Minna arrived back at the Mueller home the next day, Jake was not sitting on the porch giving Guenther an English lesson, as Erica had hoped, so that Minna's curiosity could be easily satisfied before she was on her way. Nor was he anywhere in evidence downstairs.

"So where is he, this Texan?" Minna asked, peering around her as if he might be expected to leap out from behind the horsehair sofa at any moment.

Erica shrugged. Had Jake decided he felt well enough to ride away while she was gone? She tried to stifle the anguished pang that the thought engendered. She knew better than to ask her mother where Jake was, lest by her interest Hilda decide he really did pose a danger to her daughter's virtue.

"Where are Hans and Guenther?" she asked instead after her mother, already hard at work in preparing the midday meal, had greeted her friend. "I thought perhaps they could walk Minna home?" She ignored her friend's exasperated look until Hilda turned back to the dough she was kneading.

"Invite me to dinner," Minna mouthed.

"At the moment they are not here," her mother said, "though I told them strictly they must be home for *leichtes Mittagessen*. That Texan told them he would teach them how to utter Indian war cries and something he called a 'rebel yell.' I told your father I did not approve, but as usual, he did not listen, so I said they must at least go far enough from the house that my headache would not get any worse."

"Mother, Minna and I can take over the meal preparation while you go and lie down for a few minutes," Erica said, recognizing her opportunity. "You don't mind if she stays for the meal, do you?"

"No, of course not. Minna is a good, dutiful young lady. You would do well to emulate her."

Minna winked.

Just then a wild, undulating yell, mingled with a bloodcurdling whoop worthy of a Comanche brave on the warpath, filled the air, accompanied by the thudding of hooves. It was coming from the end of the road and growing closer.

"What on earth—?" began Minna.

"*Gott in Himmel!*" moaned Hilda, covering her ears. "I told them to do that away from the house."

Erica and Minna reached the front porch just in time to see Hans and Guenther, riding Bruno bareback, come to a skidding halt by the front gate, sending dust flying.

"Ssssh!" Erica admonished, dashing outside with her finger to her lips. "Mutti has one of her headaches!"

It was hard to look stern, though, with Minna giggling beside her, for her brothers made such an amusing picture. Somehow—probably with the red stain of berries and the black of charred wood—they had managed to make warpaint that now decorated their cheeks in bold slashes. They had apparently raided the pen where Vati's geese were kept, for long gray goose quills were stuck in headbands fashioned from scraps of fabric from her mother's ragbag.

"Hello, Minna and Erica! Don't we make fine Indians?" called Hans, who sat behind Guenther on the sweating horse.

"I was giving a rebel yell," announced Guenther. "Wasn't it fearsome? It is to throw fear into the hearts of the Yankees. Jake said so."

"Hmmmph," snorted Erica. "I should think *Herr* Jake would not want to be mimicking the savages who nearly killed him."

"Oh, I don't know," said Jake, emerging from the cloud of dust that had concealed his approach on foot behind the horse. "When they're not actually after my scalp, I can admire the red men as admirable riders and fighters. They're just tryin' to protect what's left of their homeland. And who's this?" he added, catching sight of Minna and smiling politely.

Erica felt her heart speed up as it always did when he smiled. "Minna Wilhelm, I have the honor to present Herr Jake Taylor, our houseguest. Minna is my good friend." Out of the corner of her eye she could see Minna dimpling and blushing as Jake bowed.

"Miss Minna, I am charmed to meet you," he said in that honey-sweet drawl that made Erica's heart melt. "Any friend of Miss Erica's is certainly one of mine too."

Minna knew no English at all, for her parents believed in keeping their culture pure and separated from that of their American neighbors even more fervently than Hilda Mueller did. Erica obligingly translated.

"*Dankë*, Herr Jake Taylor," Minna said, then turned back to Erica and spoke in German. "Oh, Erica, I can see indeed why you're so smitten! He is the most *ansenlich* man I've ever laid eyes on! I vow, if you had not seen him first, and we were not best friends . . ." She let her voice trail off dramatically.

"Minna, it's not a matter of 'seeing him first,' because I have no such ideas, I assure you," Erica said repressively, also in German. "And you're being rude to chatter on like that, since you know he doesn't understand you—though I can imagine he has a good idea what you said, since you're batting your eyelashes around so!" She darted a glance at Jake, whose amused eyes confirmed her guess.

"Boys," she said to her brothers, who by this time had dismounted, "turn Bruno out in the pasture, and wash that paint off your faces before Mutti sees you. And hurry, it's nearly time to eat."

Chapter Ten

Over lunch, Jake had mentioned that he thought he would be well enough to ride on to San Antonio in a couple of days. "After all, I rode around a little on y'all's horse while I was showing the boys how to do the rebel yell, and it didn't hurt—very much, anyway."

It was all Erica could do to keep her face expressionless and stifle an instinctive protest. He couldn't ride out of her life, not so soon!

But Hans had no such restraint. "No, Herr Jake, don't leave!" Hans cried with all the anguish Erica was feeling. "You have not taught us to ride like an Indian yet, and Guenther still can't speak the good English!"

"Herr Taylor, you must not think of endangering your health by premature exertion," Erica's father said, and she could have kissed him for it. "It is a long way to San Antonio, is that not so? Do not be over hasty—you are welcome to stay as long as you need to."

Erica had been telling Minna what Jake said, and Minna cupped her hand around her mouth and whispered back, "No! We can't let him leave, Erica! You two are meant for each other!"

"Hush!" Erica said, hoping she was not blushing yet again. Her friend was such a romantic. Why couldn't she see that such a match would never work?

Jake smiled at each Mueller in turn. "You've all been so kind, but I don't want to overstay my welcome. I reckon it wouldn't make any difference if I stayed till Monday or so, though."

Erica was able to breathe again when she heard that she need not face losing him so soon. She blinked in surprise, realizing he had been with them for five days. It had been Tuesday when she and her father had set out for Vetter Dietrich's house in San Antonio and found Jake instead. How quickly the time had passed!

"Thank you for letting me lunch with your family, Frau Mueller," Minna thanked Erica's mother when Hilda, still pale from the effects of her migraine, descended to bid her good-bye.

"It is I who should thank you, dear Minna, for helping Erica with the making of it, and beg your pardon for not being present. But when I get these migraines, food is the last thing I can bear to think about."

"I hope your headache is better now?"

Hilda admitted it was.

"Then I expect we will see you and the family in church on Sunday, Frau Mueller? Mother has been eager to ask you for your recipe for sauerkraut. By the way, Erica and Hans are coming to the Lutheran Young Peoples' Society's Fishing Party on the Guadalupe tomorrow evening, aren't they? Oh, I'd wager Herr Taylor would enjoy it too, *ja*? He must come too, of course!"

Jake had followed them out to the porch, since Minna was about to depart, and by the slow, deliberate way he paused, then looked around, she could tell he had heard his name mentioned. Erica had been translating Minna's chattering, but she stopped before repeating her friend's last apparently guileless question.

"I—I—" Hilda stammered, turning helplessly towards her husband.

"Hilda, there can be no harm in a fishing party," Gustav Mueller said firmly. "There are always chaperones at these events."

"Oh, good, I was hoping Hans would be able to bait my hooks for me," Minna said before turning to bat her eyelashes at Erica's brother—who turned as red as a beet and grinned at the older girl like a lovesick puppy.

"I want to come too, Mutti!" yelped Guenther, becoming aware that he was not included in the plans, being too young to belong to the Lutheran Young Peoples' Society.

"Ssssh, *meine sohn*, I will take you fishing another time, just you and me," their father consoled him. "This party is for *older* young people."

Erica was stunned at how easily her friend had

managed to maneuver an opportunity for her to go away from the house with Jake. Hardly daring to look at him, Erica told Jake about the proposed party.

"But of course, if such a pastime sounds silly or tedious, you must not feel any obligation to attend," she added politely, all the while praying he would be willing to go.

"I think an evening's fishing on the river sounds wonderful, Miss Erica. Please thank your friend for invitin' me," he said.

"Herr Taylor, *auf Wiedersehen*," Minna said.

Some things needed no translation. "Good-bye, Miss Minna," he said, bowing.

Erica asked Hans to wait a moment before escorting Minna home, so she could speak to her privately, then followed her out to the gate.

"What made you think of that, Minna?" Erica demanded. "You are amazing!"

Her friend laughed triumphantly, shaking her red curls. "Erica, my good friend, it's simple. I can see by the way you gaze at him when he's not looking that you love him, and I think he's very taken with you, too. I think you would make a perfect couple! So we must create an opportunity for you to be alone together, *ist das nicht war?*"

Erica felt excited at the prospect but dubious. "At a fishing party? But how—?"

"There are always opportunities if you look for them," Minna said, waving an airy hand. "I remember now that you had not come to New Braunfels yet when we had the last one. Here's what will happen: Everyone eats together at the picnic, but afterward, when they go down to the riverbank to start fishing, you'll see—the group will break up. The unattached young men will fish with each other while the young ladies who have no sweethearts to bait their hooks will stay up by the picnic tables, pretending to clear the dishes, but all the while discussing the young men. Meanwhile, couples will find their places up and down the banks. Everyone is pretending to fish, but almost no one really is!"

"But what of the chaperones?"

"Pooh! That will be my father and Herr Pfeiffer. Once they start drinking wine and discussing politics, they will forget all about the couples!"

"But what good will it do even if Jake and I do get a chance to speak alone, Minna? You heard him, he's going to leave early next week! And Mutti would never allow—"

Minna interrupted her. "Erica, you must be bold when time is short," Minna said wisely. "You must seize your opportunities!"

Everything—especially love and romance—was so simple to Minna. But Erica had never dared to tell her best friend about her disgrace at the hands of Siegfried, nor why she was so cynical about love. Even Minna, as much as Erica loved her, would look at her differently if she knew, and Minna's parents, Erica was certain, would refuse to let their daughter be contaminated by association with a "fallen woman."

Siegfried, Erica realized with a blinding flash of clarity, was responsible for the hesitation she felt now, her lack of confidence in her own worth.

"But Minna, what if Jake has a sweetheart at

home—or even a wife?" she cried. "He is very charming, but he is that way to everyone, you have seen that!"

"Erica, he wears no ring, nor is there a white line on his finger to indicate where one had been," Minna said. "*Ja*, there could be a sweetheart, but so what?" her friend said with a careless shrug. "She is there and you are here, my dear friend! But I don't think he has one. You said yourself he didn't ask to write a letter, which he certainly would have done if he had had a sweetheart at home!" Minna insisted.

"But Minna—" Erica said, still not completely believing she could do anything to change her destiny.

"Look, Erica, the worst that could happen is that you have a charming escort to the fishing party," Minna reminded her. "And if nothing else, think how envious Gunilla will be!" she said. "Why, she will be green as grass when she sees him with you!"

"Hmmm," Erica said, imagining it, and grinned in spite of herself. "All right, we'll see what happens tomorrow night. But what a sacrifice you're making for me, making Mutti think you want Hans to keep you company at the party and flirting with him so that he thinks so, too. You won't . . . um . . . that is, Hans—" How could she tactfully warn Minna that Hans had been bedazzled by Greta Wagner?

Now Minna looked amused. "And who says it's a sacrifice? Erica, I *do* like your brother Hans. So what if he's a couple of years younger than I? I might be willing to wait for him to grow up. . . ." She winked.

Erica's jaw dropped open. "Minna? You and my brother?"

Minna shrugged, her eyes dancing. "There's no accounting for taste is there? Erica, he's really very sweet, and not at all, um . . . hard to look at. . . ."

Erica blinked at her in surprise. Minna had been sweet on her brother, and she had never suspected it? *Gott in Himmel*, this day was full of surprises!

When Minna started down the road with Hans and Guenther at her side, Erica returned to the house. Jake had apparently gone back upstairs, and she could hear her mother in the kitchen talking to her father.

"What is it, *liebchen?* Is your headache coming back?" her father was saying.

Oh, please don't say you've changed your mind about the fishing party! Erica prayed silently, freezing in place by the door and hardly daring to breathe lest her presence be discovered.

"No, husband. I was only wondering if perhaps I should say a word to Frau Wilhelm?"

"About what?" her father asked, sounding surprised.

"About her daughter. I think Minna was making eyes at that Texan, Gustav. Didn't you see it? Don't you think Frau Wilhelm should be warned to watch Minna?"

Erica could hardly believe her ears. Her mother thought Minna was the one interested in Jake? But that was perfect!

Unless, of course, her mother actually did go and speak to Minna's mother, causing her friend to be unnecessarily reproved and restricted. But Erica's father once again unknowingly came to the rescue.

"I am sure her flirting was harmless fun, wife. Try to relax. Herr Taylor will be gone in a few days, and all will go back to normal."

"And then you and Erica will complete that trip to San Antonio."

"All in good time, wife. All in good time."

Jake, who had gone out on the back porch to contemplate what had just taken place, would have given his eyeteeth to understand German. Erica was always so politely conscientious about translating the conversations so he wouldn't feel left out—except, he suspected, when the talk was about him. And he could definitely tell from the involuntary glances his way that he was the subject of the conversation between Erica and that other young lady—what was her name, Minna? But what had they been saying?

For a moment or two, during the meal, Jake had thought Minna was flirting with him, which had given him a short-lived feeling of unease, for no matter how partial he had used to be to pretty redheads, she couldn't hold a candle to Erica, to his mind.

But then Minna had started batting her lashes at young Hans, and Jake had breathed a sigh of relief. He knew then it was safe to sit back and enjoy the byplay between the youth and the slightly older girl. Hans was a goner, Jake thought with amusement, watching the boy stammer and blush as he and Minna walked off together, totally unaware of his brother's tagging along.

So if Minna were going to be concentrating her feminine wiles on Hans, that would leave the field clear for himself and Erica. . . . Did she want him to woo her? Would she welcome his trying to steal a kiss?

It was harder to read Erica than her flirtatious friend. Though she frequently blushed and ducked her gaze in his presence, for all he knew she might do so around any man besides her father. Erica Mueller was still waters, and everyone knew they ran deep. Tomorrow evening would be interesting, and that was for sure.

He had no idea how she felt about him, and yet he was falling in love with her! What sort of a fool-headed thing was that to do?

If only he could lose himself in physical activity, such as horseracing or wrestling with his friend Bowie, who was now related to him too, since he had married Jake's sister Maria. That's what he had always done before when he'd been uncertain about something. For the first time since he'd been attacked by the Comanches, Jake chafed under the restraint imposed by having busted ribs and one arm in a sling.

Since he had nothing else to do, Jake allowed himself to imagine what it would be like if Erica loved him too.

He reckoned he'd learn German quick enough if they were sharing a pillow, he thought with a grin. But that thought just made him hard and restless, since at the moment he had no way of knowing if his hot, sensual imaginings could ever be more than fantasies. So Jake's thoughts turned to what his family's reactions would be.

He was under no illusion that his father would be happy, at least initially, that his only son had fallen in love with a German girl. Frank Taylor had one opinion about the Germans who had settled in the hill country of Texas and it wasn't complimentary.

"Damned traitors and opportunists, the lot of 'em," he'd grumbled once. "If the South had won the war we'd have hung every manjack that wore blue, and shipped the rest back across the ocean where they belong. Hellfire, they don't even speak English."

But surely he'd thaw towards Erica when he beheld her blue-eyed, golden prettiness and heard the sweet way she hesitated over the *j* in his son's name. After all, the old man had learned to accept Bowie, who had been the son of his overseer, as his daughter's husband, especially since the marriage had already taken place when Maria and Bowie came home from running the cotton to Mexico during the war. Now, to hear Frank tell of it, the marriage had been practically his idea, and his first grandson a chip off the old Taylor block—despite the fact that the boy was the brown-haired, green-eyed spitting image of Bowie.

Maria, who made up her mind with the speed of summer lightning, would love Erica on sight, Jake knew. And his younger sister Kate, well, who knew if Kate would ever get to meet Erica? Jake felt the familiar ache in his heart when he thought of his younger sister, who had been just a coltish girl when he'd last seen her.

Jake was still contemplating the possibilities an

hour later when Hans returned and sought him out.

"Herr Jake—that is, Jake—" he amended hastily when he saw that Jake was about to object to his formality, "how can one tell when one is in love?"

Chapter Eleven

"How can you tell when you're in love?" Jake repeated, to buy himself time to think. He should probably steer Hans to his parents to ask such a big question, but he knew that would embarrass the youth, possibly even leave him feeling shamed.

"Please don't tell me to ask my mother," said Hans, as if he were reading Jake's mind. "She'll just say I'm too young to feel such things and I should work harder at my lessons. But it's summer, Herr Jake, and there are no lessons!"

Jake fought a smile. "But there is Miss Minna," he concluded for the young man. "That *is* who we're talkin' about, isn't it? Or do you have half a dozen sweethearts around this town?"

That drew a grin out of the boy and relaxed his tense shoulders. "I . . . I thought I was in love with this widow who lives in town, Frau Wagner. But I think she was just amusing herself with me, and it is better to love someone closer to my age, *ja*? I speak of Fraulein Minna. Isn't she the most beautiful, entrancing, kindest female that you've ever seen? Her hair is like a glorious fire, *ist das nicht war?*" Hans smiled as he said the words, and then his smile faded and he looked both fierce and worried at the same time. "But perhaps you find her so too, Herr Jake?"

The boy had it bad, all right. He was already worried about losing her. "Oh, she's quite a charmer, Miss Minna is, and yes, that red hair is very pretty, but I'm afraid there's another female who has her brand on my heart, Hans." *Your sister.* Did he dare confide in the boy, ask him if he thought Erica cared about him too? He sensed Hans liked him enough that he would be happy about the matter, but maybe that was just too big a burden for the lad to carry— especially since Jake doubted if the love that was growing in his own heart for Erica Mueller would ever be successful.

"Ah," the boy said, looking wise. "You know about love, *ja?* So how do you know if it is love you feel?"

Jake shrugged. "Well, likin' the way she looks is certainly a start, but you have to love what she *is*— inside, I mean. And you need to feel like you're willin' to die for her, if need be."

Hans pressed a hand to his heart. "Oh, I would, Herr Jake! I would walk through *Holle*—I think that is 'Hell' in English—for her! But do you think one can find the love of one's life at my age?"

Jake wanted to laugh at the boy's earnestness, but he didn't want to injury Hans's youthful, fragile dignity. "Yes, I think it's possible," he said carefully.

"But a man's got to be able to support a wife, you know. Are you prepared to do that?"

Hans's face fell. *"Nein,"* he said, and his shoulders slumped. *"Ach,* there is no hope for me then! Fraulein Minna will fall in love with some fellow who already makes a fine living, like Adel Schwartzwalder or Ludwig Josefson!"

"Now, you're not givin' up that easy, are you?" Jake asked in a bracing tone, remembering how volatile emotions were at that age, how he had felt happy as a pig in a peach orchard one moment and low as a snake's belly the next—all based on whether a girl had smiled on him or ignored him.

"Seems to me if Miss Minna's as fine a female as you think she is, she'd wait a while on you. She's only a couple years older than you, isn't she? Meanwhile, the best thing you can do to get ready to be her husband—or anyone's husband—is to work hard at your lessons so's you'll be ready to earn a living, you see?"

The boy nodded.

"Now, it doesn't always turn out that the one we're sweet on is the one we end up marryin'," Jake cautioned. "At the time they seem like they're the only ones for us, but life has a way of surprisin' us. Sometimes they're just trainin' so we'll be ready to love the right ones, the ones we were meant to be with for the rest of our lives." And sometimes the one a man marries and plans to love forever doesn't love him forever, he thought. His own parents were parted by an ocean of misunderstanding, as well as the Atlantic.

"Oh, I will love Miss Minna always," Hans insisted. "If I cannot marry her, I will remain a *Jungselle,* a bachelor."

"That's what I thought once, too," Jake said, remembering his first heartbreak when Miss Carrie Ann Moorehouse had thrown him over for some wealthy planter in Lousiana who was twice her age. Jake had thought then that he'd never get over his hurt, but now he scarcely remembered what she looked like.

"Well, only time will tell, Hans," Jake told the youth. "Meanwhile, just have fun and enjoy one another's company. Get to know her *mind,* know what I mean? Don't be in a hurry. You gonna kiss her tomorrow night at the fishin' party if you get the chance?"

Hans actually blushed. "Oh, Herr Jake, do you think she would like it?"

Jake allowed himself to grin. "I reckon so, if I'm readin' her right. Just a simple kiss, mind you!" he warned.

Hans blinked and goggled at Jake. "But I would never offer Fraulein Minna any form of dishonor!" he said, shocked.

Jake could tell Hans had very little inkling of the variety of things he could do between that first chaste kiss and actually bedding a woman. Perhaps that widow had only flirted with him, after all. Ah, to be so pure in heart again! His own innocence had ended when his father had paid the overseer to see that his son was introduced to the best whore in Miss Nora's bordello back home in Bryan at the tender age of fourteen. Bowie had gone along too and the boys had strutted around afterward like roosters, smoking cigars and trying to pretend the experience hadn't been the scariest one in their young lives.

"Oh, I'm sure you wouldn't," Jake said at last. "Just take your cue from Miss Minna—she'll find a way to let you know she'd like a kiss."

"Thank you, Herr Jake," Hans said, solemnly offering his hand to shake. "I hope you are right! *Ach*, I can't wait for tomorrow evening."

Jake shook it. That Minna had a bold eye, and she was a little older—young Hans might just receive more than a little peck on the lips if he was lucky.

"I'm lookin' forward to it too, Hans," he said, and meant it. If he had the opportunity, he was going to kiss Miss Erica, too—and try to discover how she felt about him.

You damned fool, nothing has changed, he reminded himself sternly. You preached to the boy about supportin' a wife, but you aren't ready to do that any more than he is—unless you want to give in and do it Papa's way. He knew he couldn't do that, couldn't settle for what Frank Taylor wanted for Taylor Hall. He couldn't bear to give up his dreams and watch the once-prosperous plantation reduced to sharecropping—and that meant making his own way.

Above the porch, Erica smiled to herself as she listened to the kind, wise way Jake was counseling her brother, and fell even more deeply in love with the handsome Texan for his kindness. Did he mean herself when he spoke of a woman having her brand on his heart? She had to believe he did! *Gott in Himmel*, there had to be a way she could show him that she cared about him too, so that he would not want to ride away from her in three days, or if he must leave, so that he would want to come back and brave the wrath of her mother—and possibly of her father too—to claim her!

But even if he were attracted to her—and she rather thought he might be, at least physically—it was very likely he had no such permanent plans, she reminded herself. After all, Siegfried had wanted nothing more from her than satisfaction of his sexual desire. The trouble was that after that first painful time when he had taken her virginity, Siegfried found amusement in teaching her what kisses and caresses would bring pleasure to her.

In his diabolical way, Siegfried had known that in learning how her body could respond to his artful, practiced stroking—both with his hands and with his tongue—she in turn would try even harder to please him. And even long after she knew the truth about his character and hated him for his duplicity, sometimes her body would long for the ecstasy he had taught her to feel. *Damn you, Siegfried.*

Erica let herself dream of the way Jake Taylor would make love. Instinctively, she was certain his way would be better than Siegfried's, so much so that he would make the selfish young noble look like the callowest stripling. She felt her body stir in response to her imaginings, feeling Jake's hands on her breasts, the weight of him pressing her into the bed, his knee nudging her thighs apart. . . .

It was late into the night before Erica Mueller slept.

* * *

The evening was perfect for an outing. A cool wind out of the northwest had swept away any traces of humidity so that the temperature was warm, but there was just enough of a breeze to occasionally stir a ripple or two on the placid green Guadalupe.

"Good Lord, this tops even a Texas barbecue!" Jake exclaimed when he saw the bounty spread out on the tables made by sawhorses and wide planking on the grassy sward above the river.

"We Germans like to eat," Hans agreed with a laugh.

"Miss Erica, you'll have to tell me what all of this is," Jake said. "I like to know what I'm eatin'."

She proudly set down the cucumber salad—a Bavarian specialty—which she had brought.

"This is sauerkraut pie, that is *zwiebelkuchen*—um, that is to say, onion pie. Over there is potato salad, and *sauerbraten*, meat marinated in a sweet and sour sauce, and next to it, *kurbispatete*, a pumpkin and meat pie. Beyond it is *schnizbrot*, or fruit bread, and there is bratwurst and all types of other sausages. . . . The other table is for *Nachtische*—desserts—and I can see *Nougatstangerl* and hazelnut cookies, and *Kalter Hund*, which are biscuits placed one on top of another with chocolate spread in between—"

Jake interrupted her with a groan. "I think I've died and gone to Heaven," he said fervently, making Erica and Minna both laugh.

Erica looked even more like an angel than she had that day when she and her father had rescued him, he thought, even though her hair was still in its usual sensible plait, and her skirt and waist of navy blue cotton trimmed with lighter blue piping was more practical than any plantation belle would consider wearing to a picnic.

Erica made the formal introduction to Minna's father and Herr Pfeiffer, who were serving as chaperones. Neither man spoke English, and both peered suspiciously at Jake after making stiff, correct bows. It was evident that the mayor's wife's gossip had reached even their ears. If Erica noticed the chill in their attitudes, she gave no sign. The graybeards nodded in dismissal and went back to smoking their pipes and drinking dark German beer.

The young people, for the most part, were more friendly. Though few spoke much English, the young men shook his hand amiably, while the girls seemed more inclined to smile shyly or giggle—except for one haughty miss who seemed to keep her nose perpetually in the air.

"That is Gunilla Von Hesselberg, the mayor's daughter," Erica whispered as they stood at the back of the line at the tables, after the pinch-faced girl had snubbed Erica when she attempted to present Jake to her. "I'm sorry she was rude to you. She is very proud."

Jake could not have cared less how the girl treated him, but mentally he consigned her to being staked out on a red ant hill for causing Erica a moment's discomfort. "I can't figure what she has to be proud about," he whispered back, enjoying the excuse to lean down and whisper into the German girl's ear. He thought he smelled lavender.

Erica smothered a chuckle. "Guenther calls her

Fraulein *Farblos*—that means colorless or drab."

Jake grinned back at her and whispered, "No one would ever call *you* that, Miss Erica." He was rewarded by a charming blush and a shy smile.

"*Danke*—thank you, Herr Jake. I think you are very kind."

He'd like to be a whole lot more than kind, he thought. "No more of this 'Herr' stuff tonight, at least when no one else is listening, okay? I'm just Jake."

Her flush deepened and she looked away, then met his gaze. "*Okay*," she said, smiling as she deliberately used the quintessential American word. "Then I am just Erica, *ja?*"

She was so sweet—and lucky, Jake thought, that there were so many other people around, or he would have kissed her right there and then.

"*Ja*," he said, making her smile again at his echoing of the German word in turn.

Chapter Twelve

Jake and Erica started out fishing with Minna and Hans on the grassy bank of a spit of land which was flanked by clumps of reeds and tall cottonwoods, whose branches drooped over the river. It was the perfect fishing spot, Jake told them, for the fish loved to hide among the roots of the trees that protruded into the water—and dusk was the perfect time of day to catch bass, bluegill, or perch, for they rose up to feed when the insects were buzzing low over the tranquil surface of the river.

Jake showed Erica how to cast, and she saw Hans doing likewise for Minna. They fished for a time, casting and drawing their lines in and casting again, rebaiting their hooks when the fish stole their bait. But it wasn't long before Erica saw Minna whispering into Hans's ear.

The next thing she knew, Hans strode over to where Jake was baiting Erica's hook and said shyly,

111

"Minna knows a better spot to fish. You don't mind if I go over there with her, do you, Erica? I don't think she should go by herself."

Oh, I'll just bet she knows a better spot, Erica thought, amused, but kept her face expressionless so as not to embarrass her brother. It seemed Hans had forgotten all about the Widow Wagner! Her mother would be relieved about that, at least.

"That would be all right, Hans. Just keep your ears open to hear when Herr Wilhelm blows the horn to tell us it's time to go home, *ja?* Remember, there are to be prizes for the biggest fish, and the most fish caught."

He nodded, but she could see his mind wasn't on fishing at all.

Jake's blue eyes betrayed his own amusement. "I think your brother's going to learn a lot this evening, but it probably won't have anything to do with fishing," he commented with a chuckle while Erica cast her line yet again.

She was saved from the need to reply, for just then her cork bobber plunged beneath the surface of the water and she felt a mighty tug.

"Oh, Jake, I think I have a big one!" she cried, bracing herself on the bank and gripping the pole more strongly. The cane arched with the force of the pull.

"Easy . . ." Jake said in her ear. "Let him run out with it a bit—let him think he's got it before you jerk back. . . ."

Erica was conscious of her pulse accelerating at the tingling feeling brought on by his nearness, but she was determined not to be distracted and did exactly as he advised. The line played out as whatever had taken her hook darted into open water. Her pole bent still farther.

"*Now*, Erica, now! Start reelin' him in, sweetheart!" Jake exclaimed.

Sweetheart. He had called her sweetheart! She was so happy at the endearment, but she would have to examine that emotion later. Right now she had a fish to land! And Jake had sounded as excited as she felt. It had to be a huge fish! *Ach*, he would be so proud of her!

She bent her knees and began rewinding the line. The heavy weight was still pulling at the other end, struggling. . . . In a moment it would break the surface and they would see what she had caught—

Her catch rose above the water. It was no fish, but a turtle, its clawed feet flailing in the air, water dripping from its oval shell. She had only a split second for the disappointing sight to imprint itself on her brain, and then her line broke and the turtle fell back into the water with a resounding *plosh*.

She was glad that they were somewhat isolated from the rest of the group and no one but Jake would see her embarrassment. She had been so sure she had a prize-winning fish and it was nothing but a *Schildkrote*, a turtle!

"Isn't that always the way," Jake said. "It always seems like it'll be the biggest fish you've ever seen and it turns out to be a turtle, or someone's old boot."

She tried to hide her chagrin. "And I have no more hooks. Vati said I might need an extra one, but I didn't think so. . . . I am no fisherwoman, it seems."

"That's all right, you can hold my pole," he said gallantly. "I haven't had so much as a nibble. Maybe your luck will hold and you'll have another bite. What's wrong?" he asked when he tried to hand his pole to her and saw her expression.

"I . . . You . . . that is, you called me 'sweetheart,' Jake."

He just blinked at her. "I did?"

He didn't remember? Now she wished she hadn't spoken! It had been just a meaningless word uttered in the midst of excitement, something he probably called many women.

"*Ja*, you did, but never mind. You were excited about the fish—which was not a fish. . . ." She felt her face flaming in the gathering darkness, and wished she could just disappear. "I—I . . . perhaps you should continue to hold your pole. I need to go check on Hans. . . ." She began to rise.

Jake laid his pole down and took her hand in his, effectively stopping her.

"I think your brother's doing just fine on his own," he said. "And yes, now that I think about it, I reckon I did call you sweetheart."

It was too dark to see the other fishers up and down the bank, but when she looked back, Erica could see Jake's eyes, intent on her face in the gloom.

"I know it means nothing, it is—what do you call it?—just a pet name?" she said quickly. "You might call your sister such a name, *ja*? Do you have sisters? Oh, but of course, you mentioned you had just visited a sister. Do you have more than one?"

She was babbling, she knew it, but she couldn't seem to help it.

114

He nodded, a small smile playing about his lips. "Two of them, and yes, I might call them that, but I think it meant something more when it slipped out of my mouth about you, Erica."

"I . . . It did?" she murmured, aware that he was lowering his head towards hers.

"Yes . . . I hadn't meant to say anything—I sure don't have any reason to think that you—that I—but that's how I feel, Erica," he whispered, and closed the last few inches between them and kissed her.

It was astonishing how this man, whose face was all hard planes and sharp angles, could have a mouth that was as soft as silk and as smooth as satin. And he knew how to use it, she realized, as his lips played over hers, coaxing, inciting, demanding. When she felt the spark of passion ignite within herself and would have pulled back, he framed her face between his hands and deepened his kiss, so that her instinctive response was to open her mouth and allow him inside. She leaned into him, one of her hands on his shoulder, the other settling somewhere around his waist.

"You taste so sweet," he murmured. "Somehow I knew you would. Oh, *Erica*," he said, and the way he said her name was a caress in itself.

"Jake . . ." she breathed, grateful that night had flung its dark cloak around them and they could not be seen unless someone came looking for them, for she wanted to stay here for a long time, experiencing the delight his kisses gave her. She felt him circle her waist and press her closer to him, and she felt her soft breasts meet his hard unyielding chest.

Jake groaned and Erica felt a surge of triumph, letting herself drift backward onto the grassy bank, wanting him closer, needing him to keep kissing her, aching for him to touch her. . . .

He did not disappoint her. She felt his hand inch up from her waist, shyly at first; then, when she sighed her encouragement, boldly splaying over the underside of her breast, closing over it, his thumb finding her nipple unerringly through her corset—

But just then the rude, unwelcome squawk of a horn intruded itself into their burgeoning passion, startling her, so that she stopped kissing him and began pushing against his chest, knowing the chaperones had deemed it time to go home.

"What . . . what is it, honey? Did I frighten you? I'm sorry, I didn't mean to—"

He was interrupted by shouts in German from down the bank, calling the partiers back.

The moment was incredibly awkward as he helped her to her feet. Erica didn't want to meet his gaze and see the changed way he would surely look at her. If the horn had not put an end to his lovemaking, how much further might she have gone? Would she have given herself to him, right then and there, when anyone could have walked around the reeds and seen them? No, of course not! But she wasn't perfectly certain.

"I'm sorry the time was up so quickly, sweetheart. I was really enjoying that," he murmured.

Her eyes darted upward to his, and she saw no ugly lust there, only tenderness. Dare she trust that to be real, or was he practiced in faking such an emotion?

"I also . . ."

And then Minna and Hans rejoined them and there could be no more private conversation.

Minna's eyes were overbright and tendrils of hair had escaped her braid to curl damply around her face. Hans was flushed and looking anywhere but at Erica or Minna. Erica didn't doubt they had been spending the last hour in the same way as she and Jake had.

"Did you catch anything?" Minna asked, too cheerfully, and for a moment Erica could only goggle at her, wondering what she meant.

"Catch? Oh, a fish?" She ignored Minna's knowing giggle. "No, only a turtle. Then my line broke and Jake was letting me use his pole, but no, we caught nothing," Erica said, and knew she sounded every bit as falsely animated as her friend.

"Neither did we. Oh, well, no prizes for us, then." She didn't sound as if she cared.

They watched while others, more diligent about their fishing, collected their prizes, and then they all left the riverbank together.

"See you in church tomorrow," Minna called after they had escorted her to her home in town.

Most of the partiers lived in town, so it was just the three of them walking in the moonlight to the Mueller house.

Jake strode along in a daze, carrying the pole, wishing he could hold Erica's hand but constrained by Hans's presence. If only the boy would walk on ahead a little! But now that Minna was gone, he seemed determined to be his sister's shadow, so Jake could only think about what had happened on the riverbank.

Who'd have thought his angel would be able to kiss like that, or feel so soft, so perfect in his arms? Jake had known he was attracted to her before tonight, sure, but now he needed to speak to Erica alone, to tell her that he was beginning to fall in love with her and ask her if she felt the same. And if she admitted that it was, as he was almost certain she would, he would make sure she was willing to give up her world for his.

He'd have to leave her for a little while, he'd explain. He had to go on to San Antonio so he could pick his friend John's brain about setting up his own horse-raising operation. While he was there, he'd write Maria and see if he could enlist her aid in getting Papa to accept the marriage, too—but if Erica was willing, he was going to marry her with or without the old man's approval!

He couldn't even seem to catch Erica's eye to try and convey his feelings. She seemed suddenly shier in his presence than she ever had before, and walked along with her eyes on the path ahead of them or on Hans. Was she ashamed of the ardent way she had responded to his lovemaking?

Lord, he hoped not! It seemed like a miracle that he had found a woman who looked like a heavenly messenger but kissed like a man's perfect dream of a woman.

Mr. Mueller opened the door as soon as they stepped onto the porch, which told Jake he had been watching for them.

"Good night, Herr Taylor," Erica said, and kissed her father before heading off toward her bedroom.

Surely he would get an opportunity sometime tomorrow to speak to her alone. He had to, for he had said he was leaving the next day!

Towards that end, Jake accompanied the family to church the next morning, even though he sensed Erica's mother would much prefer that he remain at home and not remind the community that the Muellers had been harboring a devil Texan—though with that old biddy the mayor's wife reminding everyone in New Braunfels, it wasn't likely they'd forget.

Naturally he understood not a word of the seemingly interminable service, so Jake figured God would understand that he'd have to meditate instead on Erica. Seated at the far end of the pew with the entire family between herself and him—Hilda Mueller had seen to that—his angel was resplendent in a pink gingham dress with a wide bow of rose satin that emphasized her slender waist and the breasts he had touched only the night before.

Forgive me my lustful thoughts, Lord, please. I'm going to marry that girl just as soon as I can.

He bowed his head when everyone else did and stood when everyone else did, and stood respectfully when they sang unfamiliar hymns, and finally the service was over and everyone was marching outside into the sunlight.

Just as at his church at home, everyone milled around outside in the churchyard, visiting with their neighbors.

Now was his chance! He'd take advantage of the

confusion to speak with Erica. He might not get a chance the rest of the day, and he couldn't count on getting it tomorrow before he departed.

"Erica!" he called softly as she was returning to her family after speaking to one of the other girls who'd been at the fishing party.

He succeeded in capturing only her attention.

"Yes, Herr Taylor?" she said, formal again in this setting.

"I—I need to speak to you. Is there somewhere here where we can speak alone?"

She looked surprised, but Jake thought he saw a flicker of pleasure cross her features at his question. He saw her look around the milling crowd, seeing as he did that her parents were engaged in conversation with the Wilhelms and her brothers were elsewhere.

"The *Friedhof*—that is, the place where there are graves," she said, jerking her head to indicate behind the church. "You go first, and I will follow in a moment, *ja?*"

He nodded to show her he understood, then set off in that direction.

Chapter Thirteen

Erica forced herself to chatter with Minna about the pastor's wife's new hat, a monstrosity with false flowers and a stuffed nightingale, before finally giving the excuse that she must go and round up Guenther and Hans. Her parents wanted to go home, she said, and the boys had wandered off. She was pleased at how nonchalant she sounded. There was no chance Vati and Mutti would be ready to go yet, of course; this was the one time Hilda Mueller permitted herself time to catch up on the town happenings, and Erica's father always liked to discuss some point of the sermon with Pfarrer Emsch, the pastor.

She had almost reached the corner of the building when a female voice called out, "Erica, there's someone who wants to see you!"

It was Gunilla Von Hesselberg, the mayor's daughter. Standing on the church steps in her expensive dress of Prussian blue *crepe lisse*, Gunilla beckoned to Erica.

Surprised that the haughty Gunilla would deign to notice her, let alone call her to her side, Erica wished nonetheless that she hadn't heard her summons. Jake was waiting! But there was no polite way to ignore the mayor's daughter, and in any case, she was curious as to whom Gunilla was referring. There wasn't anyone standing next to her. Erica couldn't believe that Jake would have enlisted Gunilla's aid, so why was she being so secretive?

"Good afternoon, Gunilla, that's a pretty dress you're wearing," Erica said pleasantly. "Someone wants to see me?"

The other young woman jerked her head towards the inside of the church. "Inside. This person wishes to surprise you."

Erica was more than a little annoyed at Gunilla's making a drama of the matter, but she supposed it would be easier and quicker to play along than to protest. She followed Gunilla back inside the church, passing through the shadowy nave before reaching the sanctuary, which was lit by the noon sun streaming through the stained glass.

At first she had difficulty discerning anyone standing there, for the man had chosen to wait in the shadowy corner between the last multicolored window and the forward-facing pews of the choir.

"*Guten Tag*, Erica," said a voice she had never expected to hear again, and Siegfried Von Schiller stepped into the light.

For a mind-freezing moment she convinced herself he was a hallucination, that she was still asleep and was in the midst of a nightmare. But then he took another step or two forward and she could smell the Hungary Water scent Siegfried had always used, and she knew he was all too real.

"Wh-what are you doing here, Siegfried?" she said, trying desperately to keep the tremor from her voice. He mustn't know she was afraid.

Siegfried turned slightly and directed his voice towards Gunilla. "Fraulein Von Hesselberg, thank you so much for bringing about this joyous reunion. I'm sure you will understand that Fraulein Mueller and I have much to say to each other, *ja?* Ah, I knew you would," he said as the other woman took the hint and started towards the nave. "And if you would be so kind, shut the door behind you?"

"Certainly, *mein Graf.*"

Erica wanted to cry out, *No, Gunilla, don't go! Don't leave me alone with this man!* But the warning in Siegfried's brown eyes assured her such a request would not be wise. Gunilla would be wildly curious about how the young noble and Erica knew each other, but it would be worse to let her remain and hear what Siegfried would say.

"I said, what are you doing here, Siegfried?" she repeated when the door creaked shut again. "In Texas?"

"Can't you believe that I have romantically journeyed across the sea to find you again, my lost sweetheart?" Siegfried purred. Coming closer, he paused, studying her. "*Ach*, but I see you are skeptical." He clucked in mock-disapproval. "When did you become so distrustful, my golden dove?" He spread his arms wide as if in innocent protest.

123

"When I learned what kind of man you really were," Erica said levelly, and backed up. "Were there no innocent virgins left in Regensberg to seduce?"

Siegfried pursed his lips. "Who would have thought you would have grown so hard, so unforgiving? I am here because I realized what a mistake I made. I have moved Heaven and earth to discover where you went, Erica."

"I don't believe you," she said. "I must return to my family." She turned as if to go, and in that instant he closed the distance between them and a restraining hand clamped around her wrist.

"All right, all right," he said with a merry laugh, as if she had been teasing him by pretending to leave. "The truth is, my father has exiled me for political plotting against the government. Ah, dear Erica, I never could keep any secrets from you."

Erica yanked her arm loose and laughed derisively. "What complete and utter nonsense, to use a polite word for it! May I express the hope you are just passing through? I cannot imagine what would keep you in such an unsophisticated backwater as New Braunfels. I would guess there are plenty of impressionable maidens in Fredericksberg, or for one of your high ambition, why not go to Austin or even farther north? I'd wager the American ladies would be charmed by your courtly manners and Old World accent. Now, if you will excuse me, I really must g—"

He went on as if she had not indicated a desire to leave. "From what I have seen, New Braunfels is a charming little hamlet! I believe I will stay here, at least for a time. The townspeople I have met seem quite impressed at having one of the nobility among them, and express themselves honored to offer me lodging until I have found housing suitable to my station. Ah, think how wonderful it will be, my Erica—we can begin where we left off," he said, and attempted to put his arm around her and draw her close.

Shaking with fury, Erica evaded his grasp and put a pew between them.

"Not if you were the last man on earth and I the last woman," she hissed.

He tssk-tssked again. "Erica, my love, by fleeing across the world, you think to have cleansed the stain from your name—"

"A stain you put there, you heartless libertine," she snapped.

"Everyone here knows you as a virtuous *fraulein*, is that not so? I see no reason why, if we are discreet in our meetings, why that could not continue. . . . But refuse me," he said, lowering his voice to a snarl as he leaned across the pew toward her, "and I will tell everyone that you are nothing but a whore, trying to pass herself off as a virgin when in truth you are damaged goods."

She gasped at his threat. "You are evil incarnate, Siegfried Von Schiller! But say whatever you wish to whomever you wish! I crossed an ocean to get away from you and what you did to me. Go ahead and tell the world. I no longer care."

His eyes glittered and his mouth, which she had once thought so sensually appealing, tightened in an ugly line. "But what of your good parents and your brothers, Erica? Is that fair to them? Think of the shame I can bring upon the name of Mueller if you remain obstinate. . . ."

Erica felt tears of rage stinging her eyes, and her hand itched to slap that smug face. Instead, she turned to walk away from him. "I am going back outside now. Leave me alone." She prayed that Siegfried would not dare to follow her and that Jake was still waiting for her behind the church.

"I don't think so," Siegfried snapped, vaulting the pew. He yanked her against him, his hands grabbing her wrists and forcing them behind her. Even as she struggled to free herself, his mouth descended on hers and forced her lips apart.

Erica did the only thing she could do, clamping her teeth down as hard as she could on his invading tongue.

Siegfried uttered a hoarse cry, swiping at his mouth. *"Whore!"* he yelled, then backhanded her, sending Erica reeling into the pew in back of her.

He shoved her down onto it, his hand reaching for the neckline of her dress. "You shrew, go ahead and fight! I'll take you right here! It will be all the sweeter—"

Before he could carry out his threat, however, a roar of rage erupted from the doorway and six feet of enraged Texan launched himself at Erica's attacker.

"Jake, no!" Erica shrieked. Jake's arm was already in a sling, he had broken ribs—Siegfried would only injure him further. He might even be carrying a derringer or a dagger!

Jake paid no heed to her cry. The first blow landed with a sickening thud and Siegfried's nose sprayed blood, but Jake didn't stop with that. Taking full advantage of the element of surprise and using only his uninjured arm, he rained blow after blow on the shrinking, shrieking Siegfried until at last the German noble covered his head and rolled under a pew in an effort to escape his tormenter.

"You—you barbarian, I shall have you arrested!" Siegfried threatened in English, his accent even thicker than Erica's. He rubbed his bloody nose on his sleeve and glared at Jake, though one eye was already swelling shut.

"For what, stopping a rape in a church?" Jake growled, his chest heaving from his exertion. "Don't you ever bother this lady again, or—"

"Lady?" Siegfried unwisely retorted with an ugly laugh as he began to clamber ungracefully out from his hiding spot. "Erica Mueller? One doesn't refer to one's former *Geliebt*—how do you say it—mistress?—as a *lady*."

That did it. Jake hauled Siegfried to his feet and slugged him, knocking the other man over the pew he had been using as shelter and into the next row.

Siegfried landed with a thud, his arms and legs sprawling. He groaned, his eyes rolling upward until only the whites showed, and then his lids shuttered over them.

Panting, Jake leaned over and felt for a pulse on Siegfried's neck. Then he straightened, turning back to Erica, who could hardly believe what she had just seen.

"Are you all right, Erica?" he asked, coming close but not touching her, as if she might shatter with the slightest handling.

Erica's body shook, as if she had an ague, as the adrenaline drained from her. She attempted to put her hair to rights and smooth her crumpled dress, but at Jake's concerned tone, the tears she had been holding back with all her remaining strength burst through, and she collapsed against him, sobbing.

"Ah, *mein Gott*, I th-thought I had escaped h-him, that I need never see him again!" What must Jake be thinking of her, finding her trying to fend off Siegfried's forcible advances, and then hearing her attacker's claim that she had been his mistress?

However chivalrously Jake had defended her, he would never look on her with respect or caring again. She could not bear to see in his eyes how she had fallen in his estimation.

"Ssssh, hush now," Jake soothed. "You're safe. He won't dare to hurt you again. Here," he said, letting go of her a moment to fumble awkwardly in his pocket to bring out his handkerchief. "He's out cold," he said shortly. "Wipe your eyes so we can walk out of here without anyone else bein' the wiser, okay? Do you think you can do that, sweetheart? Let's get out of here before the bastard—excuse my language—wakes up. He won't be stupid enough to follow, looking like that."

He still called me 'sweetheart,' she marvelled. But that was just his innate gentlemanliness speaking, Erica warned herself.

They had been naïve to hope that they could leave the church unnoticed. Both had forgotten that the lower section of the windows had been open because of the summer heat, allowing the sounds of the altercation to carry beyond the sanctuary and into the churchyard. And if the noise hadn't been enough, Gunilla Von Hesselberg's inability to keep a juicy bit of gossip would have guaranteed the audience who ringed the steps, goggle-eyed, when Jake and Erica emerged into the sunlight.

"What is going on?" demanded Pfarrer Emsch, the pastor, in German. "We heard shouting, and sounds of a struggle! I need not tell you, Fraulein Mueller and—" he peered over his half-spectacles at Jake, but obviously couldn't place him—"whoever you are, that such behavior isn't seemly in a house of God!"

Erica caught sight of her parents' and Minna's horrified faces while she translated for Jake's benefit. From somewhere her brothers had reappeared and were watching the proceedings curiously. She made herself look away and took a deep breath to calm herself. There would be hell to pay when they reached home, but she couldn't worry about that now.

"My apologies, sir, but Herr Taylor was not at fault. You see, I was accosted in the sanctuary by a-an ... old acquaintance ... and when he would have pressed unwelcome attentions on me, Ja—Herr Taylor—came to my aid."

"Tell him if he doesn't believe you," Jake added, as if he guessed what Erica had said, "he can go see the buzzard bait I left in there."

Pastor Emsch understood a little English. Blinking at Jake suspiciously, he muttered a command to one of his deacons, who slipped past him and went into the building.

Everyone waited in frozen silence under the hot

noonday sun, and then the mayor's wife cleared her throat importantly and said, "My daughter tells me a newcomer, Count Siegfried Von Schiller, approached her and requested he be taken to Fraulein Mueller, who is apparently a former . . . ahem! shall we say, sweetheart—" she filled the word with sinister meaning—"of Fraulein Mueller's back in the Fatherland. Can it be that this . . . this *American* who has been staying with the Muellers—despite my warning that he would cause trouble, I might add— saw a rival in this noble from our own country?"

The whispering, which had been a low buzz when Jake and Erica emerged, began again around the churchyard, only to be silenced by the deacon's reappearance.

The deacon whispered into the pastor's ear.

"I—I do not know what to say," the pastor said at last. "Diakon Braun says there is a stranger lying unconscious in our sanctuary. He appears to have been beaten. Clearly, we can do nothing but succor him until he comes back to his senses and we are able to hear what he has to say." His gaze fell on Erica and Jake again, and now his face was stern and disapproving toward both of them.

"Herr Pfarrer, in the interim, may I take my family home?" Erica's father asked. "My wife is understandably distressed, and I would speak with my daughter." He did not look at Erica as he spoke, a fact which made Erica's heart sink with foreboding. She looked at Jake, but he kept an expressionless profile to her. Minna was trying to get her attention, but what could she say to her?

"I suppose that would be wise, Gustav," the minister said at last. "I will speak with you when all has come to light." He cleared his throat and turned to Jake as another man came forward, a man Erica knew to be Herr Froebel, constable of New Braunfels. Apprehension stroked her spine with icy fingers.

"I'm certain you will understand, Herr Taylor," the minister said, "that until the gentleman recovers, you must be detained in our jail. Until he awakens, we have no way of knowing that you have not dealt him a fatal injury."

Jake was going to jail because of helping her? "No, surely that's not necessary! He was just defending me!" Erica cried, but everyone, including Jake, ignored her.

Jake bristled as the constable stepped forward and took hold of his left upper arm, but he did not resist. "All right, I'll go, but that fool isn't going to die. If I'd meant to kill him, he'd be dead." He descended the steps with the constable still holding his arm, then stopped and turned back to Erica.

"You go ahead home, Miss Erica," he said in a low voice. "I'll be there as soon as I can."

Chapter Fourteen

"Boys, take the horse to the barn and unhitch him," ordered Gustav Mueller, who had not said a word all the way home, as he helped his pale-faced wife down from the wagon. "You will remain there while I speak to your sister. I will come for you when we are done talking."

"But Vati—" began Guenther, looking from Erica to his father and back again. Clearly, he hadn't understood any of it.

Hans had grasped more of the matter. "Vati, you heard Herr Jake—he was just defending our sister!"

"And anyway, I'm hungry!" added Guenther plaintively.

"I have given you instructions, my sons," Gustav said in that commanding voice he so rarely used. "Go and carry them out, and remain there until you are told differently. Do you understand?"

"Yes, Vati," they said in unison, and Erica was left

133

alone with her parents. She followed them inside the house and into the parlor, her legs feeling like jelly.

Gustav helped his trembling wife into a chair and turned back to Erica.

"Daughter, what do you have to say for yourself?" he asked. His face was impassive. His voice was that of a stranger.

"Herr Taylor told the truth," Erica said, surprised at how steady her voice remained. "Gunilla told me someone was waiting to speak with me inside the church. She did not say who it was, but when I went in, Siegfried was there. He said we would begin our relationship again, that we would be discreet," she said, and now she hesitated as she remembered the count's lecherous eyes stripping her bare. She stared down at the worn carpet rather than at her father. "I tried to be . . . polite but firm, to . . . to indicate that I—I . . . had no intention of repeating past mistakes. . . . He . . . he tried to f-force himself upon me. As I said, Herr Taylor came to my rescue. If he had not, I believe that scoundrel Von Schiller would have ravished me right there in the sanctuary."

Hilda Mueller shrieked and fainted, sagging in her chair. While Gustav uselessly chafed his wife's limp hands, Erica reached into her mother's reticule and brought out the smelling salts she knew would be there.

In a moment, her mother coughed and sputtered her way back to consciousness, then began weeping as she stared at Erica. Her father had paled, and there was a shadow behind his eyes, but he straightened and faced Erica again.

"So you see, Vati," Erica continued, keeping a

wary eye on her mother, "Jake Taylor only tried to help me. He should be thanked and held blameless."

"Providing Von Schiller recovers from the beating he administered, we will see," her father said. "However, we are now in an untenable position, daughter, and we must do something or, rightly or wrongly, you will be shunned in any German community, and your family along with you. Therefore, tomorrow, we will resume our journey to San Antonio. You will allow Rudolph Schoenbrunn to court you, and once he has proposed marriage, you will wed him as soon as a decent wedding can be arranged. He has always been fond of you, and he will make you a steady husband." He stared at some point above Erica's head while he spoke.

Now Erica was sure she was caught up in a nightmare.

She opened her mouth to speak, but her father held up a hand. "Daughter, we are left with no other choice."

Her mother moaned and clutched at her smelling salts. "Gustav, you had better leave today, this very hour! Erica must become betrothed before your cousin Dietrich catches wind of the gossip about her—which will surely be flying on the wings of the wind!"

She couldn't, *wouldn't*, agree to this! "Vati, no! I am not going to San Antonio, and I will not marry Rudolph now any more than I would have before today!"

"Erica, there is no point in arguing! Your father is right—there is nothing else we can do!" her mother cried. "Now your disgrace has followed you across the ocean, and it will ruin us all! You must marry Rudolph!"

"Mutti, I love you, but I will not do it," Erica said. "I like Rudolph well enough, but not enough to be his wife. And why would it be right to involve him in this scandal? He does not deserve it! I will marry no one! This is America and you cannot force me!"

"Erica, you will not disobey your mother!" thundered her father. "Go to your room and meditate upon your disobedient spirit! And do not think to try and slip out, my girl," he added as Erica jumped to her feet. "I will be watching the door—and the yard."

Her back rigidly straight, Erica marched up the stairs and shut the door of her room behind her. *Gott in Himmel,* what was she going to do? If she went to any other German settlement—Fredericksberg, one of the smaller towns such as Comfort, or the German section of San Antonio—the gossip would follow her.

Wherever she went, she would have to find some way to support herself, such as becoming a seamstress, or teaching, or minding other families' children, but once they heard what had happened to her, who would patronize her business or hire her? That left her with no honorable options. And if she went to an Anglo town in Texas—or anywhere in the South—wouldn't she be viewed with suspicion as a foreigner, one of the hated breed who had fought for the other side in the recent civil war? Did she have the courage to journey all the way to some northern city, alone?

She could not look to Jake to rescue her again. He had done the chivalrous thing, but now that he knew that she was soiled goods, he would be only too eager to depart as he had planned, as soon as he was released from the jail!

She heard low voices below her as her parents discussed the situation, and then the sounds and smells as her mother prepared the midday meal. Through her open window she heard the back door close and saw her father walk out to the barn to bring in the boys.

Now was her chance. There was no one guarding the front door. If she wished, she could dash out the front door and have a head start before they realized she was missing. But with no time to pack and prepare, where could she go? Even if she reached Minna's house, her best friend's parents would likely refuse her entry. And what could Minna do to help her anyway?

She heard her brothers' noisy entry into the kitchen, and not long afterward, their chatter and the clatter of dishes as they ate. Her empty stomach rumbled in protest, yet she wasn't hungry.

Erica waited until her brothers had once more left the house for some boyish pursuit, then washed her face, rebraided her hair, and descended the stairs. She found her parents sitting on the back porch, her mother mending a rip in a pair of Hans's trousers, her father pretending to read some thick tome though his eyes stared, unfocused, straight ahead.

She cleared her throat and saw her father start.

"Vati, Mutti, I have decided what I am going to do. Please don't try to change my mind."

Her father stood and set his jaw. "That depends upon your plan, daughter. I am your father, and the head of this house."

She trembled within at the prospect of defying the man she had always loved and revered, but she had to do it. She would not accept an arranged marriage to Rudolph Schoenbrunn or anyone else.

"I am going to leave. I will go to some northern city—Chicago perhaps, or Philadelphia—I don't know where, but somewhere far away. I will adopt another name so that Siegfried Von Schiller can never trace me. I will become a governess. I do not doubt some wealthy American would hire a governess who could teach his children a foreign language. Naturally I will write to you, but if you do not write back, I will understand."

She had managed to deliver her speech without stammering, but now her heart sped up as she waited for her father's reply. Her mother, she knew, would remain silent until he had delivered his opinion.

"I will not permit such a thing," he said, not raising his voice, but his tone was steely. "I love you, daughter, but before I would countenance such an action, I would keep you locked in your room and you would have nothing to eat but bread and water. As your father, I know what is best."

Erica had expected such an answer, and she was prepared. "And how do you think that would protect the Mueller name? The family would be shunned all the same."

"It does not matter," her father replied. "I will do what is necessary."

"You cannot watch me twenty-four hours a day," Erica pointed out. "At some time I will escape and run away."

Her father's shoulders sagged. "This is my fault," he said wearily. "I have spared the rod, and this is the result."

"No, Vati, no . . ." Erica said, her heart wrenching at the pain she saw on his beloved face. She crossed the room to him, intending to throw her arms around him, not knowing if he would push her away or not, but before she could do so, her mother spoke.

"No, husband, it is mine," Hilda Mueller said, letting the forgotten trousers slide to the plank flooring as she stood. "Bad blood will always tell, they say. I have passed the taint along to my daughter. What I have done, she has done."

"No, wife, don't—" Erica's father began, but Hilda Mueller silenced him with a look. He walked around Erica and took his wife into his arms, his shoulders shaking.

Erica stared at her mother in bewilderment. What was she talking about?

Hilda turned until she was facing Erica within her husband's arms. "God knows I have tried to keep you from making the same mistake I did. But as I said, it must be something in the blood I have passed to you."

"Wh-what are you saying, Mutti?"

"Hilda, are you sure this is wise?"

Hilda gently freed herself from Gustav's embrace, though she retained one of his hands in hers. "I think she must know the truth, so that she will see why she must obey us in the matter of her future."

She met Erica's gaze now, her features pale but resolute. "I was pregnant when I married Gustav, Erica. He is not your father by blood, though he has been your father in every way that matters throughout your life. He has been such a good husband to me, Erica, and always referred to you as 'our daughter,' and he has never thrown my sin up at me, not even when he was angry."

Erica's eyes flew to Gustav Mueller. He was not her father? "Who—"

Her mother closed her eyes and shook her head. "It does not matter, Erica. He is long dead—he died in some senseless duel while I was still carrying you within me, though I do not delude myself that he would have married me had he lived. He was . . ." Her mother's voice faltered here, and she looked away. "Like Siegfried, he was of the nobility, and had seduced me out of boredom."

"Mutti," Erica cried brokenly. So much was clear now, especially her mother's sternness and occasional depression. She took her mother in her arms and held her, stroking her back, and felt her mother's rigid backbone finally give as she allowed her daughter to hold her while she wept.

Erica couldn't even begin to fathom the idea that she was really illegitimate, a bastard, and did not carry Gustav Mueller's blood at all. Her brothers were only her half brothers. But there would be time to think of all that later.

"Sssh, Mutti, it was a long time ago. You couldn't help it. You are human, as I am."

Over her mother's shoulder she faced the man she

140

had always known as her father, and saw the un-
guarded fear in his eyes now, and it made her heart
ache.

"You are still 'Vati' to me," she said to him. "You
are the only father I have ever known, or ever want
to know. I love you."

Gustav Mueller let out a gusty breath and put his
arms around Erica and his wife, and for a moment
they all just hugged one another.

"Thank you for telling me the truth, Mutti," Erica
said at last, releasing them. "I know it could not have
been easy."

Her mother's eyes were red-rimmed and swollen.
"Then you see why you must obey Gus—y-your father, Erica, and marry Rudolph. He loves you, and
he has chosen wisely. Rudolph will make you a good
husband, just as Gustav has always been to me."

It was so tempting to give in and agree. It would
comfort her mother, and it would assure her father
that she had meant what she said about still thinking
of him as her father and loving him. But she couldn't
do it.

"I'm happy that such an arrangement worked for
you, Mutti. My father—and of course I mean you,
Vati—is a good, honorable man, and I'm sure your
choices were limited back in the Old Country. But
don't you see that what you are proposing—to
marry me off before Rudolph is any the wiser—is
dishonest? And there's no guarantee that he's as
good and honorable a man as my father, that he
would not repudiate me if he found out, or remind
me that I was a fallen woman every time I did the

least thing to displease him. And most importantly, while Rudolph seems to be a nice fellow, I do not love him and never could."

"Then we will keep looking until we find such a man for you, daughter," her father said stoutly.

Erica shook her head. "No, Vati. It will not work. And since staying in New Braunfels or anywhere in Texas that is predominantly settled by our people means shame and disgrace, I must do as I said and leave."

"That is not the only option, you know," said another voice.

142

Chapter Fifteen

Jake watched as all three Muellers whirled to face him. He wasn't surprised by the traces of tears in Erica's and her mother's eyes. As he'd rounded the corner of the house, he had heard them talking, and of course he hadn't understood what they were saying, but any fool could guess what they were talking about. He'd caught the words "New Braunfels," "Texas," and "Rudolph," though—who was Rudolph? Any idiot could comprehend that powerful emotions heated their voices.

He was actually relieved to find them still here. He'd been half afraid of finding the Mueller place deserted because they'd already fled for parts unknown.

He was heartened to see the desperate, leaping hope in Erica's eyes when she saw him, despite the way she tried to keep it from showing.

Hilda Mueller bristled and advanced on him. "You! How dare you show your face here?"

So the woman did speak some English! He'd suspected she understood more than she let on.

"Hilda, be quiet," Gustav Mueller said, placing a hand gently on his wife's shoulder and drawing her to himself. "Herr Taylor—"

"Mr. Mueller, I've been released," Jake said, to answer the first and most obvious question in the older man's eyes. "That sidewinder Von Schiller finally came to, and when he did, he didn't seem inclined to press charges. I don't doubt he means to make mischief, though, in some other, less open way. That's the way snakes behave, and he's a snake, through and through."

"Upon that, we can agree," Mueller said stiffly. "But—"

"But what did I mean, there is another option? Easy. *I* can marry Erica. I want to marry her, Mr. and Mrs. Mueller."

Erica's cry of astonishment was swallowed in her mother's gasp of outrage. "Never, as long as I draw breath, will I allow my daughter to make such a . . . such a bad match! It is *unerhört* that you come here and say such a thing!"

Jake looked to Erica for enlightenment.

"It means 'outrageous,' " she said miserably.

Jake knew it would be her father, and not her mother, whom he needed to persuade—before he worked to win Erica herself over, of course. She would cast the final and most important vote in the matter. Therefore he transferred his gaze to Gustav Mueller.

"Mr. Mueller," he said, careful to keep his voice respectful and reasonable, "I'm prepared to marry her right here, right now. Call the preacher and see if I'm not serious. Or if you'd rather she have a traditional wedding, I'll wait for that, and get my father to come, and my sister and brother-in-law, depending on how soon you want to have the ceremony. It's up to you."

Jake saw that Mueller was about to speak, and from the set of the other man's jaw, he knew he'd better say something more to bring the man over to his side.

"The moment you agree, nothing that Von Schiller can say will matter. She'll be my wife, a married lady, and I will keep her from any form of disrespect."

"And you would carry her away from here, away from the culture and heritage she knows, to live among the Texans," Mueller said. "I believe you are not a bad man, Jacob Taylor, and you mean what you say. But despite what has happened to her at Siegfried Von Schiller's hands, Erica has grown up knowing only this heritage, and I am convinced that she does not understand the implications of leaving her roots. I believe she would be desperately unhappy."

"Mr. Mueller, I'm not proposing to take her to the ends of the earth!" Jake cried. "Taylor Hall's a fair piece from here, sure, but I'm not even positive I'm going to live there when all is said and done. Maybe we could settle near here. Even before I came here I was plannin' to see about doing something else—"

The information didn't seem to soothe Mueller— just the opposite. "*Ach*, so you would think I would allow you to take our Erica off to some uncertain existence? *Nein,* Herr Taylor, I believe I know what is best for our Erica."

Jake took a deep breath. "I know this may be an American notion, but why don't you ask Erica what *she* wants?" He'd seen her brighten as he'd talked, and he was convinced she was willing to take him up on his offer. He'd make her glad she did if it was the last thing he ever accomplished in his entire life!

"I mean no disrespect," Mueller began again, "and I appreciate the generosity that motivates your offer, but Erica will marry a German man of good family, not some . . . some *cowboy* with no means to support her!"

Jake reluctantly realized there was no changing the other man's mind. He'd just have to use another strategy to achieve his goal. What mattered was what he saw in Erica's eyes, that she was agreeable to marrying him. He'd work on having her fall in love with him later.

He looked into her eyes—those beautiful, luminous blue eyes—one more time before letting his shoulders sag in apparent resignation.

"All right. I can see that you only want what's best for your daughter, and you don't believe I'm the man who can provide it." He tried to ignore the shocked disappointment in Erica's gaze, to send her a message from his heart to hers: *Hold on, Erica, believe in me. I'm not giving up.* But he could see from the way she averted her chin that she hadn't heard the cry of his soul.

"I'll . . . be leavin' immediately, then. Just let me gather up my things and I'll be on the road as soon as I've done so. Miss Erica, whatever you end up doin', it was my privilege to make your acquaintance—and that goes for all of you. Please tell the boys I'll miss talkin' to them."

"I will do so," Gustav Mueller said. "Thank you for understanding, Herr Taylor. Our ways are not your ways, and I do not expect you to embrace them. Erica, you will remain on the porch with us until Herr Taylor has departed."

Jake edged past them to go upstairs to pack his belongings. He'd have to walk into town and hope there was a livery stable, or someone who would let him hire a mount. At least the Comanches hadn't taken the money he'd been carrying.

Before he departed he'd find some way of leaving a message for Erica so she would know the situation wasn't hopeless, that she had a way out—assuming she wanted it.

Erica had slept, but it was not a sound, restful sleep, and so she felt gritty-eyed and hollow while she watched her father hitching up the bays for the long journey to San Antonio. Her parents had been astounded but relieved when, after supper, she had announced that she had decided they were right: She should and would marry Rudolph Schoenbrunn, if he offered for her, and she would be willing to have her father arrange another match for her in the unlikely event he did not. Her mother had wept with joy; her father had patted her on the hand and told her she was doing the right thing and making him proud.

It had been harder to tell her brothers, especially

since they didn't fully understand what had happened after church, or why it wouldn't do for Erica to choose to live, unmarried, in their parents' house forever. Guenther had cried unashamedly, even though Erica had promised them she would come visit and they would visit her after she became a wife and had her own household. Hans had struggled manfully against tears, but one or two had escaped down his flushed cheeks and she had pretended not to notice when he surreptitiously swept them away.

She felt guilty to be deceiving them all, but surely a little guilt was better than a lifetime of misery if she married a man she could not love.

Erica did not deceive herself that Jake loved her—he couldn't, not after what had come to light about her past. He was offering to marry her out of a generous, chivalrous impulse, and if she had not loved him already, she would have loved him for that alone.

It would not matter that he did not really love her, Erica told herself. She loved him enough for both of them, and would make his sacrifice worthwhile by being the best wife any man could have. She would make sure he never had reason to regret marrying her.

Jake, mounted on one of his two rented horses, was waiting for them around the curve of a mesquite-and cactus-covered limestone hill about five miles north of town.

Gustav Mueller called out some German version of "whoa" and pulled his matched bays to a halt. He had to—Jake had positioned his mount plumb in the middle of the rutted road.

"*Guten morgen*—that is, good morning, Herr Taylor," Mueller called out. "I am surprised to see you here. I believed you would be most of the way to San Antonio by now."

Erica looked pale but composed, Jake noted, in her traveling dress of serviceable beige cotton. He liked her better in blue, he thought. He'd have to make sure her wedding dress had touches of blue in it.

"I would have been well on my way to San Antonio," he said. "But I've decided I'm not going there, after all. Instead, I'm taking Erica and we're going to get married."

He let his words sink in for a moment, watching the older man's eyes widen in surprise. He hoped Mueller was going to give in gracefully.

"Uh-uh, I wouldn't do that," Jake said, reluctantly pulling out the pistol he'd concealed in the back of the waistband of his trousers, when Mueller attemped to reach for the Winchester rifle that lay at his feet.

Mueller froze, going pale underneath his ruddy tan.

"Put your hands in the air where I can see 'em," Jake ordered, keeping his voice calm, though his heart hadn't pounded like this since he'd last faced a Yankee cavalry charge.

Mueller complied, watching him as if he expected every moment to be his last.

"Now, I have no intention of hurting you, Mr. Mueller—but neither am I going to let you railroad Erica into a wedding she doesn't want. So just allow her to get down from that wagon and come up here with me, and you can be on your way back home, all right?"

"Erica, you will tell me the truth," Mueller commanded, turning to his daughter but keeping a wary eye on Jake. "Do you go willingly with this man?"

Erica's eyes brimmed with tears. "Yes, Vati. I'm sorry it had to be this way, but you wouldn't listen yesterday when Jake tried to make an honorable proposal of marriage. Yes, I do want to marry Jake Taylor. Please tell Mutti I am sorry, and not to worry. I will be fine." She kissed her father on the cheek, but he made no move to lower his arms and embrace her.

"Where are you going?" Mueller demanded of Jake, watching Erica as she jumped gracefully down from the wagon and approached Jake's horse.

"Oh, I don't think I'll be telling you that," Jake said, grinning. "But we'll send word once Erica and I are safely hitched."

Mueller's jaw set and he glared at Jake. "You won't get away with this, you know," he growled.

"Mr. Mueller, I'm not going to murder your daughter, I'm going to marry her," Jake countered reasonably. "I'll take good care of her, don't you fret. Erica, do you think you can put your foot in the stirrup, and spring on up here?" he asked, patting the back of the horse.

"*Ja*, I think so," Erica murmured.

Jake kept the Colt trained on Mueller while she did so. It would be a short but uncomfortable ride for her until they reached the place about a mile away where he'd hidden the second horse. He hoped she could ride astride—he hadn't wanted to hint at his plans by requesting a sidesaddle at the livery.

He smiled when he felt her settle herself behind him and put her arm around his waist to anchor herself. Oh, yes, he was going to love being married to this woman, his brave Erica.

"*Auf Wiedersehen*, Vati. Please don't worry," Erica said again. "I will write as soon as I can."

Chapter Sixteen

"Jake, what will we do now?" Erica asked. They had reached the grove of trees where Jake had hidden the other horse he had hired, a rangy sorrel mare upon which she was now mounted. She blushed as she looked down and saw how much of her stocking-covered legs were exposed by having to sit astride.

Jake followed her gaze. "Sorry—we'll stop in the next town and try to buy you some trousers. Or we could trade for a sidesaddle, if you want."

Erica thought about it and shook her head. "To do that would slow us down. And someone might remember seeing us, and tell Vati if he tries to pursue us and comes that way. He will have to take the wagon home and round up some men to help him, of course. Where are we going, to your father's plantation?"

He reined his horse closer and reached out a hand to stroke her cheek. "That's my brave girl—you're thinkin' like a rebel guerilla! No, we won't go to Taylor Hall. I thought we'd go to San Antonio just as you planned—only I'm not, of course, takin' you to that Rudolph fella," he added with a wry grin. "Not only will they not expect us to go there—they'll assume we're going north to the plantation instead—but I have a friend in San Antonio, Dr. John Ransom, who'll let us stay with him and he'll help us get married."

Erica's heart warmed at hearing him say the word *married*. She'd believed he actually meant to go through with his promise, of course, but it helped to hear him actually say so. She smiled at him.

"This doctor—he will not mind having guests without warning? Guests for whom he must help arrange a wedding? He must be a very good friend indeed, Jake."

Jake's smile broadened. "The best," he said simply. "We've been friends since we were boys together—went off to school together, fought side by side in the war—that is, when he wasn't being the battalion sawbones," he corrected himself, then explained, " 'Sawbones' is another name for a doctor—especially during the war, when most of what they did was saw off limbs that had been shattered by bullets and cannonfire." His eyes were grim for a moment, and then he shook his head as if to clear away the memory.

He settled himself in the saddle. "We'd better get moving if we're going to put some distance between your papa and us."

They stopped only to water the horses and eat two of the sandwiches that Jake had bought before leaving New Braunfels. Finally, at sunset, Jake found a sheltering grove of live oaks and pecan trees along a little creek, and announced they would camp there for the night.

"We ought to be able to make it to San Antonio by late afternoon if we get an early start in the mornin'," Jake said as Erica raised her right leg over the horse's back and began to dismount.

He rushed forward just in time to catch her as her legs wobbled, jelly-like, and refused to hold her up. "Easy there, sweetheart, you're not used to all-day riding," he said, scooping an arm under her thighs and carrying her under one of the live oaks where he gently deposited her.

"That is the truth," she agreed ruefully. "I cannot feel my . . . my . . ." She hesitated, unable to find a delicate word for buttocks. She couldn't say that, even if he was about to become her husband!

"Backside," Jake supplied with a grin, rubbing a hand down his own for emphasis. "I know what you mean. The first few times we were in the saddle on a campaign with Hood for twelve hours straight, I thought I was goin' t' die." He dropped down on one knee and tilted up Erica's chin with one finger. "You just stay right here and rest while I see to the horses, and then we can eat the rest of those sandwiches for supper."

Wearier than she could ever remember being, Erica's eyes stung with tears at his kindness. Was this man never cross, never impatient?

"Jake Taylor, you are a good man," she murmured as he began to get up again.

He stopped, staring at her, and resumed his kneeling position. "I don't know about that, but I'm going to be good to *you*, Erica Mueller." And then he lowered his head and kissed her—just a simple kiss, but one so piercingly sweet that her heart swelled with love for him.

"I'd have liked to stop at a good hotel, one where you could sleep on a soft mattress rather than on the ground," he told her, jerking his head to indicate the sandy, sparsely grassed area under the trees. "But we can't take the chance if your papa outguesses me and comes the right direction after you. I won't let him or anyone force you into doing something you don't want."

She gazed back into those eyes of such a deep and brilliant blue, a darker blue than hers, and was touched by the earnestness in his voice.

But before she could speak, he went on, "And that goes for me too, Erica. You'll have some time to think before we reach John's house and can arrange a wedding." Jake took a deep breath and raised his head to rest his chin lightly on her head. "If you decide that what you really want is to just make a new life where you can make your own decisions and choose your own fate, rather than marryin' me, I'll understand and help you do that."

She pulled away, a cry of protest building in her throat, but he put a finger over her parted lips. "No, don't say anything. I just want you to think about the fact that you have a choice, okay?"

Erica nodded. She would show him what her decision was when it came time to sleep! He only had the one bedroll which had been tied to the back of his saddle when he had been attacked, so they would have to sleep close together. Proximity would help her convince Jake Taylor that she wanted only to be his wife!

"It's a good thing it's summer, so we don't have to chance a fire," Jake said, lying down beside her at last, after making a final check on the horses to see that they were still securely tied to the picket line he'd improvised. "Although I surely will miss my coffee in the mornin'," he added. "Perhaps we can risk a stop somewhere, just to get some. You know, your mama sure made good coffee," he said, turning to face her lying at his side.

"Jake . . ." Erica whispered. Now was the time. She was tired of talking about inconsequential things as they had all through their sandwich supper.

She rose up on one elbow and lowered her mouth to his, making sure her kiss left no doubt that she wanted him to claim her as his without any further delay.

Jake groaned and pulled her closer onto him, framing her face with those strong, long fingers, his mouth leaving hers for a few seconds to rain kisses on her neck and along the line of her jaw. Then his lips swooped down on hers again and he devoured her, pulling her closer so she was lying half on top of him.

She let her hand drift to his hip, clutching it as if it were her anchor on a storm-tossed sea. In response, he half turned so that they were both lying on their sides and pressed together along their entire lengths. Even through the thickness of their clothes she could tell he wanted her, and she thrilled at the effect she had on him.

Just when she was certain he would push her onto her back and start to remove her clothes, he moved away from her and collapsed onto his back, his breathing ragged.

Erica stilled. What had she done wrong?

"It would be so easy to make love to you now, Erica," he said. "I—I *want* to . . ."

"Then—" she began, not understanding why he would stop when he was clearly aroused and wanting her.

"But when I make love to you, sweet Erica, I want to do it as your husband. I guess you could say I don't want to do anything the way that . . . that sidewinder Siegfried did it."

"But I don't think you're . . ." she began, and then her voice trailed off and she turned on her side away from him so he wouldn't sense that her cheeks were flaming with embarrassment. As much as he clearly desired her, Jake thought her experience with Siegfried had made her into a wanton woman, and he was going to teach her to act like a respectable wife!

He put an arm around her waist and pulled her against him so that her back was against his chest. "We'll be married in a few days, Erica. And then believe me, I'll make love to you so much you'll beg me to leave you alone!"

Erica smiled through her tears in the balmy darkness, appreciating the thoughtful words that were meant to salvage her dignity. She was very sure she could not imagine ever begging such a thing.

But the fact that he could hold back now, when she was so obviously offering herself to him, assured her that she was right—Jake Taylor did not love her, and he was only rescuing her from an unwanted marriage. And while he would claim his husbandly rights once they were wed, and undoubtedly give her a child or two, in time the fact that he did not love her would begin to tell.

Eventually he would begin to spend more and more time away from home. Maybe he would have a mistress in town and set her up in a modest house that Erica would never see. Maybe he already had such a woman!

Could she love him enough to bear that? Yes, she would, she vowed fiercely. She would be his wife, and she would always be there for him to come back to, because she would love Jake Taylor until the day she breathed her last.

"There it is, that's John Ransom's house," Jake said, pointing at the handsome three-story stone edifice in the King William district of San Antonio. It was now dusk, and across the street, the lamplighter was making his appointed rounds. ·

They were arriving much later than he had hoped, but a Texas thunderstorm waits for no man, or even an eloping couple. In the early afternoon an ugly gray thunderhead had arisen over the valley they were riding through and, before they could reach any sort of shelter, it had dumped a gully-washer on them.

Both of them had been soaked to the skin by the time they'd found an abandoned shack nestled against a limestone hill. Since there seemed to be no sign of recent human habitation, they dismounted and pulled the horses in with them.

Then the full fury of the storm struck. A series of lightning bolts sent zig-zagging fire zinging ground-ward, some of them frighteningly close. It was all Jake and Erica could do to calm the horses so that the frightened beasts did not inadvertently step on them or plunge back into the wall of water pouring down just outside their shelter. Neither of them had wanted to have to walk the rest of the way into San Antonio!

In true Texas style, the storm had gone as quickly as it had begun, but the humidity that it left in its wake prevented them from fully drying out before they reached the city.

"Don't worry, John will see that we get baths and some dry clothes to put on," Jake assured her as he helped her dismount.

"I wish I did not have to meet your good friend looking like a drowned *Ratte*," Erica said, gesturing ruefully towards her sodden braid and mud-splashed skirts. "He will think you pulled me out of a river!"

Jake chuckled. "I sure don't look any better," he said, pointing at his own muddy, wet shirt and trousers. If only she knew how much he wanted to kiss her, drowned rat or not. He'd been tormented all afternoon by the way the rain had molded her beige cotton bodice so completely and transparently to her breasts: she might as well have been wearing just her thin, lace-trimmed camisole.

He'd already been suffering the tortures of the damned after his foolishly chivalrous refusal to surrender to her sweet kisses the night before. He'd lain awake most of the night, tormented as she'd nestled closer to him in her sleep, unconsciously settling her soft backside against his groin. He'd had to grit his teeth and clench his hands into fists so as not to push up her skirts and wake her just as he plunged deeply inside her. . . .

Erica had been a little shy and guarded around him all day, no doubt because he'd been such a high-principled fool. Was it possible she didn't realize he found her the most desirable woman he'd ever met? Well, with any luck, very soon they'd have a lifetime for him to show her that she was!

"Your friend must be very wealthy, *ja?*" Erica asked as Jake tied the horses' reins to the wrought-iron fence that formed a perimeter around the imposing, mansard-roofed, gingerbread-trimmed mansion. In the front there were stone arches over a broad gallery.

Jake followed her gaze and shrugged. "Yeah, I reckon he is. I never noticed when we were growing up together because Taylor Hall was just as big and prosperous as John's family's property there. His parents are dead now and John was an only child, so after the war, he sold the plantation up on the Brazos to pay the taxes on this place. But people will always need a doctor, so John's managed to outsmart the carpetbaggers and do pretty well for himself."

Erica didn't know much about carpetbaggers, but she forgot all about that subject when she saw the front door open. A man emerged, clearly dressed to go out for the evening in a black frock coat and trousers and immaculate white shirt. A shaft of late evening sunlight illuminated the dark gold of his hair.

He halted on the step when he saw them standing outside his fence and peered at them curiously. "May I help you? Do you need medical care?"

Erica watched as a grin spread over Jake's face. "No, but we sure could use some dry clothes and a couple of rooms, John."

The tall, elegant man's jaw dropped. *"Jake?"* And then he was running to them, and in a flash the two men were embracing and clapping one another on the back.

Chapter Seventeen

Jake released his friend after a moment and beckoned Erica into the circle of light cast by the streetlamp.

"John Ransom, I have the very great honor to present you to the woman I'm going to marry, Miss Erica Mueller."

The tawny-haired man looked from Jake to Erica and back again, his smile even broader than before.

"So my best friend has been struck by Cupid's arrow at last!" He bowed, then raised Erica's hand to his lips, the gesture as polished as that of any European courtier. "Miss Erica, I am so very pleased to make your acquaintance," he said, sincerity lighting his dark eyes. "I can't wait to hear how you captured him!"

The well-meant statement threw her into confusion. What could she say to that? She was sure her grasp of English wasn't quite up to explaining to a stranger—even if he was Jake's best friend—how she

163

had come to be Jake's intended. She threw Jake a look full of appeal.

Jake cleared his throat. "Um, well, that's quite a story, and one I'll be happy to tell you, but right now Miss Erica's feeling a little self-conscious about the soakin' we sustained this afternoon—do you suppose you could provide us with baths and a loan of some dry clothes?"

Erica spoke up. "Oh, but I'm certain Herr Ransom would not have clothes for a woman! Perhaps if I could just wrap up in something—a bedsheet, maybe?—until my clothes have dried? And Jake, I'm sure your friend was about to go out for the evening. Perhaps we should let him be on his way, and we should find a hotel? We could return to see him in the morning, if that is convenient for him?"

John Ransom blinked and turned to his friend as if a further explanation were needed, and Erica realized he hadn't realized from her name that she was a newcomer to America. Or had she made some horrible grammatical mistake?

"I should have told you that Miss Erica is from New Braunfels," Jake said. "To be correct, I suppose I should actually have introduced her as 'Fraulein Mueller.'"

"Did I say something in bad English?" Erica asked.

"Not at all, Fraulein," John assured her. "Your accent is charming. And I wouldn't hear of you going anywhere for the night! Don't you worry about me— I'd thought to go out to find a poker game and a drink, but I assure you those plans were only made for lack of anything better! I'm so glad I hadn't actually gone already, though I'm sure Jake knows me well enough that he would just go inside and ask my housekeeper for anything y'all needed to be comfortable till I returned." He studied her for a moment and added, "I'd be honored for you to make Ransom House your own for as long as you're in San Antonio. And I'm sure Señora Velasquez—that's the housekeeper—can find something among her daughter's things that you could borrow." He started back toward the house and beckoned. "Come on inside, y'all, and we'll get you settled. And while you're gettin' cleaned up, I'll have my cook, Rosita, make some of her famous enchiladas!"

Erica was shown by Señora Velasquez into the ornately furnished dining room, with its long, rectangular table of polished mahoghany, silver candlesticks and gilt-framed portraits, to find the men cozily ensconced there with a crystal decanter of wine. Both men stood as she entered, and suddenly she was all too aware of how the low- cut, ruffled white blouse loaned to her by the housekeeper's giggly daughter revealed the tops of her breasts, even though Erica was also wearing a shawl of a rose-colored lacy weave over her shoulders. But at least her hair was once again neatly braided and wound in a coronet at the back of her head, so she felt more composed than she had an hour ago when she had first met Jake's elegant friend.

"Miss Erica, how lovely you are, even in borrowed garments," John murmured, but it was the admiration in Jake's eyes that curved Erica's lips upward.

"Please, come sit down," John added, bringing

her to a chair between himself and Jake and pouring her a glass of the ruby-colored wine. "I hope you like this—a sea captain friend brought it all the way from Bordeaux. I've been told your countrymen transplanted to Texas are fine vintners too, though."

She nodded, though she didn't think she'd tell this cultured, polished friend that she'd never tasted any of their efforts. Mutti didn't hold with serving wine to children, even full-grown ones. In fact, Erica realized she hadn't tasted wine since she'd experienced Siegfried's campaign of seduction.

"Excuse me," John Ransom said, rising. "I'll just tell Rosita we're ready to dine." He left the room.

"Sweetheart, I went ahead and told John a little about how we came to know one another," Jake told her. "I hope that was all right. I thought it would make it easier."

Erica smiled gratefully. "*Ja . . .*" she said, but her face must have reflected her uncertainty, because Jake quickly added, "Oh, don't worry, I didn't tell him about that no-good scorpion Von Schiller, of course—though I know John, and I'll guarantee you he'd say the only one who has anything to be ashamed of is Von Schiller. Not you, Erica," he said, kissing her forehead as if to emphasize the truth of his words. "I just told him that your mama and papa didn't like the idea of you marryin' an Anglo, so we eloped."

He might have gone on, but just then John Ransom returned with a rotund Mexican woman close on his heels, bearing a huge tureen.

"I don't know whether you've ever had gazpacho, Miss Erica," John said as Rosita began ladling out the light green soup. "Bein' as it's summer, it's too hot for hot soup, but this always tastes good because it's cool."

"I have never known anything but German cooking, but it looks good," Erica said, then tried it. "Mmmm," she said appreciatively, "She can give me the recipe for this soup, *ja?*"

"Oh, I imagine so," John said, clearly pleased. "Miss Erica, Jake's told me how y'all have come down here to get married, and why, and I have to admire your pluck—that is, your spirit," he explained, when Erica again looked to Jake in confusion.

"And I'm right pleased t' help y'all arrange a weddin'," he went on, taking a spoonful of his gazpacho. "We can use my church, St. Mark's. It's really a lovely place, and one of the few Protestant churches in the town. I have a suggestion t' make, however—though I want y'all to feel free to tell me to jump in a lake about this one if you want."

"He means you can feel free to ignore his opinion about what he's going to say if you're so inclined," Jake explained wryly.

"I see. . . ." she murmured. *Gott in Himmel,* was Jake's friend about to suggest they should go home and try again to persuade her parents? If so, she was going to have to tactfully refuse!

"Now, I could help you get married tomorrow morning if that's what you really want to do," John said. "But what I was thinkin' was that you ought to write and invite your parents to the ceremony, Miss Erica, and Jake will invite his papa, too."

"Oh, no, Herr Doktor Ransom, I cannot do such a thing," she began, trying to find the right words to explain that her parents would never soften their stance towards Jake and his suit. "We have a proverb in German, Herr Doktor Ransom," she began as Rosita brought in a steaming tray of enchiladas giving off a savory aroma and began to serve their plates.

"Please, just call me John, Miss Erica," Ransom murmured.

She nodded her acceptance. "John, I cannot translate it exactly into English, but it means roughly that my parents will let me marry Jake, I believe, when sinners can iceskate in Hell."

Ransom chuckled and shook his head. "Their minds are made up, hmmm? But still, I think it's worth tryin'. I'd send messengers with your letters—we wouldn't wait on the mail. If we succeeded in gettin' them to come, it might go a long way toward achievin' better relations between them and your Jake."

Your Jake. How she loved the sound of that! She had to shake her head, though, about the likelihood of Ransom's idea succeeding. "John, you don't understand. . . . I—I do not think ever they will change their minds. . . ."

Ransom did not seem dismayed by her doubt. "It might not, but at least you'd have the peace of mind that you tried. But then again, it might. They're probably worried sick about you right this minute, and don't you think they'd like to see their little girl walk down the aisle?"

Erica hesitated, swayed by the powerful word-picture he painted.

John must have sensed he was convincing her, because he added persuasively, "And if y'all were to wait just a week or two until they could get here, we'd have the time to have a beautiful white wedding gown stitched up for you by San Antonio's finest seamstress."

Erica closed her eyes to hide her conflicted feelings from both Jake and John. How wonderful it would be to walk to Jake at the altar wearing a white gown of a virgin bride! But she had no right to such an innocent hue, and Jake knew it. But she didn't want Jake's friend to know Jake had agreed to have her as his wife despite her less-than-innocent status.

She opened her eyes to see Jake looking at her. He took her hand and gave it an encouraging squeeze. "Erica, we'll do whatever you say, but I'd purely love to see you in a gown like John's talking about."

She tried to explain her ambivalence with her eyes. "But . . ."

"But nothing," he said, and his own eyes were steady and sure.

She looked down at her hands, her heart so full of love for this man that it would surely burst. She would give her life to making this good man happy!

"All right, Jake," she agreed.

But Jake Taylor would not settle for less than a full surrender. "And I agree with John that we ought to try invitin' your parents—and my papa."

"But what if Vati arrives with several men and tries to force me to leave you? For that matter, this district is populated by wealthy Germans, including the father of the young man with whom my parents wanted to arrange a match."

"I told you, I'm not lettin' anyone take you away

unless you want to go, Erica," Jake reminded her. "It doesn't matter if he does bring a posse—a search party—armed to the teeth."

"Nor would I allow such a thing," John added with calm certainty. "I'm not without powerful friends in this city. Who is that German father and young man you were talkin' about, by the way?"

Erica hesitated. Perhaps if she said the banker's name, John would say he was too powerful a man to cross! But she could see Ransom was not going to let her elude the question.

"It is Dietrich Schoenbrunn and his son Rudolph," she said at last.

John nodded. "I know the man. He helped arrange the purchase of this house for me, as a matter of fact. I know his boy too. They're good enough fellows. But Jake's right, he's not the man for you, Miss Erica."

"The worst your parents could say is no, honey," Jake said.

It was the unexpected endearment that won her. "Very well, we will send the letters tomorrow, *ja?* And if it would be all right, I will send one to Minna too—not that she could come, but I want her to know I am all right."

Jake grinned. "And then we're goin' to take you to that seamstress John was talkin' about. I want you to have a weddin' gown fit for an angel!"

John raised his wineglass. "I'd like to propose a toast—to the most beautiful bride San Antonio will ever see!"

Erica felt the tears escape down her cheeks as both

men raised their glasses in her direction. If this was a dream, she never wanted to wake.

Jake scooted his chair closer and took her into his arms. "Better stop cryin', or my friend might think you're scared of marryin' me after all," he teased. "And then he'd try to steal you away from me." He lowered his voice to whisper into her ear, "and I'd have to teach him a lesson just like I did Siegfried, friend or not."

His sally elicited a watery smile from her. "I know you are only making a joke, *ja?*"

John hadn't heard the part about Siegfried, of course, but he responded to the part he had heard. "If my friend ever disappoints you, Miss Erica, you just come runnin' to me, all right?" he promised gallantly. "I've had to straighten him out when he's been wrongheaded before—though not, of course, about a lady," he added. "This is the first time my friend has ever lost his heart that *I* know of."

"It is," Jake confirmed.

"And now we'd better get busy with these enchiladas, or my cook's going to worry we don't like them, and sulk for a week," John announced, lifting his fork. His eyes danced with pleasure at Erica's agreement.

Perhaps it was partly the wine speeding through her veins, but bathed in Jake's warm regard and his friend's generosity and hospitality, Erica felt all at once full of optimism and joy. Perhaps everything would work out, after all!

It was not until she was saying good night to Jake at the door of her bedroom, though, that she asked

171

Jake the question that had occurred to her sometime during the meal. She had been sure this was not something she dared to ask John himself, however.

"Jake, why has your friend never married? He seems like such a nice man, and well-favored— though I have eyes for no one but you, of course!" she added quickly. "And he is wealthy. . . . I would think the ladies of San Antonio, and even all of Texas, would be lined up outside the door trying to attract his attention."

Jake grinned. "Oh, they've been tryin' to hook John since we were barely old enough to go to the dances, believe me. But John's always been rather fond of my sister Kate, even though she's a good deal younger than he is."

"Kate? But . . ." Erica paused, wanting to make sure she remembered correctly. "Is she not the sister who left for England with your mother at the beginning of your war? Did you not say she still lives there?"

Now a shadow of regret tinged Jake's eyes. "Yeah, that's the one. And I purely hate to see my friend longin' for somethin' he can't have," he said honestly, "because I don't believe Kate's ever comin' home. Maybe after we're all married and settled, you could introduce John to one of those pretty *frauleins* back in your hometown? Looks like your friend Minna's spoken for, though, if your brother has anything to do with it," Jake added.

"Perhaps," she agreed thoughtfully. She wouldn't mind playing matchmaker, but there was something about John Ransom that told her he had already given his heart away and couldn't get it back. Had it gone to Kate Taylor, so long ago? Ah, it was all too much to consider, when she was so tired and had her own wedding to think about!

Chapter Eighteen

"There," Erica said, her hands on her hips. She stood on John Ransom's pebbled driveway watching the two youths, hired to carry their letters about the wedding to Erica's parents, Minna, and Jake's father, gallop off.

Please, God, soften Mutti and Vati's hearts towards Jake, she prayed. And Herr Taylor's, toward me. Jake hadn't said much about how his father would feel about their marriage, but she guessed his disapproval would stem from the fact she was a foreigner, and a German foreigner at that.

"The die is cast," murmured Jake, standing beside her.

"You have crossed the Rubicon," added John, who stood on the other side of Jake.

Jake looked confused. "The what?"

Erica was amused. It was high time Jake had to have something explained to him—it was usually she who had to ask for clarification.

"It is from Shakespeare," she told Jake loftily before John could supply the answer. "From the play, *Julius Caesar*. It means there is no going back, *ja*? Just as your quote from Caesar's writings did." She laughed when John as well as Jake blinked in surprise. "Did you think we Germans were ignorant of all but our own literature?"

"You're full of surprises, sweetheart," Jake said with a laugh, giving her a hearty kiss. "I can see our children won't be ignoramuses."

She colored at his casual mention of children, *their* children, then pretended to pout. "*Ach,* so now you use an American word you know will be unfamiliar to me, just to get your revenge!"

"Guilty," he said with a grin, and gave her a playful kiss on the forehead.

John cleared his throat as a landau, drawn by a pair of matched black horses, pulled up in front of the house. "Ah, right on time," he murmured. "Well, if we're done quoting literature, and if you can bear to let her out of your sight for a while, Jake, I've arranged for a friend of mine to take Erica to the foremost modiste in San Antonio. Hello, Henri," he said, greeting the lady who sat in the back of the open carriage, holding a ruffly parasol. "Jake Taylor and Miss Erica Mueller, I'd like you to meet a long-time friend of mine, Mrs. Henrietta Hilliard—Henri for short."

Henri Hilliard was the sort of woman generally referred to as "handsome," with a long face and striking, strong features rather than classically beautiful ones, but the general effect was pleasing.

"You'll notice he doesn't dare call me an *old*

friend," Henri said with a smile as she leaned forward to shake Jake's and Erica's hands. "Oh, John, she's just as pretty as you said she was in your note," she said, studying Erica. "Mr. Taylor, you're a lucky man."

"I think so too, ma'am," Jake agreed as Erica murmured her thanks. He turned back to his friend. "John, old friend, you don't waste any time arrangin' things!"

"I was fortunate Miz Henri was available to help us on short notice," was John's modest reply.

"I'm happy to help," Henri said, "since time is of the essence, Mr. Taylor! John's note said y'all wanted to be married within the fortnight, and a good wedding dress isn't made at the drop of a hat, sir!"

"It's just Jake, ma'am."

"I am pleased to meet you, Frau—that is, Missus Hilliard," Erica said, wondering what the relationship was between Ransom and this pleasant woman who seemed so familiar with him. "But—Jake is not to come along?" she said, looking back at him and feeling a bit uncertain. Since she had left New Braunfels, she had not been anywhere without him.

Henri Hilliard's trill of laughter was not unkind. "Bless your heart, darlin,' your groom can't see the dress before you come down the aisle—it's bad luck! Besides, a man is as useless at a dressmaker's as a milk bucket under a bull, don't you think so?"

Erica couldn't help but smile at the absurd comparison, although she didn't really know—she had never had a dress that either she or her mother hadn't made.

"Now come on up into my carriage, honey, and

we'll be off to Madame LaFollett's. She's expecting us, and she doesn't like to be kept waiting!"

"Don't worry about Jake, Erica," John said. "I'm takin' him to see some fine bloodstock, since he'd expressed interest in settin' up his own horse farm," John called. "Then we'll all meet for supper back here!"

Feeling like a fairy-tale princess meeting her fairy godmother, Erica allowed herself to be handed up into the carriage and swept off in the direction of Madame LaFollett's establishment.

"Your fiancé is a handsome thing, isn't he, if you don't mind my sayin' so?" Henri Hilliard remarked with a smile as the carriage rolled through the live oak- and cottonwood-lined streets. As they left the King William district, the architecture became distinctly Spanish in flavor. "I mean, with those blue eyes and dark hair and all . . . Even better-looking than John Ransom, and that's sayin' a lot!"

Erica found herself warming to the woman with her easy, chatty friendliness. "I think he's very *ansehnlicht*—handsome, *ja*. But Herr Doktor Ransom is very good-looking too!" she added hastily.

The older woman's laughter was like music. "Yes, John's not hard to look at, not that he ever uses his looks to his own advantage! And I'm sure you're wonderin' what we are to each other, aren't you?" She didn't even wait for Erica's admission of curiosity, but went on, "Well, I'll tell you. John and I are just good friends. When I need an escort to some big 'do,' I know I can count on him. I'm a war widow, you see."

"Oh!" said Erica, startled. "I'm so sorry!" she

added, peering at the other woman to see if she had missed some trace of mourning wear, such as a black ribbon-trimmed brooch with her late husband's hair. Clearly, since the woman wore a dress of red-sprigged muslin, her loss had not been recent.

"Thanks, but I lost George early in the war," Henri replied calmly, "and I must be honest and admit I didn't love him—at least, not the way a wife should love her husband. You see, he was about a hundred years older than me."

It was impossible not to laugh at the woman's droll recital of the facts, especially when Henri rolled her eyes.

"I don't know what I was thinkin' to marry him, but George gave me a comfortable, if childless, life and left me securely provided for when he died, bless him. John and I, well . . . we keep each other company, and by havin' him as my escort, I'm not plagued by fortune-hunters, and he's not bothered so much by matchmaking mamas."

Her next words completely surprised Erica. "But I'm under no illusions, dear Erica. I know John's always been in love with your Jake's little sister Katherine."

"You—you do?"

Henri's smile was open and genuine. "Yes, I do. Or at least he believes he is. Perhaps he's just a born bachelor, and Kate Taylor represents an ideal—you know, like the knights of old who worshipped some unattainable lady?" She laughed at her own fanciful comparison, then went on, "Anyway, I'm not lookin' to get married again, you see, so I'm not jealous. I just wish John would realize Kate Taylor's apparently never goin' to come home to Texas. Then he could go on with his life and marry some nice girl. It'd be a shame for John never to marry, I think."

Erica wondered why, if Henri felt that way, she didn't try to deepen their friendship to something more. But apparently she really was comfortable with the way things stood between her and John, and in any case they had arrived at Madame LaFollett's establishment. She would have to forget her questions and concentrate on choosing a wedding dress.

Madame LaFollett made no secret of the fact that she felt San Antonio was fortunate she had deigned to bless such a backwater with her sophisticated presence. But seeing the Frenchwoman looking down her sharp little nose at Erica's borrowed Mexican garments, Henri Hilliard lost no time in making sure the Frenchwoman did not think to intimidate Erica with her opinions.

"Madame LaFollett, my friend Miss Mueller needs your finest wedding dress," she said as soon as she had introduced Erica. "And some everyday wear as well."

The Frenchwoman's eyebrows rose.

"It's the most romantic story you can imagine!" Henri went on gaily. "Miss Erica and her fiancé, who's as handsome as any French prince, have eloped from the town of New Braunfels and she arrived with just the clothes on her back, didn't you, sweet Erica? So, you see, she'll need everything!"

"Vraiment?" inquired Madame LaFollett. "And is her so-handsome *beau* to pay the bill?"

Erica darted a worried look at Henri.

"No, send the bill to Dr. John Ransom," said Henri. "He's the very good friend of Erica's fiancé, and he said it was to be his wedding present to the happy couple. Isn't that sweet?"

"*Vraiment*," the French modiste said again. "*Eh bien*, let me show Mademoiselle some designs that I think would suit her well, *oui?* And when is thees wedding to take place?"

"In two weeks, Madame," Erica said.

The Frenchwoman fluttered her hands. "Oh! *C'est impossible!*" she shrieked. "I cannot possibly make one of my wedding dresses in less than a month! There are fittings to arrange, and if she needs also other dresses and undergarments, well, you see my difficulty, *n'est-ce-pas?*"

Erica was reluctantly willing to agree that she did think that they were asking too much, but Henri Hilliard drew herself to her full statuesque height and shook her head firmly. "No, two weeks is the limit. You wouldn't want to make lovers wait, would you? Of course not."

"*Mais non*, but—"

"Dr. Ransom is prepared to pay your price, my good Madame LaFollett, with a little something extra thrown in for the necessary haste, but I know you have some dresses for everyday that would only take a minimum of alteration to fit my friend here, isn't that so? I wouldn't want to tell anyone Madame LaFollett couldn't rise to the occasion!"

The Frenchwoman blinked, and apparently knowing herself beaten, said, "Never let it be said that

Madame LaFollett was not up to a challenge, especially one made by Cupid himself, eh? Come then, come into my fitting room, Mademoiselle Mueller, and I will take your measurements, and then I will show you designs for wedding gowns straight from Paris!" She kissed her own fingers in an extravagant gesture. "Ah, they are *magnifique!*"

Erica, accompanied by Henri, was gestured through a curtain into a spacious room with mirrors on all four walls.

"Now then," the modiste said briskly. "You will remove your outer garments. Come, come," she said when she saw Erica hesitate. "No modesty, please. It is necessary that we lose no time!"

Henri nodded encouragingly, and in moments, Erica was standing on a small pedestal in just her chemise and drawers while the Frenchwoman circled her bust, waist and hips with her tape measure.

"Ah, such a tiny waist, but a generous bosom, and good hips!" Madame LaFollett praised, straightening after she had measured Erica's hips. "This girl will have no difficulty bearing children, eh?" she said to Henri.

Henri Hilliard merely nodded, amused.

Erica reddened from her scalp to her toes at the frank assessment.

The Frenchwoman cackled. "Ah, she blushes, the shy virgin! She is *très belle, n'est-ce pas?* Her man will not be able to resist her, dressed in my creations!" she crowed.

"I don't think he can resist her *now,*" Henri responded dryly. "You should have seen how he looked at her, Madame!"

The two other women shared delighted laughter, while Erica maintained a frozen smile. *If they only knew that Jake is marrying me out of kindness, and that to my everlasting regret, I am no virgin. . . .*

But once she had donned her borrowed clothing again and was poring over Madame LaFollett's Parisian fashion magazines, she forgot her secret regrets and gave herself over to the delight of choosing her wedding gown.

In the end, she decided upon a dress made of white *peau de soie*, with a high-necked basque trimmed with ivory satin and Valenciennes lace, and a long white veil of Swiss muslin to be trimmed with orange-tree flowers fashioned of silk.

"Erica, honey, you're going to be such a beautiful bride!" Henri exclaimed, and Erica beamed, thinking that if Jake didn't love her, he would at least be proud to call her his on their wedding day.

"And now you will come back to my showroom and I will display for you the dresses I have ready-made, *oui*? I can deliver one or two of them ready for you to wear by tomorrow morning."

At the same time that Erica was trying on all manner of dresses at Madame LaFollett's establishment, Siegfried Von Schiller was emerging from his rented lodgings, his bones and muscles still aching from the beating that Jake Taylor had administered three days earlier, his ego still stinging from Erica Mueller's foolish rejection of his renewed attentions.

His thoughts centered on vengeance. No woman would be allowed to treat him as if he were some foolish peasant who had been passed over in favor of another swain! He, Siegfried Von Schiller, did the rejecting, not the woman!

He had killed men in duels over far more trivial causes than that rude lout of a Texan had given him. Jake Taylor would die for being so free with his fists! And then he, Siegfried Von Schiller, would have Erica Mueller in his power and begging for his favors. When he had degraded her to the point that she was fit only for the gutter, perhaps he would kill her too!

Chapter Nineteen

For the next four days, Erica relaxed and enjoyed her days in San Antonio. She knew it would take the messenger at least two days to reach New Braunfels, and as long again for the messenger to return so she could learn whether or not her parents had written a response. She had decided that at least for these four days, there was no point in worrying. She could do nothing more to affect the outcome, and what would be, would be.

It would take much longer for the messenger riding to Taylor Hall to reach his destination. Because of the greater distance, the messenger had been given an extra sum of money to send a telegram with Jake's father's response, for they had decided if Frank Taylor unexpectedly gave his blessing, they would wait until he could be present at the ceremony. But although Jake said little about it, Erica already sensed that he wasn't counting on a miracle.

That fact troubled her, but Jake refused to consider changing his mind about marrying her.

Every day was spent pleasantly. Dressed in one of the two new dresses Madame LaFollett had delivered the morning after her visit to the modiste's shop, Erica spent the mornings strolling the tree-lined streets of San Antonio with Jake, getting to know her fiancé better and learning the ways of the Americans. Her English—or, rather, the drawling Texas version of that language—improved daily.

Twice they met Henri for dinner at a café and then Jake left her in the older woman's company so he could keep visiting nearby ranches, for he still hadn't found the right stallion and mare to be the foundation sire and dam for his horse farm. Henri took Erica back to her own home during these afternoons. She said it was really too hot to do anything outside, but she refused to waste an afternoon by napping as many Southern gentlewomen did. She and Erica talked and shared recipes, going into her kitchen to try them out. Erica learned how to fry chicken and cook Mexican dishes like enchiladas and tamales, while Henri, to her delight, learned how to make such traditional German dishes as sauerbraten and Wiener schnitzel.

In the evenings, once Ransom returned from his last house call of the day and Jake was back from his ranch visits, all four of them would have dinner together, either at Henri's house, to taste the results of the women's cooking lessons, or at Ransom House, where John's cook demonstrated her versatility, treating them to sumptuous feasts as apparently effortlessly as she cooked her Mexican specialties.

Juan, the messenger boy who had gone to New Braunfels, was waiting for them on Sunday when they returned from services at Ransom's church. Erica listened with some trepidation as he began to deliver his report.

The elder Muellers, he said, had heard him out in complete, tight-lipped silence and had declined to send a reply or indicate in any way their opinion of Erica's upcoming wedding. He said both of them had turned a bit pale and had begun chattering to each other in German as soon as Juan turned to go. He'd been waylaid at the front gate by Erica's brothers, however, and eagerly questioned about their sister's welfare.

Erica felt tears sting her eyes and a wave of guilty homesickness sweep over her. She missed them all so much, and she might never see them again if her parents remained obdurate.

Jake put a consoling arm around her. "It'll be all right, sweetheart, you'll see. Your letter would have caught them by surprise and they probably didn't know what to say just then to Juan. Thanks for going, Juan," he said, handing the youth a tip for his speediness.

Erica was grateful for Jake's kindness, but doubtful that they would hear anything further from her parents. Perhaps when Hans and Guenther were older, the boys would seek them out. . . .

Juan, the messenger, had looked on sympathetically as he'd delivered his report about the Muellers, but now he brightened and pulled a folded piece of paper from his pocket. He'd had better luck with Miss Minna, he announced. He had found the young woman alone on her porch and so had not had to risk being turned away by her parents. Erica's friend had asked him to wait and had immediately written a letter back to Erica, which he now handed to her.

Erica eagerly unfolded it and read,

My very dear friend Erica, I am so relieved to hear from you that all is well and you have run off with your handsome Texan to get married! It is such a romantic story, and I must confess I envy you completely! If I did not feel that your brother Hans and I are destined to be husband and wife someday, I would ask you to beg your Jake to find such a dashing Texan to come and steal me away too! The Mexican boy who brought your letter tells me your parents did not send a response. Try not to worry about this, my dear friend, as I fear you will do. They will be reconciled to the idea in time, especially when you send news that their first Enkelkind is on the way! I hope to be able to come visit you someday, and please let me know where I may write to you in the future, for I will assuredly find a way to do so. Your devoted friend, Minna.

Would her parents forgive her when she could write that a grandchild was on the way? Erica could only pray that it would be so.

"I'll have Juan take a note to the rector that the wedding will proceed on schedule next Saturday, all right?" John asked, and Jake and Erica nodded their assent. "Meanwhile, since it's Rosita's night off, I thought we might go out to the Menger Hotel for a nice supper tonight."

"What a good idea!" Henri crowed. "Erica, you wear that lovely gown Madame LaFollett delivered yesterday, the one in rose grosgrain with the flounces that shows off your lovely shoulders so well."

Erica smiled at the other woman's enthusiasm and felt her apprehension lift a little. If only life were as simple as having a beautiful dress to wear!

Supper in the dining room of the Menger was delicious. They all had the special that night, prime rib of beef so perfectly aged and marinated that it practically melted in their mouths, accompanied by green beans almondine and baked potatoes.

"Will *messieurs et mesdames* care for dessert?" inquired their pinched-nosed, supercilious waiter. "I have an elegant *gâteau au chocolat* to offer you, truly a sumptuous delight for the palate—"

"Yes, we'll have the chocolate cake," John Ransom said, winking wryly at his companions.

"Then you can have my slice, dear John," Henri insisted. "I declare I dare not eat another bite! It's all very well for young ladies like Erica to eat dessert, but as a woman of mature years, I—" She broke off as all of them noticed the doctor's distraction. "Why, John, whatever is the matter?"

John looked down at his plate, muttering, "I just spotted Mr. Schoenbrunn coming in the door, and unfortunately he's seen me."

Erica looked around for somewhere, anywhere, to

hide. She had no desire to speak to her father's cousin the banker, the father of the young man her parents had wanted her to marry!

It was worse than Ransom had first said—not only was Dietrich Schoenbrunn heading right for their table, but behind him followed Rudolph, a youthful copy of the stolid, florid-cheeked banker.

"Herr Doktor Ransom, Frau Hilliard, it is a pleasure to encounter you here," said Schoenbrunn, adjusting his pince-nez to focus on Erica and Jake. "You have guests with you tonight, *ja?*" he added, so sharply that Erica could tell he already knew who they were. Behind him, his son stared unabashedly at Erica.

"Why, Dietrich, how charming to see you," Henri put in warmly, and Erica guessed she was trying to distract the older Schoenbrunn. "And Rudolph, you . . . um, look more like your father every day."

Ransom had stood up when the banker approached, and now he said, "Dietrich, Rudolph, I believe you already know Miss Erica Mueller, a relative of yours? I would like to present her fiancé, my very good friend Jake Taylor—"

"Yes, Herr Doktor, I have heard from my cousin in New Braunfels, and when I saw you and Erica I guessed who he was," the German said, his posture as ramrod-stiff as any Prussian general. "Courtesy forbids that I express my feelings on the matter, *ja?*" he said, and swept on past.

"Why, that pompous windbag," growled Jake, clenching his fists and glaring at the banker's back as he walked away. "I ought to give him the same drubbing I . . ." His voice trailed off as Ransom laid a restraining hand on his friend's arm.

Erica stared after Schoenbrunn, ignoring the way his son continued to goggle over his shoulder at her. She wished she had the courage to pursue her father's cousin and ask if he knew what, if anything, her parents planned to do.

"Never you mind, honey," Henri said bracingly. "If that young man's the one you told me you were supposed to marry, you just thank your lucky stars the good Lord sent Jake Taylor into your life instead!"

"*Ja*, I do, Henri, oh, I do!" she said, so fervently that everyone laughed.

"Erica, sweetheart, come down and let me show you what I've bought! He's back at the barn!" Jake called up the stairs late Thursday afternoon as he returned to Ransom House from his latest expedition to the San Antonio area ranches. "John said this fellow named Maverick had some good horseflesh, and sure enough, he did! Wait till you see the lines of this silver dun stallion, sweetheart!" he went on enthusiastically, his voice coming closer as he dashed up the long curving marble stairway. "He's got barb in him—I can tell from the shape of his head—and thoroughbred, too—wait'll you see the long legs on him! But he's quick as a cat—"

"Jake, don't come in!" Henri called, laughing, as she leaned against the door to prevent him from entering, just as the doorknob had started to turn. "Your bride's dress was just delivered by Madame LaFollett and she's trying it on."

"Ah, her lover has come, her prince!" cooed Madame LaFollett, who was once again kneeling to inspect the hem to assure herself of its correct length. "See how she blushes! She will be the most beautiful bride in Texas, yes?" she said to Henri, who naturally agreed.

"I'll be down in a few minutes, Jake!" Erica promised, unable to take her eyes away from the mirror, which reflected a vision of herself she wouldn't have believed a couple of weeks ago when she'd first ridden into San Antonio with him, damp and disheveled and saddle-sore. Now she couldn't wait for Jake to see her in this fairy-tale gown on their wedding day!

"Did you find a good mare too?" she called through the door as she turned her back to the modiste so she could undo the line of tiny pearl buttons that ran from her neck to below her waist.

"I sure did!" came his response. "She's as black as midnight, except for this white blaze that runs down her nose, and a couple of hands shorter than Shiloh—that's the stallion, Erica. Meet me downstairs as soon as you change your clothes, okay? John said they were an amazing bargain!"

"Isn't that just like a man?" clucked Henri in amusement as the sound of Jake's boot heels faded back down the stairs and she left the door to assist Erica in lifting the dress over her head. "The wedding's in two days and he gets so excited about a horse."

"Yes, but if he wants to breed horses for a living, it is very important—" began Erica, then she paused as she heard the sound of a conveyance pulling into the driveway below her window. Usually Ransom, when he returned from the day's doctoring visits, drove his black one-horse buggy directly back to the stable rather than stopping in front for Señor Velasquez to lead his horse back.

Curiously, still clad in just her petticoats and chemise, she went to the window to see who had come—and froze. Her father was just handing her mother down from the family buckboard, and behind the high perch, her brothers were jumping down to the ground.

Chapter Twenty

Jake too had seen the Muellers' arrival through the etched-glass upper half of Ransom House's front door. Now he paused and took a deep breath, as he always had right before Hood had sounded a cavalry charge. In truth he felt as if the coming encounter might be just as fraught with a different sort of peril. Not that he was afraid for himself—he didn't think Erica's father would offer him any violence, and he was more than prepared to restrain the older man without hurting him if need be. The important thing was that Jake didn't want the woman he loved to go through any more conflict and unpleasantness than she already had. She tried to make her parents' disapproval of their marriage sound as if it were something she was resigned to, but Jake could tell that it had hurt her terribly.

He'd never known such a feeling of protectiveness as Erica Mueller aroused in him. It must be a part of true love, he mused. Planning to use all the diplomacy he could muster, Jake opened the door.

Hilda Mueller saw him first and ran from her husband's side, launching herself at him. "Where is my daughter? What have you done with my little girl?" she demanded, taking hold of Jake's shirtfront.

"Good evenin', Mrs. Mueller," Jake said as normally as he could with her clutching at him. "And Mr. Mueller. Howdy, Hans and Guenther," he added, letting himself smile as he saw that, whatever the elder Muellers felt about him, they hadn't managed to change their sons' minds. Guenther bounded up to him like a gangly puppy, throwing his arms around Jake's waist and hugging him with abandon while he babbled away in a combination of German and heavily accented English. Hans, more dignified in his adolescence, just grinned at Jake and fervently pumped the hand Jake extended.

"Erica is fine, and I'm sure she'll be down in just a minute or so," Jake said. He'd heard her rapid footsteps over his head and guessed she had seen her parents' arrival. "I know she'll be happy to see y'all."

"She had better be fine," growled her father as fiercely as any enraged bear. "Herr Taylor, I am taking her home with me even if you have an army at your back. Has the wedding taken place yet?"

"No, it's still to be on Saturday, as she told you in the letter," Jake said, relieved to see that Hilda had released his shirt, although she was still glaring at him as if she expected him to sprout horns and a tail. "I'm pleased you could make it to San Antonio in time to be there."

Hilda opened her mouth, obviously to contradict him. But at this point, Erica, now wearing one of her everyday dresses, hurtled through the door. She was instantly enveloped in her parents' embrace. For a moment there was a torrent of German words as father, mother, daughter and sons all talked at once.

So engrossed in each other were the Muellers that they didn't hear John Ransom pull up in his buggy, but Jake did. He crossed the driveway, his boot heels crunching on the gravel.

"Ah, this must be Miss Erica's family, eh?" John said, nodding at the hugging, gesticulating quintet.

Jake nodded.

"Well, no one seems in need of my medical services as yet," John said dryly. "So it must be going fairly well. Oh, *buenos noches*, Señor Velasquez," he said as his stablekeeper came around the side of the house. "Since it seems we have guests, would you mind seeing to my horse for me? *Gracias*." He jumped down, handing the reins to the old Mexican.

"Good evening," John said, walking over and extending a hand as Erica's father looked up. "You must be Erica's father. I'm John Ransom. And this must be Mrs. Mueller?"

Jake saw Gustav Mueller release his daughter and turn to face the newcomer. "*Ja*, I am Gustav Mueller and this is my wife Hilda, and these are my sons, Hans and Guenther," he said, indicating each in turn with a stiff nod of his head.

"You are the doctor who is Herr Taylor's host?"

"Yes, and I would say I am Jake Taylor's good friend, as well. Welcome to Ransom House. I hope you are planning to stay here while you are in San Antonio for the wedding? I assure you, there is more than enough room."

"There will be no wedding," Gustav Mueller said, and Erica looked stricken, but Jake noticed his tone had been moderated somewhat in the face of John's hospitable geniality.

"*Dankë* for your offer, sir," Gustav went on, "but we have made plans to stay at the house of my cousin, Dietrich Schoenbrunn. We will be leaving as soon as we have persuaded Erica that her plans to marry Herr Taylor are *verrückt*—madness."

"Papa, I am not going to change my mind—" Erica began, but broke off when John Ransom held up a hand calmly.

"Miss Erica, I'm sure your mother would be purely delighted to see your bridal gown, wouldn't she? Why don't you take her up and show her, since as your mother, she's one of the few mortals who can see it before you come down the aisle. Oh, Henri, I'm glad you're here too," John added as Henri, who had been hovering at the door, stepped onto the gallery. "Mr. and Mrs. Mueller, boys, this is my good friend, Mrs. Henrietta Hilliard. Henri, would you mind going to Rosita and telling her there will be four more for dinner?"

Jake didn't exactly know what his friend intended to do, but he figured it was best that the Mueller boys not be part of the audience.

"Hans and Guenther, if you'd like to follow Dr. Ransom's stablekeeper, yonder," he said, pointing to where Señor Velasquez was leading John's horse, released from his traces, back to the barn. "I bet if you ask him real nice he'll show you the stallion and mare I just bought today. They're real beauties, I think, but I'd be interested in your opinions," he added when Hans hesitated, clearly torn between the desire to stay with his sister and his love of horses.

Jake winked at him in a man-to-man way, and that worked. Hans said something in German to his younger brother and in a flash both boys were running to catch up with Señor Velasquez.

"Now, why don't we gentlemen come inside and have a drink?" John said, beckoning to both Jake and Gustav Mueller. "I have several bottles of Rhine wine that Dietrich Schoenbrunn assures me is among the best that the German vintners can produce."

Mentioning the banker was the trump card. "Ah, so you know my cousin Dietrich?" Gustav Mueller said, already following John through the door.

Once inside John's study, Jake and Mueller arranged themselves in chairs opposite one another while John poured the wine.

John looked at Jake. "Jake, why don't you make a toast? Something we can all agree to?"

Jake thought for a moment. He couldn't make a toast regarding the wedding, because Mueller would be bound by his stubbornness not to agree. Finally, he held up his glass. "To peace between all Texans, no matter what their country of origin." How could Mueller disagree with that?

Evidently Mueller knew he couldn't, and after an endless moment he too raised his glass and echoed Jake's words.

All three men took a drink, then Jake and Gustav looked at one another, each hoping the other would say something to open the discussion.

"Did you have a good journey, Mr. Mueller?" Ransom inquired. "I trust you encountered no hostile Indians or bandits, no inclement weather?"

"We had no problems, thank you. We broke our journey at my aunt's house which lies about halfway between New Braunfels and San Antonio."

"Good, good . . ."

"Herr Doktor Ransom, it is very kind of you to offer your hospitality, and I am grateful that you have given my daughter shelter during her stay in your town. But as I have said, I am opposed to this marriage, and I have come to take her home. Herr Taylor informs me that no marriage has taken place, so I see no impediment to my doing so—immediately."

Jake jumped to his feet. "No impediment except the fact that I won't allow it to happen," he said, and was aware that his voice had taken on a dangerous edge.

John ignored him. "Well, it seems mighty late in the day to be thinking of starting a journey," he said mildly.

"Naturally, we will stay with Cousin Dietrich tonight, and start home in the morning."

John refilled the older man's glass so smoothly that Jake thought Mueller hadn't even seen him do it. "Now, Mr. Mueller, Jake had already told me you had some serious reservations about the marriage. But don't all fathers feel a little suspicious about the men who are to wed their daughters?" He took a sip of his wine and went on. "But be reasonable, sir. Your Erica is a beautiful girl. Do you wish your beautiful daughter to be an unmarried, childless woman the rest of her life? What a waste that would be!"

Mueller made a strangled sound in his throat. "*Nein*, of course not. But I would have wished for her—"

"To marry one of her own," John finished smoothly for him. "Certainly. Any father would do the same."

Jake held his breath. Ransom was so convincing— it almost sounded as if he were a father too. But what if Mueller asked him if that were indeed the case, and refused to listen further because John had never been married, let alone fathered a child?

Ransom apparently sensed he had Mueller's ear, though, for he pressed his advantage: "Realistically, sir, what chance is there of making a match for your daughter, after all that has happened, with another German immigrant? Jake told me what happened in your town just before he and your daughter left it— I'm referring to the incident with that Siegfried Von Schiller. And by now it is known that your daughter has eloped with Jake."

Gustav shook his head. "I have been very careful to keep it quiet. Our pastor has agreed to be silent on the matter. To those who have inquired, I have said that Erica went to visit an aunt in Comfort."

John spread out his hands. "But, sir, think about it. A scoundrel like Von Schiller will talk—you know he will. And then how long do you believe your acquaintances will believe the polite fiction of your daughter's visit to her aunt's? And then, even if Jake agrees to part with her—"

"Which I won't," Jake snapped.

"What chance do you think she has of making a good marriage?" John went on persuasively. "You will just have condemned her to being an old maid."

"No!" Gustav Mueller said despairingly.

"Yes," Ransom countered, politely insistent. "The truth will come out, sir, that she ran off with Jake. And to be frank, Mr. Mueller, how many people are going to believe Jake didn't touch her before they reached my home?"

Jake couldn't believe his ears. Had his friend lost his mind, saying such a thing?

Mueller jumped to his feet and advanced on Jake, his fists clenched. "Herr Taylor, if you have offered my daughter the least bit of dishonor—"

Jake jumped to his feet too, and in a heartbeat only a scant few inches separated the two men's flushed faces. "I didn't dishonor your daughter, Mr. Mueller, as God is my witness." *Though it took every bit of self-control I had.*

John Ransom arose too, his movements slow and easy. "Gentlemen, gentlemen. Please sit down again." He waited until both had done so, and then went on, "And if all that weren't enough, we encountered your cousin Dietrich—and his son Rudolph—when we were out dining the other night, so they have seen your daughter in Jake's company too."

Now Gustav buried his head in his hands and groaned as if he knew his cause was lost.

"What I'm saying is, you have virtually no chance

of marrying your daughter now to one of your own countrymen. And as Jake has told you, he *does* desire to marry your daughter. He has been my friend all my life, and I can tell you he is a good and honorable man, and will make a faithful husband to your Erica—and he will provide for her. Why, Jake served alongside me in the Confederate Army, and I can tell you there is no better man—"

Now it was Jake's turn to groan, though he did it inwardly. It had been a tactical error to mention the rebels to a man whose allegiance had been to the Union.

Gustav Mueller bristled. "That is no recommendation, Herr Doktor, to remind me that the two of you served in the same army whose officials murdered so many of my fellow German immigrants, just because our consciences did not permit us to wear the gray of rebel slaveholders—"

Ransom, however, was wise enough not to take offense at the term. "Pardon me, perhaps I shouldn't have used that in my argument. However, I will tell you that I—and for that matter, Jake—have never owned a slave, although Jake's father did. But I will still insist he is a good man," he said, putting his arm on Jake's shoulder, "and you would be a fool not to let him marry your daughter."

Mueller was silent, studying Jake as if his life depended on it.

"I love Erica, sir," Jake said. "I'll be good to her, I swear it."

Gustav's shoulders sagged, and Jake knew he had won.

"All right. I will agree to the wedding," Mueller said simply.

"Wonderful!" John said. "Why don't we call the ladies to join us? We can all toast to the bride and groom!"

Chapter Twenty-one

"I now pronounce you man and wife. You may kiss the bride."

The words had been spoken an hour before in the beautiful sanctuary of St. Mark's Anglican Church. The kiss had been unforgettable in its sweetness and promise—not only of passion, but also of happiness in their future life—and had provoked sighs from several of the onlookers. But Jake still had trouble believing his good fortune—that the golden angel now sitting next to him at the wedding breakfast back at Ransom House could really be his wife, Mrs. Jacob Taylor.

He was sure there wasn't a more beautiful woman in the world than the one sitting next to him, clad in a wedding gown so dazzling that the cloth must have been spun by celestial beings. His heart had pounded as Erica walked down the aisle of the church on her father's arm.

Erica Taylor. Jake and Erica Taylor. Mr. and Mrs. Jacob

Taylor. He tried the names out in his mind as he watched his bride pick at the delicacies Rosita had cooked.

She's nervous, Jake realized. She's already thinking about the wedding night to come, and she's apprehensive. Does she think I'll turn into a monster like Von Schiller when I make love to her?

It didn't help that that oaf Dietrich Schoenbrunn had made a needlessly awkward toast citing the bride's duty to provide her husband with the delights of her body in the marriage bed, and that all the time Dietrich was talking, his son Rudolph had leered, satyr-like, at Erica. Jake would have preferred that John not invite them, though he was sure his friend had done it out of his innate courtesy, in order to give the Muellers someone of their own culture to sit with. He was fairly certain father and son were both drunk when they arrived at the wedding breakfast, if not at the wedding ceremony itself. Now they seemed intent on preventing the return of sobriety, endlessly tilting glasses of champagne to their lips.

It was now early afternoon, and everyone had eaten heartily. Gustav Mueller arose.

"Herr Doktor, my wife and I thank you for your hospitality," he began. "But we must be going."

"Vati, no, must you leave so soon?" Erica protested beside Jake, her color fading.

"You don't have to leave already, do you?" Jake said, getting to his feet too. "Why not stay another night and leave in the morning, when you'll have the whole day to travel?"

"*Ja*, why not stay at my house tonight, as you had

206

originally planned? Doctor Ransom stole you away, so I have not been allowed to welcome you into my home," Dietrich Schoenbrunn put in, with drunken truculence.

"I thank you," Mueller said, barely glancing at his prosperous cousin, "but I believe it best that we start out now. We have been away from our home for many days, and it is time that we allow the bride and groom to begin their new life together."

Jake left his place and extended his hand to his new father-in-law. "Thank you for coming, sir, and bringing your family. I'm glad y'all could be with Erica on our special day."

Gustav shook his hand.

"I promise I'll be good to her, sir," Jake said.

Gustav nodded. "Yes, I believe you will. Erica," he said, extending his arms to his daughter, who was waiting uncertainly next to Jake. She flew into his embrace.

Hilda Mueller surprised Jake by embracing him and giving him the broadest smile he imagined she had bestowed on anyone in years. "Blessings on you and Erica, *mein sohn.*"

"*Dankë*, Mrs. Mueller," Jake said, grinning as he used the German word to please her.

She beamed back, but also corrected him, "No, it is 'Mutti' now, *ja?*"

"Mutti," he agreed, pronouncing the new word carefully, and kissed the top of the older woman's head. Then Hans and Guenther were there, also wanting to welcome Jake to the family.

Jake got a lump in his throat, realizing that this

was now his other father and mother, and wishing his own cantankerous sire, Frank Taylor, were there too. But there had been no word from Taylor Hall, although the telegram had come back indicating that the elder Taylor had received the message.

Jake sighed. Evidently, as he feared, his father was going to be a tougher nut to crack. He'd have to take Erica to meet him, for he was sure the old man could not remain opposed to his son's new wife if Erica just smiled at him once.

"We will take your rented horses back to the livery stable for you, Jake," Gustav added, startling Jake out of his reverie.

"Much obliged, sir."

The Schoenbrunns, father and son, left while the Muellers were still loading their wagon, and Jake, for one, was not sorry to see them go.

Henri Hilliard departed next, after kissing Erica and Jake and saying, "I told you you would be the most beautiful bride ever seen in San Antonio, Erica dear, but you are even lovelier than I had predicted. Much happiness to you both. Now, no tears, Erica, honey. I know Jake will take good care of you."

Now, in mid-afternoon, there was only John standing next to them, and Jake was realizing he probably should have made some arrangements for a suite at the Menger. Somehow it seemed awkward to contemplate staying in Ransom House with their host on their wedding night, that most private of times.

"John, I can't thank you enough for all you've done for us," he began, wondering how to broach the matter without hurting John's feelings. "You're the best friend a man could ask for."

"*Ja*, John," echoed Erica. "We are indebted to you more than we can say."

But John seemed to have thought ahead to this difficulty. "You're more than welcome, both of you. But I hope you won't mind if I leave you two alone here. I have some pressing business up in Austin to take care of, and the sooner the better. I hadn't wanted to leave while you required my assistance, but you won't mind now, will you? My household staff stands ready to meet your slightest need, and I want you to feel free to stay as long as you like. I plan to be away at least a week."

Jake looked deeply into the other man's eyes and let him see the gratitude he felt. He knew there was no "pressing business": Ransom was fabricating the story to give Erica and Jake some much-needed privacy among familiar surroundings.

"Thank you, John," Jake said, embracing the other man. "I hope as soon as we're settled that you'll be our first houseguest."

Evidently John had already discussed his plan with the servants, for the Velasquezes' son was already bringing down Ransom's bags, while outside, his father was backing the buggy horse into the traces.

"Jake, when you leave, take that other carriage in the stable, and there's two horses you can use too, since we don't know if those two you bought have been broken to driving. And don't worry about sending them back—I'll get everything when I come to visit y'all."

"You've thought of everything, it seems."

In just minutes, Ransom's buggy had rolled off down the street, the servants had retreated to their quarters, and Mr. and Mrs. Jake Taylor were alone together.

Jake cleared his throat, which had suddenly, inexplicably, become as dry as dust. "Erica, honey, why don't we go upstairs and I'll help you out of that gown? Surely you'd like to put on something more comfortable."

He watched as Erica's cheeks paled again and she seemed to have as much difficulty swallowing as he did. Both of them knew it was an excuse; she wouldn't be putting on any other clothes any time soon.

"But it's the middle of the day," she pointed out, looking like a frightened deer.

He tipped her chin up with one gentle finger. "So we'll see each other without lighting candles. Erica, you know I won't hurt you, don't you?" he asked softly.

"Y-yes, husband," she said at last, and turned towards the stairs.

He didn't want her blind obedience, damn it, he wanted her love. "Erica, wait," he said, and pulled her into an embrace, kissing her until he made her forget about her apprehension and the touch of his lips on hers set them both aflame. Then, without any further hesitation, he scooped her into his arms and carried her up the stairs to the bedroom which until then had been occupied by Erica alone.

Ransom's servants had seen to everything here

too, for the bed was freshly made and turned down, and a bottle of costly French champagne stood chilling in a silver bucket amidst vases of roses that filled the air with their heavy, sensual fragrance.

Neither of them paid any attention to these things, however, for they only had eyes for each other.

Erica trembled as Jake made short work of undoing the score or more of tiny buttons that fastened the gown in the back. He slid the soft fabric down over her slender hips so that it pooled in a gleaming white puddle at her feet. She stood before him now in a low-cut corset, lace-trimmed chemise and petticoats, and she was conscious of his eyes caressing the exposed tops of her breasts even as he strove to unlace the confining corset and untie the tapes which held the numerous petticoats around her waist.

She wanted to reach out to him, to push the frock coat from his shoulders, to begin undoing the row of buttons that extended down his snow-white shirtfront. She was hungry for his fingers to begin touching *her* and not the fastenings of her underwear, but she forced her hands to remain at her sides.

She must not be bold. Jake must not be reminded of the fact that she was no virgin bride, that she had been undressed by another man, touched by another man. Jake must not be forced to remember that Siegfried Von Schiller had seen her naked before he had, so she must act as if this were the first time, despite the way her hands ached to touch him and her

211

body kept urging her to show Jake every form of lovemaking she had ever learned.

She closed her eyes as if to shut out the sight of his eyes, gleaming as he took in the sight of her, clad in just her chemise and pantalets.

"Help me," he whispered, his face so close to hers that she could feel his warm breath softly brush her cheek. "I seem to be a little overdressed, compared to you."

She opened her eyes to see what he meant, and Jake made a gesture toward the shirt and trousers he still wore. When had he shed his frock coat? Or had she done what she had imagined and pulled it off herself? Somehow it had come to rest on the chaise longue sitting at a right angle to the canopied bed.

Well, since he had asked her to help him undress, she had the perfect excuse to do as she had wanted, didn't she? She would merely be complying, not acting like a wanton woman.

He backed up, making her follow him closer to the bed, as her fingers reached out to remove his shirt. She was grateful, as she moved closer to him under his watchful gaze, that he hadn't removed *all* her clothes and then compelled her to stand naked while she obeyed his command.

Still wearing the last filmy barriers between his hands and her nakedness, she raised her lips to his and kissed him while she undid his shirt. She wasn't acting when her hands shook as she unbuttoned the fly of his trousers, and then she was pushing the trousers down over his lean hips and he was standing before her wearing only his under-drawers.

"Erica, you are the most beautiful creature I have ever seen," he said, pulling her the last little distance between them and falling backward onto the bed, taking her with him.

The sheets felt cool under her bare shoulders.

Remember, you have never done this before, Erica commanded herself, and forced herself to close her eyes as Jake began to unlace the chemise in the front so that it fell to her sides, held on only by the narrow straps over her shoulders, baring her breasts.

He began to stroke them and she went still, achingly aware of her nipples peaking with pleasure at his touch. She gasped, relieved to hear that her cry could be interpreted as maidenly shock though it was actually an expression of ecstasy. And then his lips closed over one of her nipples. He drew it into his mouth and her body arched, taut as a bow.

"Oh, Erica, I want you so much I ache with it," he said, his voice husky with passion. "Your skin feels like satin, sweetheart."

She thrilled at the need she heard in his tone, yet she tried to remind herself it didn't matter to a man which woman lay beneath him—any comely, well-formed female would do once he was sexually excited. Hadn't Siegfried always told her that, laughing when he saw that he had hurt her with his brutal truth?

She couldn't deny to herself that she was aroused, and became more so when she felt him push the

213

pantalets off her hips and the heat of a Texas afternoon touch her bare body. She felt a dampness between her legs, and was aware that her hips turned naturally towards his as Jake turned on his side and yanked off his drawers impatiently.

Remember, you are a virgin! You should be frightened, not eager to feel him inside you! She lowered the hand that reached out to stroke his rigid length and made herself cross her arms over her breasts as if she were shy of his gaze.

Jake must have seen it, too, for his voice was harsh when he whispered, "Erica, love me. Love me! Relax, please, sweetheart!"

She hesitated, not knowing for sure if he had guessed what she was trying to do, and then she felt him touch her, his fingers gentle but insistent as he caressed her, stroking her until her legs parted as if they had a will of their own, allowing him full access.

A moan escaped her lips as she felt his hand cupping her.

"That's it, honey, let me hear how that feels. Let me know you want me. . . ." he said, and she knew she was losing the battle. Her eyes flew open to find him gazing down at her, and the tenderness there, where she had expected only a raging lust, was her undoing.

"Erica, tell me what *you* want," Jake said. "Tell me what feels good to you, sweetheart. . . ."

How could she do that? How could she say, *touch me here, touch me there, softer, faster, more slowly*, without exposing herself as a sexually experienced woman? No man wanted his new bride to be well versed in the arts of love—he wanted to be the one to teach her!

"I do not know. . . ." she whispered back. "My English . . ." She shook her head, as if she just couldn't find the words. She hated herself for the falsehood—but it wasn't as bad to lie that she didn't know the words, was it, as it was to deny that she knew exactly what she needed him to do to bring her to that same fever pitch of excitement as his ragged breathing and the flush on his cheekbones showed he was beginning to feel?

He smiled down at her. "Then I'll have to try everything I know until you show me what you like, Erica."

It was a promise, not a threat, but one which made her quiver with anticipation.

"Do you like this?" His finger entered her, then retreated, stroking that spot of exquisite sensitivity on the outside.

Her outcry seemed to be all the confirmation he needed, and his encouragement to continue. In little time her head was tossing restlessly back and forth on her pillow and her arms had encircled him of their own volition. As she felt his manhood join his hand in tantalizing her, her fingers raced up to tangle in his hair and she was murmuring endearments—but at least she remembered, even in the haze of passion that was beginning to cloud her brain, to use German instead of English, so that he would not know she was calling him "darling" and crying out, "I love you!"

She wasn't even aware when her hands cupped his buttocks, urging him inside. But Jake had evidently been awaiting just such an indication of her readiness, for he surged inside her in one smooth stroke, smothering her cry with his mouth on hers, and then she knew nothing but wave upon wave of flame until at last she felt a flooding of joy and they were consumed together.

Chapter Twenty-two

Afterward, Jake lifted himself off of Erica and collapsed on his back, his breath coming in hard panting gasps as he felt the warm afternoon air cool his fevered flesh.

"That was . . ." He searched his brain, trying to come up with the word, as if his native language were as foreign to him as it was to her. "Wonderful," he said at last, and knew the word was woefully inadequate.

"I . . . I pleased you?" she asked, and he opened his eyes to look at her and found his bride, his Erica, gazing at him with a shy smile.

"Oh, yes, honey, you pleased me," he assured her, and leaned over to bestow a quick kiss on her forehead, smoothing away a curl that had plastered itself to her skin. Then, because he had to know, he asked, "Did I please you, Erica?"

The question seemed to startle her, for her blue

eyes widened in surprise. "Please me? Of course you did, my husband."

Of course? Was she just saying that because she knew he needed to hear it? There was no "of course" about the matter, even though he had felt the spasms inside her that signaled her climax.

But had he touched her *heart*? Had he pleasured her in a way that Von Schiller could not, because Von Schiller hadn't loved Erica when he had taken her?

"Erica, I want the truth between us, always," Jake said, wishing desperately she would know what he meant, because he didn't know how to say it. "Nothing dishonest, do you understand?"

She nodded, her eyes clear and direct. "Yes, Jake."

"I don't want you to hold back."

Erica blinked. " 'Hold back'?"

"Don't be afraid to be yourself, sweetheart. Tell me what you're feeling—don't pretend. About anything."

"All right," she agreed slowly, but he was convinced she really didn't understand.

And who was he to demand such a thing of her when he wouldn't be completely honest with her? But how could he tell her the truth, that he loved her, when she had only married him to escape an intolerable disgrace? Knowing it would be an unwelcome burden to her.

Oh, Erica liked him, he knew that well enough; she found him good company, amusing, and she valued his courage. But did she love him? He couldn't bear the idea of telling her he loved her, only to hear it parroted back to him because she knew that was what he wanted to hear.

But the gift of her passion was enough for now. They were compatible sexual partners, if not lovers in the strictest sense of the word. She would welcome his advances in the future.

It had been a long day already, full of stress and tension, and now, in the wake of their lovemaking, drowsiness swept over him.

He pulled her to him, cradling her head on his chest. "Let's sleep now," he murmured.

She woke sometime after darkness had fallen. The house was quiet, and all Erica could hear was the hoot of an owl somewhere on the grounds and the steady, comforting beat of Jake's heart beneath her ear. And then the bell in some nearby church began to toll the hour, and she realized it was midnight.

Erica wasn't sure Jake was awake too until he yawned, then chuckled softly as his stomach began to growl.

"You are hungry, husband?" she asked, smiling against his chest as his arm came down from above his head to rest around her upper back.

"Yeah," he admitted. "The wedding breakfast seems another lifetime ago, and I reckon we slept through supper. It's a long time till breakfast."

She knew they could pull on the cord by the head of the bed and summon Rosita from her bedchamber, and the cook would uncomplainingly fix them something to eat, but neither of them would be so inconsiderate.

"Perhaps," Erica murmured, "if we are very quiet, we could steal down to the kitchen and find something to . . . what is the word for *knabbern*—nibble?"

"I think I'll just nibble on you," Jake said, then suited the word to the deed by mouthing places on her head until she giggled and he laughed into her hair.

How she loved the feeling of him stretched naked, full-length, against her. Siegfried had never stayed with her for long after he had taken his pleasure; he always seemed impatient to be elsewhere once he had been satisfied. She could not imagine him sleeping with her for hours as Jake—her *husband*—just had. And she would have a lifetime of sleeping with Jake, she thought happily, smiling into the darkness and feeling a return of the desire that had so overwhelmed her just hours ago.

He had said she was not to hold back, hadn't he? Then perhaps he would not mind if she acted on his instructions right now? The worst that could happen was that he might want to postpone further lovemaking until they found something to eat.

"Ah, but Jake, there are better places to nibble," she said, raising herself up on one elbow and nibbling on his lower lip. "Here, for example," she said, then moved down so her teeth could close lightly, briefly, over his earlobe.

Erica felt him shiver in pleasure.

"Ah, delicious," she murmured, and trailed her teeth down the side of his neck, never causing pain, then licked his nipple to see if that excited him as it had when he had done it to her.

It did.

She could feel him growing hard once more against the thigh she had thrown over his leg, and knew a heady feeling of feminine power.

"Oh, but you said you were hungry, husband. I'm sorry, I forgot," she said with patently false regret as she pretended to pull away. "We'll go down to the kitchen and find something for you to eat, *ja?*"

"No," he growled in her ear, his arm suddenly like iron, holding her to him. "I think I've found a feast right here," he added, pushing her gently onto her back.

After they had made love again, they found robes hanging in the closet and went to the door, ready now to sneak downstairs for something to fill their stomachs, but they found Rosita had anticipated them.

Sitting on a tray just outside the door were several covered dishes. Jake brought the tray inside and they uncovered the dishes to find fried chicken, a bowl of spicy rice, and apple pie.

Arranging the midnight supper on their bed as if it were a picnic field, they fell to it as if they had been denied food for a week.

They hardly left the bedchamber the next day except to go down for meals.

Jake and Erica remained at Ransom House for the next five days. Then, one morning after breakfast, Jake turned to her and said, "I think we should leave tomorrow."

"All right," Erica said, for she knew they could not remain in this dreamlike existence, immersed in each other, forever. "But where are we going?" She wouldn't mind if Jake said Timbuktu, as long as they were going together.

He looked a bit startled. "I guess I haven't said

what I've been thinking, have I? I think we need to go to Taylor Hall, Erica. I want Papa to meet you."

To learn to love you as I do, he thought, though he still couldn't bring himself to say the words— because *she* hadn't.

"It hurt you that he didn't come to the wedding," Erica said, and she was so unexpectedly correct that his first response was, "Yes." Then he tried to take it back, thinking he sounded too much like a little boy in need of reassurance. "No. It's not that. I don't know. . . ." he said, and threw his hands up in the air. It was too late to take it back.

"I just want him to get to know you, Erica. . . ."

"He does not like it that you married an immigrant woman."

"Yes. No! Well, who knows what he thinks, since he didn't even write a letter?" Jake asked, frustrated. "I just think he'll learn to like you, if he meets you . . . but it won't matter if he doesn't," he added quickly, not wanting her to think he might repudiate her if his father chose to remain stubborn. "And I want him to see the stallion and mare I bought . . . and I need to see what he's decided about Taylor Hall. When I left there, we'd quarreled about what we were going to do with it."

She looked troubled. "You had an argument with your father?"

He nodded. "He wants to keep Taylor Hall anchored in the past, before the war, when it was a cotton plantation. He can't own slaves anymore, though, so there's no way he can make a go of it except by sharecropping—having tenant farmers."

"And you want to make it into a horse farm, my husband?"

He loved it when Erica called him that. She sounded so . . . wifely.

He nodded. "It's set in prime country for horse raising." He wasn't aware that his eyes had gone dreamy and unfocused. "Rolling green pastureland, good soil and water, more rain than here . . . But he wants to rent it out to a bunch of sharecroppers and let cotton keep sucking the life out of the soil." He sighed. "I'll buy another place if I have to, but that'll take time, and I'd have to work for someone for a while to earn the money to do it. My sister Maria's husband Bowie would hire me, until I had enough to buy a ranch elsewhere."

"But Taylor Hall is home to you," she said.

"I wouldn't mind living at Taylor Hall with Papa, if I could convince him that raising good horseflesh is the best thing—much better than wearin' out the land raising cotton. . . . Eventually, of course, Papa will be gone," he said, acknowledging a bleak, painful truth he'd rather not have thought about at all. "But he's an old man, Erica. He shouldn't have to be alone."

He looked to see if he had bored her with his musing, because she was so quiet, but she was just watching him intently, waiting patiently for him to finish saying what he wanted them to do. She wasn't making demands that he prove to her how he was going to provide a roof over their heads and food for their table, that he take her to visit her parents. . . .

Had there ever been a woman like this one? Did

she have no wants of her own? That quality in her made him want to please her even more, and provide her with everything.

"You're right," she said. "Your father should not be alone. We will travel to Taylor Hall and you will make him see that your way is the best way."

"We won't stay if he's not willin' to be nice to you, Erica. I won't tolerate that," he promised her. "I'll work for Bowie and we'll buy a place halfway between his place near San Marcos and New Braunfels."

"Jake, you must—how do you say it?—'mend your fences' with your papa, *ja?* I think your father will come to agree with you. And he will learn to like me, too. I will cook for him, *ja?* Then he will see that you have found a good wife."

He pulled her to him and kissed her. "*Ja.* He'll be putty in your hands, Erica." He hoped it was true. He couldn't bear for anyone to cause this woman any more pain.

"It shouldn't take us any more than a week, assuming the weather is good. And we're going to spend the nights in hotels whenever possible, not camping out."

"Ah, that will be nice." Erica rolled her eyes. "No more thunderstorms, *ja?* I shouldn't like to arrive at the home of your papa looking like . . . like a rooster under the rainspout again, okay?"

He laughed at the image, and at her unconscious use of the quintessential American word "okay." His German wife was becoming Americanized. "Okay. But perhaps some of the journey you'll want to ride your new mare, just as I'll want to try out Shiloh.

Perhaps we'd better go back to that seamstress and buy you something better to wear for riding?"

She clucked at him. "Is that not just like a man, to assume one can snap one's fingers and expect a modiste to produce a riding habit? But don't worry, I thought ahead, husband. One day while you were napping I sneaked out with Rosita and paid a visit to Madame LaFollett and ordered a riding skirt that is divided in the center, like wide trousers," she said, gesturing to indicate what she meant. "But there is a panel in the front that hides the split when a lady dismounts—it is such a practical garment for a Texas woman!" she said proudly. "Madame LaFollett was scandalized, of course, that I would not wear a riding habit, but I explained I must have such a thing when we left San Antonio, so we can go pick it up today. She sent word yesterday it was ready."

"You constantly amaze me, Erica," he said, caressing her cheek.

"A good wife should be prepared, *ja?*"

Chapter Twenty-three

Siegfried Von Schiller departed from New Braunfels at about the same time Erica and Jake left San Antonio. He was feeling profoundly disillusioned with life in America—especially in the German parts of Texas. After a week or two of free lodging in the most prosperous homes, the practical, hardworking settlers of New Braunfels had seemed less and less welcoming to a man who was too noble a personage to soil his hands with work.

He decided to shake the dust of the place from his boots and go north to Austin. He was embarrassingly close to being out of money—he'd used most of the paltry sum his father had given him upon his departure from Bavaria to buy his passage to New York and from there to Houston, but no matter. Thanks to an American cardsharp returning from a visit to Berlin aboard the same steamer to New York, Siegfried had learned card games like monte and poker without losing too many more of his pfennigs.

Until he could find some rich American widow who wanted a European count on her arm and in her bed, he could support himself by fleecing the gullible in the saloons of the Texas capital.

No matter what he did to keep the wolf from his door, it was all destined to be temporary, Siegfried knew. As soon as he had amassed enough wealth, he was going to hunt down Erica and take her back— back into his bed and eventually, back to Europe. They'd settle in Paris or London, however, not Germany. He was done capitulating to his father's iron will.

He knew that Erica had married the damned Texan who had beaten him within an inch of his life. The ceremony had taken place in a fancy church in San Antonio and they had been staying with a wealthy physician who was Jake Taylor's friend. That much Siegfried had gleaned from talking to the mayor's homely, gossipy daughter, who'd gotten it from Erica's gullible friend Minna. But neither Minna nor Erica's parents, whom Gunilla had also pumped for information, seemed to know where Erica and her new husband were going to settle after their honeymoon.

No matter—he'd find them. Money removed all obstacles, and by the time he was ready to search, he'd have plenty of it. It troubled Siegfried little that Texas was an enormous state—bigger than Germany, he'd heard someone boast. There were always ways of finding out what he needed to know. And when he found Mr. and Mrs. Jake Taylor, he was going to make Erica a widow. No one took anything from Siegfried Von Schiller that he wasn't ready to give up.

Jake called out, "Whoa," to the carriage horses on a grassy hill and pointed into the Brazos River valley below. "There it is, Erica—Taylor Hall," he said, indicating a white Greek Revival–style house set amidst tall live oaks and surrounded on all sides by cottonfields—barren, all but a couple of them. Papa must not have had too much luck getting tenant farmers so late into the growing season. Maybe that was good—maybe it would cause the old man to begin to see reason about the impracticality of his plan.

They could have ridden on and arrived at Taylor Hall late the last evening, but both of them had thought it best to spend the night in Bryan for a variety of reasons, not the least of which was that Jake knew his father wasn't at his best at the end of a long day. He might even have overindulged in his whiskey. In addition, since it hadn't always been possible to find a decent hotel along the way, they wanted to wash the last of the trail dust away. But most importantly, they had tacitly agreed they wanted to have one last night alone together. One last night of honeymoon, or *Hochzeitsreise*, as Erica told him it was said in German.

The passion which existed between them astonished Jake. They had made love every night, whether they spent it in a hotel bed or under the stars—and they had even sometimes stopped during the day when a look or a touch ignited desire. He had never, in his wildest imaginings, believed such a fierce fire could burn so continually between a man and a woman, even if they were married. *Especially* if they were married, he thought, remembering his parents' acrimonious relationship. Had Frank and Constance Taylor ever felt this inability to keep their hands off one another? *Dear God, please don't let our relationship ever become like theirs!* He felt like the luckiest man in Texas to have found such a woman.

And yet the word "love" had still not been spoken between them. Jake knew that he loved Erica, and the love grew more every day. He also knew that she thought him a skillful lover, because she had praised him more than once when they lay spent in each others' arms.

There were times when he could have sworn that the next words out of her mouth would be, "I love you, Jake." But so far, it hadn't happened, and so he hadn't said it either.

Was he just being stubborn? Maybe he had inherited that trait from his father, Jake mused, and the thought didn't make him happy. But somehow he thought it was more than that. Maybe it was just that he couldn't bear to confirm his secret fear that the most Erica felt for him, when they were not actually coupling, was gratitude for rescuing her.

The previous night when they had undressed, Erica had folded away her divided riding skirt and laid out one of the new dresses Madame LaFollett had made, a light blue Swiss muslin dress which made her look pretty as a picture. He marveled at her feminine wisdom in the choice. How could his father resist her?

"Do I . . . do I look all right, Jake?" Erica asked.

He turned to look at her, and saw that her lovely face was a trifle pale under her new flower-trimmed hat.

Jake reached out a hand to caress Erica's cheek. "You look lovely," he said. "Try not to worry. My father's not going to bite you."

She smiled, but it didn't reach her eyes. "I know he will not, Jake. But I am afraid. It is so important that you and your father are reconciled—I do not wish to come between you."

He locked her gaze with his and said, "I'm a man, Erica, and I make my own decisions, not my papa."

She blinked, and he saw at once that she feared she had offended him. Before she could open her mouth and voice an unnecessary apology, he put a finger gently on her lips. "I'm just saying that if the old coot acts too bullheaded today, it's not going to change my mind about you, Erica. Like I've said before, I wouldn't mind buying some land for our horse farm in the hill country near your parents."

Erica shook her head vehemently. "If you do all you can to make peace and he still will not listen, perhaps then we will speak of other places to live."

Jake leaned over to kiss his bride. He loved her even more for her determination to help him make things better with his father, even though she didn't, as yet, have a clue about how impossible that task might be. He hoped he wasn't leading her into the lion's den by bringing her here.

His father could be a cranky old lion, but even from here, Jake could see the dilapidation of the "den." He had to find a way to turn things around, or Taylor Hall was going to be falling down around their ears before the next generation inherited it.

"Well, come on then, let's see how it goes," he said, wheeling his horse to start down the hill that led to home.

He should have known he couldn't sneak up on old Vespasia, the housekeeper. She must have been sitting out on the front porch shelling peas or something and seen them coming down the hill, because by the time they entered the long, tree-lined lane that led up to the house, she was running towards them, moving surprisingly fast for a woman who had to be sixty if she was a day. Her calico skirts flapped as she held them up out of her way.

"Mist' Jake! Mist' Jake! De Lord be praised! Y-you're home!" she called, waving.

Gesturing for Erica to follow, Jake spurred his horse to her. A woman of her size and age shouldn't be out running in this heat.

He jumped out of the saddle and, keeping hold of one rein, hugged the excited woman who had been more of a mother to him than his own. "Vespasia, I'm so happy to see you!" he said, giving her a hearty kiss on both cheeks.

"And this must be yo' beautiful bride!" Vespasia cried as Erica drew abreast of them on her mare.

"Erica, this is Vespasia, the best cook in Texas— no, make that the world!" Jake cried, still hugging the old woman. "Vespasia, my wife Erica."

"Aw, Mistah Jake, you go on!" said the old woman, beaming at Erica. "Ain't he the silver-tongued devil, though? But you, Miz Erica, you're a golden angel an' no mistake. No wonder Mist' Jake fall in love wit' you. Mist' Jake, you din't tell us in yo' letter jes' how pretty she was!"

Jake was fairly sure he had mentioned Erica's beauty, but since Vespasia couldn't read, his father might have left that part out when he'd read the letter aloud.

"Hello," came Erica's shy reply as Jake helped her to dismount. "Thank for you for the compliments. You are very kind."

Vespasia scooped her up in a hug. "Honey, kindness don't have nothin' to do wit' it. It's jes' purely th' truth. An' ain't it pretty how she talks, Jake? Like no one I ever did hear."

"She's from Germany, Vespasia," Jake reminded the old woman, amused. "That's across the ocean from here."

Vespasia reached out a hand and swatted his shoulder. "I know dat, boy, I'm not ignorant, even if I don't have no idea *where* across the ocean. But let Mose take your horses—this my husband Mose, Miz Erica," she added, nodding to the elderly black man who'd come down the lane in her wake. "Y'all come on into the house. I cain't wait for yore papa to see her, Mist' Jake!"

Jake wished for a second he could speak to Vespasia away from Erica's hearing so he could have some warning of how his father was going to react to the introduction. But he couldn't, so as they walked towards the house, he contented himself with asking, "So how has he been, Vespasia? Having any more of those chest pains?"

"He's been tol'able, Mist' Jake. Tol'able. He been frettin' 'bout you," the old woman said. But she

233

added with her customary optimism, "Now you be back, he'll be better. Don't you worry 'bout the explosion—that's jes' his way an' he'll come 'round," she concluded, and Jake knew she was obliquely referring to the way Frank Taylor had felt about the letter and how he was apt to behave.

Jake squared his shoulders as he crossed the threshold.

"I think he be in his office, Mist' Jake," Vespasia said, leading the way up the stairs. "He's been fussin' over th' accounts all mornin'—when he wasn't peerin' at the newspaper wit' dat magafyin' glass."

Erica followed a step behind on the wide marble staircase, looking around her at the faded splendor of the plantation house's interior—the ornate but threadbare carpet, the burned-down candles in the sconces, the chipped gilt of the frames around the family portrait.

Jake had his father's determined chin and high cheekbones, she saw, pausing by the picture, but it was his mother, the lady sitting next to the man in the portrait, with her children standing or sitting around them, from whom he had inherited the shape of his eyes and the intensity of their blue hue.

His sisters were lovely, even though one of them had been but an adolescent girl when the portrait had been painted. That must have been Kate, the younger daughter who had gone to England with her mother when the war began, the one whom John Ransom had never been able to forget.

The place needed a good cleaning, Erica saw. There were cobwebs festooning the upper parts of the dusty chandelier hanging in the hallway and the tops of the picture frames. Vespasia probably couldn't see them due to her age, or perhaps it was simply that she couldn't manage the big house without help anymore. Jake had told her that Vespasia and her husband were the only servants left at Taylor Hall these days. A younger woman who had been his sister Maria's maid had left to marry. If Vespasia were the only one cooking and seeing to Jake's father, she wouldn't have time to keep the big house spotless too.

No matter, Erica thought, straightening her own shoulders in unconscious imitation of her husband. She would make it her business to see that despite its age and the Taylors' financial limitations, the house sparkled with cleanliness. It didn't take money to dust and clean, it only took energy, and she, Erica Taylor, had plenty of that—

If only Jake's father did not turn them away on sight.

Vespasia led them to the last room to the left of the staircase and knocked, then pushed open the door.

"Mist' Taylor, Jake's home!" she called, preceding them into the room. Erica had a brief impression of a pleasantly masculine, if slightly musty, chamber with books lining the shelves of one wall and a French door opening onto a gallery.

Then she focused on the hunched-over figure at the desk. He was asleep, his chin tucked into his chest, and snoring.

"Papa," Jake said softly, then more loudly, "Papa, it's Jake. I'm home."

Chapter Twenty-four

As Erica watched, Jake gently shook the old man's shoulder and said, "Papa," again.

Frank Taylor coughed, sputtered, and then, apparently realizing who was calling him, started to leap out of his chair, but he didn't have his feet squarely under him and nearly tipped the chair to the side. Jake quickly stepped close and helped him to right himself.

"Jake! Son, is it really you?" he cried in a gravelly-with-age echo of Jake's own voice. Using the silver-headed cane propped against the desk, he pushed himself up and embraced his son, slapping him on the back. "Well, it's about time! Let me look at you!" Erica knew he hadn't seen or thought about her yet, but she was touched to see a tear escaping down the old man's cheek.

Perhaps it was the light blue of the dress that drew his eye in the midst of all the masculine furnishings, but Erica knew the moment he became aware of her presence, for he stiffened and his eyes narrowed.

Jake could no doubt feel the change, too. "Papa, I'd like you to meet my wife, Erica. Erica, this is my father."

"So you went through with your foolishness. Jake, there weren't enough Texas gals for you—you had to marry a foreigner?"

"Mist' Taylor, you be nice now, hear?" Vespasia cried, hands on her ample hips.

Erica's heart sank. So he wasn't going to pretend for politeness's sake to be welcoming. *Ach*, well at least his disapproval was out in the open.

"Papa," Jake's voice was cold with warning, "I'll expect you to be civil and give Erica a chance, or we'll ride on out of here as fast as we came."

"And I'm your father and I'll expect you to remember that!" Frank Taylor snapped. "No need to be a hothead, boy, but I've asked you a question."

"About why I didn't marry a Texas girl? Maybe I was taking after you, Papa!" Jake retorted. "As I recall, Mama wasn't American either, she was British."

"Ha! And you see the wisdom of that, don't you? She's gone right back across the ocean and she took Kate with her!" his father roared. "At the very least, if you had to marry a damned foreigner, you could've married one whose people weren't a bunch of traitors in our midst!"

"That's enough, Papa!" Jake roared back, his face livid. He turned and saw Erica just as she knuckled away a tear. "Come on, Erica honey, I'm sorry, this

238

was a mistake—" He took her hand and started to pull her from the room.

But Erica had seen the elder Taylor sit back down and clutch his chest, his face paling. "No!" she cried, pointing and refusing to budge. "Can't you see he's sick?"

Taylor was already pulling open his desk drawer and taking out a little box which he opened to reveal tiny white pills.

Jake, tight-lipped, strode back to the desk and poured water into the cup which sat by a pitcher. Whatever was happening to his father, it appeared to Erica that Jake had seen it before.

"It's his heart," Vespasia explained. "When he get excited, he need dat med'cine. He be okay in a minute."

Her assurance did much to calm Erica.

Just as Vespasia had said, it wasn't long before the pink color returned to Frank Taylor's face and he was able to mop his forehead with a much-used handkerchief he pulled out of his pocket.

"Better now?" Jake asked, and his father nodded wearily.

"Good. Vespasia, why don't you show Erica where our room is? Papa and I are going to talk a while. Erica, sweetheart, I won't be long."

Erica opened her mouth to protest, since Jake's set face promised the conversation might not be pleasant, but Vespasia touched her wrist and shook her head in warning. Erica let herself be led out of the room.

"Doan' you worry none about that stubborn ol'

man," the servant said as soon as she had closed the door behind her. "His bark worse than his bite."

"But if his heart is bad, surely Jake should not argue with him? *Ach*, I knew he would not approve of me for his son. Maybe we should leave, as Jake said."

"Dat man been gettin' his way 'cause a' his heart for years," Vespasia said, her wide hips swaying from side to side as they walked down the long hallway. "Oh, his heart bad all right, an' one of these days it be the death a' him, but chile, we all got t' die some time. I doan' reckon it be today for him."

"But if they start arguing again and 'some time' *is* today, Jake will never forgive himself," Erica fretted, just as the woman stopped at a door at the far end of the hall.

"Jake knows how to handle him," Vespasia said as if that were the end of the matter. "Now, ain't dis room nice? It was Jake's when he was growin' up and now he done brought himself home a wife. My, my . . . You jes' make yourself at home, an' I'll bring up some fresh water so's you kin wash. My Mose bring your trunk in directly. I'll unpack while you bathe."

Erica looked around the pleasant room with its four-poster bed and crocheted canopy and cherry-wood chest of drawers. Just as Frank Taylor's office did, it boasted a French window that let out onto the gallery that ran around the front of the house.

"Perhaps you should just leave the rest of the clothes in the trunk," Erica said uncertainly.

"Jake . . . wasn't sure we would stay, because of how his father feels about . . . our marriage." She felt awkward about explaining all this to a servant, even one who clearly loved Jake too.

Vespasia snorted. "Men! Doan' you fret none, Miz Erica, it'll all work out. Now you just relax an' after I bring up the water and yo' things, I'll go fix dinner. It's gonna be late gettin' on th' table, what with all dis 'citement."

"Oh! Just let me wash my face and rebraid my hair, and I will come to help you!"

Vespasia looked alarmed at the offer. "But you Mist' Jake's wife. You doan' have t' help me."

"I was not raised to be idle," Erica told her, and added, when the old woman seemed inclined to object again, "Jake told me how his sister Maria helped to pick cotton during the war, as well as helping to cook, so I think it will not be the first time a Taylor woman enters the kitchen, *ja?*"

Vespasia looked amused. "You got spunk, Miz Erica. I see why dat Jake love you."

"Oh, but—" Erica began, then shut her mouth. The pragmatic reason for their marriage was certainly nothing the housekeeper needed to be told, and if she knew the truth, Erica feared Vespasia might lose her goodwill to Jake's new wife.

"Papa," Jake began after Erica had left the room, and after he had poured two fingers of brandy for each of them. It was only midday, but he thought this one time it might help to ease his father into a more agreeable frame of mind. "I think you ought

241

to know that Erica's father didn't fight in the war—they didn't even arrive in Texas, from what Erica said, until two years ago. Not that it would matter," he said quickly, when he saw his father was about to open his mouth. "The war's over, Papa. It's time to start letting go of all those old prejudices. That'd be like someone holding a grudge against you for holding slaves."

"Hmmmph. There'll be plenty who'll do that, including your bride's people, I'll wager," Frank Taylor said, "but they were mighty glad to marry their girl off to a planter's son, weren't they? Poor as church mice, I'll bet."

"It's time to stop acting like we're wealthy aristocrats, Papa, because the truth is, we're the ones who are poor as church mice. I have eyes—I can see how down-at-the-heels Taylor Hall is! Erica's father is a clockmaker, and they seem to do just fine. Their house is neat as a pin. And don't forget what I wrote in my letter, Papa, they saved my life, coming along when they did after those Comanches attacked me. For that alone, you ought to be grateful to them. If they hadn't come along, if those Indians had come back before Erica and her father found me . . ." Jake shook his head.

"So they played good Samaritans," his father grudgingly allowed. "Good Samaritans who just happened to have a daughter to marry off."

"Papa, I'm a foreigner to them, and they'd have preferred to marry Erica to one of their own kind. They weren't in favor of the marriage—"

"But I suppose you'd already put her through her paces and thought you couldn't live without her in your bed. Boy, you enjoy those women, you don't marry them," his father scoffed.

Jake took a deep breath, holding onto his temper with difficulty. If this man hadn't been his father, and not in good health, he'd have knocked him off his chair.

Jake stood and put his face inches from his father's. "Not that it's any of your business, Papa," he said, keeping his voice low and controlled, "but I never made love to Erica until she was my wife, and I'll thank you to remember she's a lady." It was a good thing his father didn't know about Von Schiller, Jake thought.

Frank Taylor sat there, unblinking, studying his son.

"So why didn't you get married in that town fulla foreigners? Didn't they think you were good enough for their daughter?"

Jake allowed himself a wry smile. "As a matter of fact, no. And they didn't seem apt to change their minds, being as stubborn as you are, Papa, so Erica and I ran off to San Antonio together."

"And went to your old friend Johnny Ransom."

Jake nodded. "I felt like Erica deserved more than some hole-in-the-corner marriage and I knew John would help us arrange it. It was his idea to write you and Erica's parents, Papa."

"That boy always did seem to have a good head on his shoulders."

"I'm sorry you weren't there. Erica was beautiful in her wedding gown."

Frank Taylor looked away. "I . . . I don't venture far from Taylor Hall these days, boy," he said at last, then pointed to his chest. "The old ticker won't let me."

Jake nodded. "So we've come to you. I want you to get to know my bride, Papa. Give her a chance."

Frank Taylor snorted again. "We'll see, boy. I can tell you think she hung the moon. Well, she'd better feel the same about you—I'll be able to tell if she's just putting on a show!"

Jake remained silent. He couldn't say that while Erica liked him, she didn't love him. He just had to hope that what she felt for him turned into love over time.

"You still thinkin' you're gonna make me see my way clear to makin' this place into a horse farm, boy?" Frank Taylor asked, probably relieved to leave the topic of his son's marriage behind for a time.

Jake was happy to change the subject too. "I'm hoping to, Papa, and wait'll you see the prime stallion and mare I bought in San Antonio to be the start of my herd. . . ."

It had been a long day full of tension, and Erica was grateful to escape from the parlor, where they had gone after supper, to the haven of their bedroom. Vespasia had offered to bring up bathwater to fill the copper tub so she could bathe.

Jake and his father had come down to the midday meal arm in arm, she had been relieved to see, so they must have achieved some sort of understanding. But while Frank Taylor didn't offer her any more overt hostility, he seemed to talk around her rather than to her.

After lunch, Jake had told her he was going to take his father out to the barn to see Shiloh and Mitternacht.

" 'Mitternacht'?" Frank Taylor had said, his nose wrinkling as he said the word. "What kind of a fool foreign name is that for a horse?"

"Papa—" Jake began in a warning tone.

"It . . . it means midnight, Herr Taylor," Erica said, hoping her voice didn't shake as much as the hand she'd put in her lap before replying. She was determined not to let him see that he bothered her.

" 'Herr Taylor'? I'm an American, girl, so that'd be 'Mister Taylor,' " the man said, derision plain in his voice, "if you must be so formal. Of course, you could call me 'Papa Taylor' if you wanted to sound like a real American woman."

"Now, why would she want to call you somethin' nice when you bein' as mean as a bulldog on a gunpowder diet?" Vespasia put in as she brought in the dessert, an applesauce cake, apparently not inhibited by the fact that she was but the housekeeper.

"That will be all, Vespasia," Frank Taylor said, not looking away from Erica.

Erica recognized a challenge when she heard one. "Very well, if you prefer, *Papa Taylor*, Jake told me I could name the mare anything I wanted."

"Hmmpph. She'll always be 'Midnight' to me," Taylor retorted, but his tone had softened just the slightest bit.

"I will help you do the dishes," Erica said to Vespasia when the men had left the room for the barn.

"You'll do no such thing," Vespasia said. "You

take yourself upstairs, Miz Erica, and take a nap. You can do anything you want to tomorrow, but right now you lookin' tired from the trip and from that old coot's bullying," she said, making shooing motions with her big hands. "Who knows, maybe you even carryin' Mist' Jake's baby already, and that make you tired, sho' nuff. Go on, now."

The idea had made Erica flush scarlet and flee up the stairs. It was too soon, of course. Even if Jake's seed had taken root within her womb on their wedding night, they couldn't possibly know yet.

She had slept and awakened refreshed just before supper, and Jake had helped her do up her dress in the back.

Wouldn't it be delightful, she thought now as she relaxed in the bathwater and felt her tense muscles relax. Wouldn't it be wonderful if she became with child quickly? Surely if she gave Jake a son or daughter some nine months after their hasty wedding, it would give them more in common? She let her head rest against the back of the copper tub, imagining what a child of theirs might look like.

There had been wine at dinner, and the glassful she had drunk must have caused her to drift off, for she woke with a start when Jake pushed open the door and entered the room.

"Erica . . ." he began, and she saw the way his eyes roved over her, especially at her breasts, whose nipples were barely submerged in the cooling water. She had come to know that look, and she felt her pulse begin to accelerate as he came toward her.

"I must have been asleep," she managed to say. "Is it late?"

"Late enough," he said with a chuckle as he held out a towel. "Come on, let's get you dry. . . ."

Chapter Twenty-five

Jake swallowed hard as he held out a towel and Erica rose from the bathwater—like Venus emerging from the sea, he thought. Had there ever been a woman as beautiful as this? And she was all his, he reminded himself wonderingly. *His*.

It was no wonder he could hardly wait to join her here in this room where he had once dreamed boyish dreams of being a knight rescuing a damsel in distress from a dragon. He'd been polite and remained while his father had raved on and on about what had been happening in town while he'd been gone, how the the carpetbaggers had arrived and were making life miserable. He'd kept one eye on the grandfather clock ticking away the minutes over Frank Taylor's head, and made sure his father's glass of whiskey was refilled. He even followed the old man out onto the veranda while his father smoked one of those smelly old cigars that he favored—but Jake was careful to stay upwind of the direction the stinky smoke was drifting. It wouldn't do to go up to his bride smelling worse than a wet dog.

"Well, go on to bed, boy," his father had said as he stubbed out his smoke and headed for the door. "I can tell you're itchin' to. Oh, to be young again and as randy as a stallion in a field full a' mares!"

Jake had ignored the gibe and bid him good night.

"You were very brave today, Erica," he said now. "I'm proud of you. It couldn't have been easy putting up with my father."

"Thank you. 'Putting up'?" she repeated the unfamiliar phrase, wrapping herself in the towel as if it were a shield from his bold eyes.

"Tolerating his nonsense without telling him he's an ornery old cuss."

"You Americans, you have such funny words," she said. "But I would not speak so to your father!"

"He'll come around in time, don't worry," he said, "and then he'll l—then he'll be fond of you too," he amended. He'd been about to say, *then he'll love you as I do.* "Here, let me dry your back, sweetheart."

He'd meant to slow himself down by facing her back and rubbing the towel over her shoulders, for he didn't want to frighten Erica with his hunger for her, but drying her back led him down to her trim waist and then to her sweetly curved buttocks. She must have put some sort of scent in the water, because she smelled so clean and fine all over, like a princess who'd been lying in rose petals.

"I believe my legs are dry," he heard her say, and realized he'd been mesmerized by the curve of her calves.

"Are you wet anywhere else?" he said, turning her around, and he couldn't miss the invitation in her slumberous gaze.

"*Ja,*" she said, "But I think you will not mind." She held out her arms to him.

His arms went around her waist, and she went into them, snuggling close. Her skin was still damp, the heat of her breasts radiating through his shirt front. He tightened his grip, molding her to him at every point. He didn't doubt she could already tell how much he wanted her, for her eyes had lost their sleepy look and widened, the pupils dilating before she closed them. She raised her lips to his for a mind-drugging kiss.

He would have begun unbuttoning his shirt as a first step to becoming as naked as she was, but her fingers stayed his hand and she began unfastening the buttons herself. Her lush mouth never left his as she made short work of the shirt and pushed it off of him.

The trousers came next, but by this time he was so eager to have her he had taken over the unfastening. He groaned as Erica pushed them down over his hips. If he didn't take control here and now, they were never going to make it to the bed!

"Erica, honey, you make me want you so bad. . . ."

He heard her soft laugh. "*Ja,* I can see that," she said, but when she came into his arms again, he could stand no more and picked her up, laying her gently on the bed.

Jake lay down beside her, intending to continue to lead in their lovemaking, but he found his bride had other ideas. When he would have raised up over her, she pushed on his shoulder.

"No, Jake, you will allow me, please . . ." she murmured, and covered him with the body he had grown to love so well.

It was the first time she had taken charge like this, and Jake found himself surprisingly willing to lie passively, waiting to see what she would do.

She began by kissing him, and when he filled his hands with her breasts and stroked her nipples, she moaned, "Jake, *liebling* . . ." and then added a flood of German words, her words broken and shaky. He could feel her pulse pounding beneath his hand.

He didn't know what she was saying, but she obviously took great joy in what he was doing and he rejoiced in that. He'd heard young ladies were taught that they were not expected to enjoy their husbands' lovemaking, merely to tolerate the crude expression of their baser natures for the sake of begetting children. He thanked God Erica apparently hadn't heard such a dictum. If ladies believed such things, give him a real woman like Erica every time!

And just when he thought it couldn't get any better, she positioned herself over him and took him so deep inside her that they both gasped. And then there was nothing but a wild vortex of heated pleasure until they shattered together into a shower of golden stars.

Jake woke with the morning sun sneaking past his eyelids through a crack in the curtains. Without opening his eyes, he reached out a hand, but instead of encountering his wife's warm satiny flesh, his hand touched nothing but empty sheets. He opened his eyes. She was gone.

He frowned. Tarnation, he wanted her to be there. He wanted to kiss her good morning, to see her yawn and wrinkle her nose the way she did when she was trying to wake up. He wanted to make love to her again! Where was she?

He smelled coffee, and turned to see that someone had left a pot of it on the bedside table along with a cup and a few lumps of sugar. God bless his wife!

After fortifying his brain with the strong brew, Jake dressed and left the room. He didn't have to look far.

Erica was standing on a chair on the landing, attacking the frames of the family portraits with a feather duster. She was wearing some old brown dress that Jake suspected had once belonged to one of the slaves and her golden hair was tied up in a kerchief.

"Good morning," he said, and startled her so badly that he had to dash over and steady the chair. "What are you doing?"

"I am cleaning, husband," she said. "I hope you slept well?"

He nodded. "I can see you're cleaning. But *why* are you cleaning?"

"That's what I asked her too," his father growled, coming out of the dining room with a crust of toast in his hand. "Jake, your wife needs reminding she's your wife and not a housekeeper!" He snorted as he passed them on the stairs.

She looked at the old man's retreating figure, then

back at Jake, her eyes troubled. "I am cleaning because Vespasia needs help," she said simply. "Jake, it's a big house, and she is not young. She has much to do already with all the cooking, and there is no one to help her. You do not mind? I do not like to be idle when there is work to be done."

Jake looked down, then shrugged. "No, of course I don't mind—I just wish it wasn't necessary, that's all." He could remember that when he was a boy, his mother wouldn't have dreamed of lifting a finger to do anything more strenuous than a bit of embroidery. She was the mistress of a grand plantation, and there were slaves to do such things! But then as Jake reached manhood, the war had come and his mother and Kate had departed, and his sister Maria, once the foremost belle of Brazos County, had helped the few slaves still there pick cotton. Times had changed, and the belles had to change with them.

"I thought we'd have breakfast together," he said, and was disgusted to hear how disappointed he sounded. Would his need for this woman ever slacken? Remember, she doesn't love you, he reminded himself.

Erica smiled at him. "I suppose I could use another cup of coffee before I go back to work."

The smile encouraged him. "Then maybe I could help you a little? Is there anything you can't lift, can't reach?"

She blinked in surprise but quickly recovered, and now her smile was luminous with approval. "*Ach*, but it would be wonderful if you could find a ladder and a bucket of soapy water and wash that—I do not know the word for that big light," she said, pointing to the chandelier. "It is dusty and so full of cob-webs."

That was how Vespasia found them, a couple of hours later: Jake standing on a ladder, washing the dangling glass crystals of the chandelier, Erica mopping the cracked marble floor.

"Lord above, what a sight. Mist' Jake, come down from there. Miz Erica, you better take dat kerchief off yo' head. Y'all got a caller. I tried to tell her to come back another time, but—"

"But I took refuge in the fact that I was an old friend and came on in," said a female voice behind Vespasia, and Jake looked down from his ladder to see a female figure with ginger-colored hair, wearing a black-trimmed lavender dress.

It was Lilybelle Harris Moorehead, the widow whom his father had been encouraging him to call on all those weeks ago when he had just returned home, before he had left to go visit Maria. It already seemed like ten years ago.

She came closer and peered up at him, completely ignoring Erica. "Rebecca Sue—that's my sister, you'll remember—said she saw you ride into town day before last, so I figured you'd come back from your visit to your sister and I thought I'd come pay a call. Your father had promised me you'd come see me when you came home from the war, but you never did, you naughty man, and the next thing I knew you were gone again!" She gave a little tinkle of laughter and fluttered her eyelashes at him.

She meant to sound and look coquettish, Jake figured, but her simpering only confirmed his wisdom
in not seeking her out as his father had pushed him
to do. At least now that he was married, he was reasonably sure the old man wouldn't be making promises for him to unattached females like Lilybelle.

"So I just took the bull by the horns and decided
to come beard the lion in his den!" Lilybelle went on.
"But Jake Taylor, whatever are you doin' up on that
ladder?"

"Cleaning," Jake said, just as his wife had explained to him earlier. In his peripheral vision he
saw Erica watching the interchange uncertainly. He
beckoned her forward now. "Mrs. Lilybelle Harris
Moorehead, I'd like you to meet my wife Erica," he
said.

Lilybelle's green eyes widened, her cheeks went
pallid and her jaw dropped open. She reminded him
of a fish gasping for air after it had just been pulled
out of the river. She whirled to face Erica, her worn
black-trimmed skirts belling out around her booted
ankles as she took in the sight of Erica in her dust-
smudged dress with a strand of cobweb draped
across the top of her kerchief.

"Y-your wife?" Lilybelle said disbelievingly over
her shoulder at Jake. "I—I'm sorry, I saw her out of
the corner of my eye when I walked in and I thought
you'd hired some help for your old mammy!" She
walked forward and grandly extended a hand, almost as if she expected Erica to kiss it, Jake thought,
wondering how soon he could shoo this woman out
of the house.

"Hello, I'm Lilybelle Harris Moorehead. Your husband and I have been friends just forever!" the woman gushed.

Erica shook her hand uncertainly. "I am pleased to meet you, Mrs. Moorehead," Erica said, her accent more pronounced than usual, as it usually was when she felt unsure.

Lilybelle's eyes narrowed. "Oh, you're a foreigner. That accent isn't . . . French, is it?"

She knew damn well it wasn't, Jake thought, irritated. He saw Erica's chin go up and her back straighten.

"No, I am German by birth," she said proudly. "I was living with my family in New Braunfels when I met Jake."

"I see," Lilybelle said, and her face hardened. Jake could tell she was remembering which side the German settlers had taken during the war. She turned back to Jake. "Well," she said with false gaiety. "Aren't you just the slyest dog, Jake, gettin' married while you were gone! And you found a woman who likes to clean—aren't you just the smartest thing?"

"She's not afraid to do what needs to be done, that's true," Jake said evenly, but he made sure that Lilybelle saw the warning in his eyes. "Miss Lilybelle, was there something you needed help with? Something I—we—could do for you?"

Lilybelle chewed her lip and shrugged. "No, I guess not, after all." She shrugged. "I'd come to invite you to a barbecue, but I suppose now that you're a married man that's out of the question." She gave a tinkle of laughter again, and the sound grated on Jake's nerves. "Oh, but if you were in San Antonio, you must have seen your old friend, that handsome Dr. John Ransom? I never did understand why he left these parts! Is he still a confirmed bachelor? A shame, him bein' a doctor and all, not havin' a wife. You think he might ever come back for a visit?"

Jake shrugged. "You just never know."

Lilybelle chewed on her lip again, patently frustrated that Jake wasn't being more forthcoming.

"Well, I'll just be going," she said at last. "Nice meetin' you, Miz Taylor. Oh, and if you're ever interested in taking on more housework, I'd be happy to hire you. Ever since my slaves ran off I just can't seem to keep up with the housework, and it bores me to tears!"

He saw the shock in Erica's face at the woman's rudeness, and his temper snapped. "Miz Lilybelle, you have a good afternoon, you hear? But don't come back," he called after her.

The widow had been stomping angrily to the door, but now she stopped and turned around. "Oh, don't worry, I won't," she said. "I wouldn't soil the hem of my skirts crossing the threshold of Taylor Hall again. And you, Jake Taylor, you ought to be ashamed of yourself! I'm sure my Billy Wayne is turning in his grave at the news that you married one of those traitors to the South!"

Jake waited until the sound of the front door being slammed reached their ears, then crossed to Erica, putting his arms around her.

"I'm sorry, sweetheart. If I'd had any idea that woman was going to talk to you that way, I'd have turned her away the moment I saw her." He hoped they weren't going to get this reaction wherever they went. They'd go back to New Braunfels or San Antonio if that was the case!

Vespasia had been hovering in the background the whole time, and now she came forward, bristling. "Dat woman gonna perish of her own pizen one a' dese days! She ever come 'round here again, I'll drive her off myself!"

Erica sighed and looked up at Jake and then Vespasia, and he could see that though she was flushed with anger, there were no tears in her eyes. "It is all right," she said. "There are women like her everywhere, *ja?* In fact she reminds me of Gunilla Von Hesselberg!"

Chapter Twenty-six

"I could've told you that was going to happen," Frank Taylor said from the second floor.

Erica looked up to see the old man looking over the railing at her and Jake, contempt in his eyes—contempt for her.

"Is that right?" Jake said, sounding irritated.

"Yep, sure as God made green apples," his father went on, ignoring his son's tone. "You marry a foreigner, one of them traitor Germans, and that's how you'll be treated. And the rest of your life depends on what you do about it."

"What's that supposed to mean?" Jake said, his chin jutting out, a pugnacious glint in his eye.

"It means you can either run or you can learn to lie in the bed you made. And I don't think I raised you to run. You didn't run from those damn Yankees, did you?"

Jake shook his head, still staring up at his father.

"I've given you enough to chew on about that.

You'll have to make your own decision. Now if you're about done playing housemaid," Frank Taylor said, jerking his head towards the chandelier, "suppose you come upstairs and tell me how you propose to make a go of a horse farm here, if I'm tomfool enough to let you do it. I reckon you ought not to let that fine gray dun stud go to waste."

Erica couldn't follow all that Jake's father had said, but she recognized a change, a willingness to listen to Jake's dream. She gave her husband's hand an encouraging squeeze. "Vespasia and I will make the dinner, *ja?* One of us will come get you when it's ready."

He leaned over and kissed her cheek, whispering, "If we haven't come to blows by then." He winked before turning to climb the stairs to join his father.

"You a good woman," Vespasia said softly, watching them go, then beckoning Erica to follow her into the kitchen. "I seen a lotta belles, befo' the war. You know what a belle was, honey? They used t' be the prettiest of the planters' daughters, an' they didn't lift a finger t' do any work. Well, most a' them would've collapsed into a weepy puddle after meetin' up wit' a witch like dat Lilybelle Moorehead. Not you."

"Thank you, Vespasia."

"Dis here biscuit dough be raised," the big black woman said, holding out a bowl with a cloth on top. "You break off pieces big enough for biscuits and drop 'em on dis baking pan. Now, back to Miz Lilybelle—she ain't no pillar a' society or nothin', but she the first one from Bryan that met you. And she gonna go back and tell her sister and everyone within the sound a' her carpin' voice what she thought a' you."

"*Ja*, so I imagined," Erica said, aware of a sinking feeling in her stomach at the thought.

"Well, you got to show the rest a' them that she not only wrong, she crazy."

"And how do you suggest I do that?" Erica asked, following the woman's soft, drawling speech with some difficulty.

"You got t' get out dere, show 'em what a nice lady you be. You hide out here at Taylor Hall, they goin' t' start thinkin' Lilybelle right."

" 'Get out there'? Where?"

Vespasia uncovered a ham she'd brought up earlier from the smokehouse and started slicing it. "Go t' town. Meet people. Invite 'em here."

"*Here?*" Erica said faintly, sure she had misunderstood. "But . . ." How could she tactfully tell this woman Taylor Hall was much too *baufällig*—dilapidated—to have guests see it?

"Yep, dis place seen better days," Vespasia said, as if she had read the doubt on Erica's face. "But if I help you redd it up, by the end a' the week it be lookin' better."

" 'Red' it? You mean we should paint it red?"

Vespasia chuckled. "No, honey, I mean clean it, like you begun t' do this mornin'. And you think these folks 'roun' here got palaces to live in? We all got hit by the war, honey. You act hospitable, though, they'll all be glad t' come. Now, tomorrow, you go inta town wit' Jake an' pay a call on th' minister, invite him to Sunday dinner. That's a start. You make a good impression on him, you find all kinds a' doors open to ya."

Erica nodded slowly. "You think that will work?"

The old servant nodded so emphatically that both her chins wobbled. "I'm sure of it. I seen it work. I'm an old woman, honey. I'm old enough to remember when Mist' Taylor brought home dat Englishwoman, Jake's mother. Dat exactly what she did."

Erica hadn't considered that Jake's mother might have met the same prejudice as she was meeting. But she had a new thought as she popped the biscuits into the already heated oven and wiped her brow. "But there had not been a war then, *ja?*"

"No, but Mist' Taylor tol' me 'Merica used t' belong t' England not too long befo' dat, an' it fought fo' its freedom, an' had to beat England again, a few years after dat." She finished slicing the peach pie she'd pulled from the oven just before Lilybelle had arrived. "Now, why don' you carry dese plates out to th' dinin' room please, an' we set the table. . . ." The two women worked in silence for a few minutes, setting out plates and silverware.

"I'm thinkin' we need Jake's sister Maria here. Everyone like Miss Maria. Dis afternoon, befo' I have t' start supper, we goin' t' write her an' invite her an' Bowie to come in th' fall, when it be cooler, say in October. We goin' t' have a barbecue an' a horse race to celebrate Jake's sister's visit, invite everyone. Jake's horse will win the race."

Erica's head was whirling with the ideas Vespasia was spouting. "He will win? How do you know this?"

The woman crossed her hands over her apron and smiled broadly. "I seen dat hoss. He got legs on 'im. An' when he win, everyone goin' to want to bring their mares to him. An' he goin' t' give your mare a fine colt, and wit' the stud fees Mist' Jake goin' t' buy mo' mares, and befo' you know it, Taylor Hall be a horse farm t' boast about." She clapped her hands in glee. "Dis ol' woman full a' ideas, huh?"

Erica found her enthusiasm infectious. "Good ideas, *ja.*" Suddenly, however, she was assailed by doubt. "But Jake's father—you must see he does not like me. Why would he agree to such a thing?"

The old woman rubbed her chin thoughtfully. "You got a job dere an' no mistake, Miz Erica. But he don' hate you—he doan' even properly know you yet, to my mind. You jes' keep standin' up t' him, but be nice to him too. He jes' a lonely ol' man, honey. He be nice back afore too long."

"And Jake's sister? She will agree to come and visit? Does she not have little *kinder?*" She pantomimed a baby being held in her arms.

"Chil'ren? Sure, she got two now. Just had a little girl, in fact. But she ain't been back home since she married an' I bet she be right curious about you, honey. She'll come. Lawd, that'll be good to hol' dat lil' Olivia baby and spoil dat Jefferson boy. An' den, by 'n' by, I'll have yo' baby to rock."

Vespasia laughed as the color flooded Erica's face.

"But maybe she will not approve of me, either," Erica pointed out.

"Oh, Miss Maria always did have her own mind, an' it wasn't her daddy's mind, or she wouldn't be Mist' Bowie's wife. An' she always did dote on her brother. She see you make Jake happy, she'll purely adore you."

That, Erica thought, was the crux of the matter—making sure that despite the fact she was not the one Jake would have picked, she made him happy. But what if he was beginning to get restless by then? *Ach*, it was all so complicated!

"I will take your advice," she decided, full of resolve.

"You won't never be sorry," Vespasia promised.

"You're a dab hand at cards, I'll give you that, Dutchman," the other man said as Siegfried scooped the pile of coins and paper money toward himself across the scarred pine table in the saloon in Round Rock. "You done won all my money."

Siegfried stifled the impulse to snap back, once again, that he was German, not Dutch. He had made the mistake of saying "Deutschland" rather than "Germany" when Grits Hanley had asked him where he was from, and he'd been "Dutchman" ever since. He suspected the saddle tramp didn't believe he was really a count, but it didn't matter. If Hanley would teach him the things he knew, it would not matter that he did not bow and scrape and call him "Your Lordship" as social-climbing Americans were apt to do.

"I will give it all back to you if you will teach me how to be as fast with a gun as you are," Siegfried said, injecting fawning admiration into his voice. And the admiration wasn't totally feigned, either. He'd seen the drifter gun down a man he'd claimed had cheated him at cards. Grits Hanley was fast—

lethally fast. Siegfried was glad he was the man's friend and not his enemy.

The drifter eyed him consideringly. "I reckon I could," he drawled in that slow way that Siegfried found maddening. Why couldn't Texans just come right out and say their words? "Who're you tryin' t' git even with, Dutchie?"

"I wish to kill the man who took my woman," he said, letting the other man see he was deadly serious.

Hanley whistled. "You jes' come right out an' say what you think, don't you? But I ain't sure a female's worth lettin' daylight into a man. There's plenty a' females. Jes' find you another."

"You are right that there are plenty of women. I will, perhaps, have many others—once I'm finished with her," Siegfried replied. "But the man who dared to take her from me—to marry her, when she was mine—he must die. As slowly and painfully as possible."

The man grinned, tipping his chair back and taking a big swig of the whiskey Siegfried had bought him. "He really chapped yore hide, didn't he? Waal, it might be amusin'. This man, he good with a gun?"

Siegfried shrugged. "I am told he was a soldier in your war."

The other man snorted. "That don't necessarily mean nothin'. It jes' means he was lucky. Where's the happy couple livin' now?"

"Somewhere in the Brazos valley, I believe. I am making inquiries." He'd already found that the lovesick mayor's daughter was quite a correspondent. In the short time he'd been living in the rooming house of the little town north of Austin he'd already received two letters from her. He'd skimmed over the drivel about how much Gunilla loved him and looked forward to the day she would be his countess, living in splendor with him in his Bavarian *schloss*. The silly idiot! As if he would ever marry a drab girl from a backwater like New Braunfels! He'd skipped down to the paragraph where Gunilla related her conversation with Hilda Mueller. She had found out that Erica and her new husband had planned to journey toward Taylor's old plantation home to visit his father.

"Waal, if you want to be a real gun-totin' desperado, we best stop tippin' glasses and go start practicin'," Hanley said suddenly, slamming his glass down and swiping at his mouth with the back of his sleeve. "Come on, I know a place outside a' town where we won't be bothered."

"What's this stuff?" Frank Taylor asked suspiciously the next evening, as Erica began to pass the platter laden with the savory-smelling beef she'd marinated all day in a sauce made of vinegar, garlic, peppercorns, onions, and bay leaves. "And why did you do the cooking? Where's Vespasia? That's what I pay her for."

Jake forbore to point out that as far as he knew, actual wages had never passed from his father to his former slave, now his housekeeper. Vespasia had lived with the family since before Jake had been born, and she would no doubt die of old age at Taylor Hall, but his father had never given her more than enough to buy whatever the plantation didn't grow or raise.

"It is called sauerbraten, Papa Taylor—a traditional German dish. And the dumplings are called spaetzle," she added, passing the bowl to Jake. "Vespasia is sick today, so I did the cooking. Oh, she has nothing that should last too long, only a summer catarrh," she added quickly when Taylor's face registered alarm.

Jake smothered a grin. He was in on the secret: there was nothing wrong with Vespasia. Vespasia and Mose were eating the same food right now in their cabin. Erica had just wanted to show off her culinary skills in her campaign to win over the old man.

His father sniffed the meat as he took the plate from her. "Nothing wrong with American food, girl—you remember that."

"Ah, but Vespasia tells me you are a very adventurous diner, always willing to try new things. She was afraid you had grown bored with the same old dishes she knows how to make."

"Fried chicken and steak and ham—that's all I need," Frank grumped, but Jake noted that he heaped his plate with the meat and dumplings and later went back for seconds.

Jake winked at Erica while his father was looking down.

Later, when they closed the bedroom door behind them, Jake said, "I think you're making headway with my father. What do you bet he tells Vespasia to have you teach her how to do German cooking?"

Erica smiled as she sat in front of the mirror and began to undo her braid. "It was a pleasure to watch him enjoy his food, especially after he insisted he wouldn't like it."

"You'll have him eating out of your hand before long, sweetheart," Jake promised, then laughed as Erica's eyes grew wide with alarm. "Oh, not literally!"

His wife smiled at her own mistake. "Your papa is full of—how do you say it?—bluster, *ja?* Inside he is soft as butter."

Jake couldn't begin to tell her how much he appreciated her efforts to win his father's approval—especially since Taylor's approval seemed to benefit Jake too. The old man had agreed to Jake's plan to try making Taylor Hall into a horse farm, at least for a couple of years. Since he couldn't find the words to thank her for what she had accomplished with his father thus far, he decided to praise her about something else.

"And you charmed the rector this morning when we paid him a call. If you have Reverend McDowny on your side, Erica, Lilybelle Harris can blather all she wants and you'll still be the toast of the town."

He took pleasure in the way Erica beamed with delight as she began to comb through the rippled gold of her unbraided hair.

"It was actually Vespasia's idea," she said, always honest.

"She's a wise old woman. And what else did you two plot between you? If I know both of you, you sure didn't stop there."

"No, we didn't. This is what she said we should do to combat the gossip of that Lilybelle." Erica told Jake about Vespasia's plan to invite Maria for a visit, then celebrate it with a barbecue and horse race that would make them the talk of the Brazos valley—and make Jake's horses in high demand.

"What a great idea. I'd sure like it if Maria and Bowie would come," he said.

"Will you write the letter to her? She does not know me, after all."

"I'll do it first thing tomorrow," he promised. "Maybe we could even interest your parents in visiting."

"*Wunderbar*, husband!" she said, and the word needed no translation. She came and sat beside him on the bed.

"You're a good woman, Erica," he said, which was as close as he dared come to saying *I love you*. "You've done a lot in a short time to make life good here. Is there something I can do for you?" He'd give her a pair of stars for earbobs if she but said she wanted them.

Her gold-tinged lashes fell over her dazzling blue eyes, and when she raised them again, her eyes were shining. "*Ja*, husband. I would like a baby."

"Is that all?" he drawled lazily to hide the delight he felt. A baby. She wanted his baby. And if she had a child to love—*their* child, thought Jake in a daze, might Erica not learn to feel more than gratitude for him, the man who had fathered that baby? If giving her a baby would help Erica learn to love him, really love him, then surely she would never leave.

Chapter Twenty-seven

Erica knew she had conceived that night, knew in the space of one heartbeat that another life had been created within her, a life made by Jake and her. But two months had passed until she had been sure enough to tell him, and now, as she listened to Jake saying grace over supper, she had decided the time had come.

They were already celebrating the arrival of Jake's sister Maria and her husband Bowie, their lively toddler son Jefferson, called Jeff, and their three-month-old baby daughter, Olivia Grace. Erica had liked Jake's sister, so like him with her black hair and sparkling blue eyes, at once, and had seen immediately why Maria had fallen in love with her handsome husband Bowie, with his chestnut-brown hair, green eyes and devil-may-care smile. Their children seemed to have inherited the best features of both of them. Jeff was a copy of his father, with brown hair and green eyes; little Olivia Grace had Bowie's green eyes, but the downy fuzz that was growing in was the same sable hue as her mother's.

"And lastly, Heavenly Father, I'd like to thank you for the blessing of family, both the family I was born into," Jake said, "my father and sister Maria, my mother and Kate across the ocean in England, and those who have been added to it—my brother-in-law Bowie, my mother-, father-, and brothers-in-law in New Braunfels, and last but not least, my wonderful wife Erica."

"Amen to that!" Maria had said, and they all laughed, even old Frank Taylor, as the platters and bowls full of food began to be passed around.

Erica opened her mouth to speak, to tell her husband and her family the momentous news that she was with child, but before she could do so her father-in-law spoke.

"Just wait till you taste these new dishes our Erica has taught Vespasia how to cook," he said. "I can't believe I'm sayin' this, but them foreigners do know some new tricks with beef and potatoes and such! Wait till you taste the potato salad—Erica calls it some German name I can't ever remember. . . ."

"That is *Kartoffelsalat*, Papa Taylor," Erica said, surprised and pleased that he was boasting about the traditional German recipes she had shared with Vespasia.

"Yeah, that's the word. And that's onion pie yonder, but there's some outlandish name for it—that's my favorite."

"*Zwiebelkuchen*." She was so full of joy she felt her heart might burst when she saw Jake wink at her. Frank Taylor had come a long way since that first day she had met him. He still scoffed at her foreign ways, but now he was bragging about her!

The only way she could have imagined being happier was if her parents and brothers, and maybe even Minna too, had been there, but they had written saying that they thought it best to wait until the Christmas school break to travel so far, since the boys would fall behind in their schoolwork if they came now. But she could wait, she thought, relieved that they were at least willing to come.

"It's a durn good thing you don't have to be able to pronounce it to like it," Bowie remarked, his eyes dancing with amusement. Jake had told her how Bowie had once suffered the old patriarch's disapproval, too.

Erica stood, and suddenly all eyes were on her. "I would like to add something to the thanks my husband gave to God," she began, and everyone paused, some of them with their forks halfway to their mouths—except for little Jeff, who had been fed earlier and who was now prattling at his mother's feet as he played with a wooden horse on wheels.

"My husband Jake called me 'last but not least' when he said the blessing," she said, shyly smiling at all of them. "It is not his fault that this is not completely true, because he does not know what I am about to tell you, that I am not the last of the family. If it pleases God and all goes well, we will be adding a baby to the Taylor family next May."

All around the table there were shouts of congratulation and expressions of joy, which Erica could hardly hear because her husband was hugging her so tightly.

"Are you sure, Erica? Are you all right? Uh—maybe you should sit down!" Jake said, much to the amusement of everyone else.

"Enjoy this solicitude now, Erica. By the second baby husbands decide you're not made of glass after all," Maria said wryly.

"That's real fine news, Erica," Frank Taylor said, and it was the glint of a tear in the old man's eye that had Erica all at once tearing up and weeping on her husband's shoulder. But they were happy tears.

I'll tell Jake the rest tonight, Erica thought. It is more than time that I tell my husband I love him. I don't care if he can never honestly say he loves me the way I love him, but I want him to know!

"Vespasia, bring that French champagne from outta the cellar!" Frank Taylor bellowed in the direction of the kitchen. "We need to make a toast to the newest member of the family!"

Then everyone was talking and laughing at once. The champagne was brought and the toast made, and as they ate, Jake and Bowie and Frank had finished off that bottle and called for another. Maria was full of advice on everything from giving birth with the least amount of discomfort to the best way to wean a baby to solid food. Vespasia joined in with tales of how Jake and Maria had behaved as babies, and her own tips on child-rearing, and before anyone noticed, it had grown quite late and Bowie, Frank and Jake were all happily drunk.

It required the combined efforts of Erica, Maria and Vespasia to get the three men safely upstairs to their beds.

There would be no telling Jake anything tonight,

Erica thought with amusement, looking down at her huband as he snored softly in their bed.

It didn't matter. There would be another night to tell him she loved him. Perhaps she would tell him three nights later, after the combined barbecue and horse race that Bryan folk were already talking about as the "biggest social event to be held in the Brazos valley since before the war."

"I'd say your first attempt at entertaining Brazos valley society was a huge success," Maria commented right after the horse race on the quarter-mile track Jake had laid out. "These folks don't even seem to mind that the host's horse won by three lengths, with his brother-in-law's stallion taking second!"

It was a rare moment of solitude for the two women, now that the race was over. So many ladies of Bryan and the surrounding valley had been curious to meet the German beauty who had captured "the hand and heart of the area's handsomest man," as one matron had phrased it. Erica had scarcely known a moment of peace to consume some of the delicious food she and Vespasia and Maria had worked so hard to prepare. It certainly didn't seem that anyone had paid attention to the viperish ramblings of Lilybelle Harris Moorehead, who was nowhere near Taylor Hall on this momentous day.

"*Ja*—Jake's already had half a dozen men come up to him and ask to have their mares bred to Shiloh," Erica said. "And some rich man offered him a thousand dollars for the stallion's first colt, but Jake told him the colt wasn't for sale. Imagine such a thing— we just found out Mitternacht was—how do you say it?—'in foal' and already someone tries to buy the colt not born yet?" She laughed. "This man talked so fast and so strangely, I could barely understand him."

"That's because he was a carpetbagger from up north," Maria explained. "Jake would never sell to the likes of them. Neither does Bowie."

"*Ach,* I see."

"Why don't we go have some lemonade and sit down under that big live oak yonder?" Maria suggested. "Jake and Bowie will be busy talking horses to those fellows for hours yet, and you probably ought to get out of the sun—though I've never seen a woman who's enceinte look better. What's the German word for expecting a child?" Maria asked, steering Erica towards the shade, where Vespasia had been keeping little Jeff entertained and out from underfoot while she rocked Olivia Grace. Vespasia gratefully allowed Maria to take over, saying that she needed to go into the kitchen and bring out more of Erica's *Kalterhund,* the dessert dish made of chocolate frosting layers between stacked biscuits.

"*Schwanger,*" Erica supplied. "I do feel well, hardly any of the sickness my mother told me to expect! I am blessed in that!"

"Such a funny word, 'schwanger.' But you deserve to be blessed, Erica, it's only fair, since you have really been a blessing to Taylor Hall. I've never seen Papa looking so well, and Vespasia told me he hasn't tried to sneak a cigar in a month! He's really getting mellow in his old age! And Jake—it's plain to see he adores you, sister—"

She broke off as Erica stopped still in her tracks.

"He does? Oh, Maria, do you really think so?" she said.

Her face must have reflected the overwhelming, incredulous rapture she was feeling at this moment, for Maria gaped at her and said, "You mean you didn't know?"

"*Nein*—I mean no," Erica said, and it was plain from the confused, unbelieving look on her sister-in-law's face that nothing would do but that she hear the whole story. So Erica told her—hesitatingly at first, starting on that first day when she had been on the way to San Antonio with her father to see the young man with whom her father had hoped to arrange a match and had found Jake instead, wounded and left for dead under the carcass of his horse.

"Dear merciful Heaven!" Maria exclaimed, paling. "Jake might have died! Papa didn't write us that part! No doubt he didn't want to worry me. But how romantic," she added with a smile. "You nursed him back to health—a sure recipe for falling in love."

"I had fallen in love, *ja*, and I thought perhaps Jake was attracted to me, but my parents were opposed to us marrying, because he was not German," Erica went on. "He might have ridden away and we would never have seen each other again if Siegfried Von Schiller had not come to New Braunfels!"

"And who is that?" Maria asked, intrigued.

Erica began to explain, all the while wondering if it was wise to confide in Maria the entire truth about her seduction by Siegfried back in the Old Country and her coming to Texas to begin anew. But somehow she felt she could tell Jake's sister anything, and the whole story came tumbling out.

"I . . . I hope you will not think less of me for being such a stupid, gullible *fraulein*," Erica said, hardly able to meet Maria's gaze when she had finished. "Please don't tell your papa. It has been so hard to get to know him, to gain his approval—I should not wish to l-lose that," she said, faltering at last.

Maria threw her arms around her. "Oh, Erica, of course I don't think less of you! We all make mistakes, especially in love! And your secret is safe with me—I won't tell Papa. He hasn't any room to criticize, mind you, the way he carried on after Mama left. But how wonderful of my brother to come to your rescue like that!" she said, her eyes shining.

"He is like a knight in shining armor, *ja?*" Jake seemed like a hero right out of chivalry. "But you can see why I cannot believe what you are saying, that he *adores* me? He only did the honorable thing, Maria—he married me to save my good name."

Maria stared at her, her jaw falling open. "Sister, I've come to adore you too in a short time, but I can't believe what I'm hearing! Why, it's as plain as the nose on your face, honey! I've seen the way my brother looks at you, and if that isn't love, I'm first cousin to a monkey!"

Erica sighed. "*Ach,* if only I could believe it," she said wonderingly. "But what if you're wrong, Maria? Then things will be so awkward between us. You know how kind Jake is—he would never want to hurt my feelings with the truth."

"You'll never know unless you ask, will you?" Maria said sagely, rising to go over to where Olivia Grace was beginning to fuss in her cradle, wanting her dinner.

"I think we should attack them tonight, as soon as everyone's asleep," Siegfried said, staring at Erica from behind a row of cane at the edge of the grounds of Taylor Hall. He'd kept to the edges of the celebration all day long, fearing recognition, even though his disguise as an aged graybeard made that unlikely, and now he hungered to wipe the happy smile off Erica Mueller Taylor's face.

"Keep your britches on, Dutchie," growled Grits Hanley in his ear. "It'd be plumb fool stupid to hit the house tonight."

"Why? The Taylor men will likely be *betrunken*, celebrating the winning of the race."

"How many times have I told you to speak English, Dutchie? I don't understand your foreign lingo," Grits complained.

"It means intoxicated—drunk, I believe you would say," Siegfried replied stiffly. He couldn't wait to snatch the newly widowed Erica and flee across the sea with her, where with any luck he'd never have to hear English spoken again—American English, at any rate.

"Yeah, mebbe they'd be drunk, and mebbe they wouldn't. And maybe they'd have half a dozen or so guests sleepin' off their likker in and around the house tonight—fellas who will have taken their sore heads home by noon tomorrow," Grits argued. "So ya can see why it wouldn't be prudent-like to attack tonight, when they'll have more help to fend off the 'wild Comanches.'" He guffawed at his own joke. "Besides, our 'Injun braves' are probably gettin' likkered up themselves, back at the camp."

Siegfried cursed. "Damn them if they are! I told them they needed to remain sober until after Jake Taylor was dead and I have Erica Taylor safely in my care!"

Grits Hanley took a swig of the whiskey flask he'd brought with him. "'Safe in yer care'?" he mimicked. "What a joke!"

Siegfried imagined what he was going to do to Erica and smiled grimly. "*Ja*, I am one funny fellow, am I not?"

Chapter Twenty-eight

"I'll see you upstairs when you are finished, Jake," Erica said when the last carriage had been driven away from Taylor Hall. Maria and Bowie had already gone upstairs to make sure their little ones were settled for the night. "Do you think you will be long?"

Jake stood in the entrance hall and looked up at her as she paused on the stairway.

"I hope not, but I want to make sure those yahoos that drowned themselves in our beer and whiskey are all safely bedded down in the pavilion. I don't want any of 'em wandering into the barn, drunk as they are, with their lanterns for one last check of their horses—or a last look at my stallion. It just takes someone dropping a lantern . . ."

He didn't have to finish his sentence. Erica shuddered at the thought of a barn fire.

"That was smart of you to send their ladies and

children home with other families when you saw how tipsy they were getting. In fact, the success of the whole day is largely due to your efforts, sweetheart. Thank you."

He was so proud of her. The fact that Maria Taylor Beckett, the former belle of the Brazos valley, had returned for a visit had caused many of the couples to accept the invitation for a day of feasting and horse racing at Taylor Hall, but it was Erica who had unexpectedly delighted them most with her cheerful hospitality and the delicious food that had been kept in plentiful supply in the pavilion all day. She had seemingly been everywhere at once, and yet she had the gift of making each person she met feel as if he or she were the most important guest at the party. She mingled with the husbands as easily as with their wives, and she didn't neglect the children who came, using the older ones to help organize games for them that enabled their parents to enjoy themselves freely. She'd seemed tireless, and no one who didn't already know would have suspected, looking at her still-slim figure, that she was in the early stages of pregnancy.

But now fatigue shadowed her face, and Jake realized how exhausted she must feel after being the perfect hostess all day.

"Don't try to wait up for me, sweetheart. You've had a busy day, and you need to take care of yourself," he said.

She gave him a radiant smile, as she always did when he referred, even indirectly, to the child she carried. "I am all right, husband. I probably could not sleep for a while—I am still walking on air, I think, about how well things went. I am very glad Maria and Bowie came. We could not have done it as well without their help."

"That's a fact, but you carried the day, Erica. I'm grateful for all you did. Now get to bed," he ordered her with mock ferocity. "If you're asleep when I come in, I'll try not to wake you."

She nodded in agreement, but he could tell, as he watched her go, that she was planning to be awake when he joined her. But he was convinced she would fall asleep as soon as her head hit the pillow.

Many envious looks had been cast at his gray dun stallion, especially after Shiloh had beaten all comers in the race, but Jake had seen envy on many more male faces after they were introduced to his wife.

She was a treasure, no doubt about it. The day he'd been attacked by the raiding band of Comanches and found by Erica and her father had turned out to be the luckiest day of his life.

Was she happy here? He thought so, especially after she had conceived. He was glad. And perhaps her loving his child would make a bridge to loving its father.

He'd tried to show her that he loved her by what he did—by looking out for her comforts, by riding herd on his cantankerous father, especially when they had first arrived, by showing appreciation of the myriad of things she did for him. Had she sensed through these things that he loved her, even though the words wouldn't come?

He wasn't sure. At times when they coupled, it seemed as if there were something she searched his face for, something she was just about to say. Well, one thing was sure—now that they had held the party, and once all the guests had gone home, he was going to declare his love for her, or die trying.

Maybe he'd even wait until Maria and Bowie departed, the day after tomorrow. As much as he loved them and their children, their presence was distracting. One of Maria's and Bowie's children or the other was always waking during the night and needing comforting, and the sound of their wails carried. Now that he had waited this long, Jake wanted everything to be perfect and peaceful when he told Erica what he should have told her so long ago.

Yes, he'd wait until they had the house relatively to themselves again. He'd pour his father an extra finger or two of whiskey and wait until the old man had gone to bed before he and Erica went to the haven of their room.

Once he'd closed the door and the humid night heat closed around him, Jake was surprised to find Bowie already out on the terrace in the back of the house, sitting in a chair, his booted feet propped up on a table that had been groaning with food only hours before. He was staring broodingly out at the moonlit barn.

At the sound of Jake's step, however, he looked around.

"What's the matter?" Jake asked. "Too hot to sleep?"

Bowie shook his head, his gaze going back to the barn and the surrounding paddocks.

"You worried about our overimbibing guests gettin' into mischief out in the barn? Don't worry, I'm goin' out to make sure they're all bedded down, Bowie. Go on up to bed."

Bowie got to his feet, but he still seemed ambivalent about going. "No, it's not that. . . ."

"What then?" Jake asked.

Bowie shrugged. "I dunno. Maybe nothin'. I just can't put my finger on it. But the hair on the back of my neck keeps pricklin'."

Jake studied him. Bowie had been a cotton runner during the war, taking a dozen or more trips from the Brazos valley to Mexico, shepherding a fleet of wagons laden sky-high with cotton. During the blockade in the Gulf, they couldn't get it to market any other way besides overland to Matamoros. He'd survived attacks by Indians, bandits and Yankees, and on one occasion he'd had to keep Maria, who'd followed him, safe too. If Bowie thought there was the potential for mischief, Jake knew he'd do well to pay heed to the other man's instincts.

"There were times during the race, and while we were eatin', that I felt like we were bein' watched."

"Well, we probably were," Jake said. "We were the host family, after all. You and I both were riding handsome horses fast as cats with their tails on fire. And we're married to the two most beautiful women in Texas," he added, trying to add a note of levity so Bowie's tense features would relax.

Bowie grinned, though the alertness in his eyes never waned. "That's a fact, brother-in-law. But I thought I saw some fellows out in the cane by the river, looking up at the goings-on."

Jake straightened. "You think they plan to steal my stud?"

"Maybe."

"Okay. I'll take the first watch. You go on up to bed. Just tell Maria what we're doing so I won't startle her if I have to knock on your door."

There would be no sleeping tonight, Jake thought. Even later, when he traded places with Bowie and went upstairs to bed, he could only lie there rigidly, watching Erica sleep.

"The last of 'em finally gone?" Grits Hanley asked at midmorning when the man assigned to keep a watch on Taylor Hall rode back into the camp.

"Yeah. This last wagonload looked like family, the way everyone was huggin' and kissin' and wavin'," the saddle bum said disgustedly.

Grits went back to the campfire and poured himself another cup of coffee.

"They're gone now, so what do we wait for?" Siegfried demanded. "Let us don our Indian disguises and attack!"

The others snickered. "Whoa, there, Dutchie. Take it easy!" Grits said with a laugh. "You'll be pokin' that woman soon enough! But you don't go raidin' a place in broad daylight, not 'lessn you want to end up swingin' from a rope! No, we're gonna wait till nightfall and sneak up gradual-like."

Siegfried scowled, resenting the need to wait and humiliated that he should be shown for the amateur raider he really was.

"Look at it this way, Dutchie, you'll have all day to perfect your warpaint!" guffawed one of the others, and he was answered by a chorus of hoots and cat-calls.

"This place better be worth the trouble—besides the female, I mean," growled one of their recruits, a fellow with a patch over one eye whom the others called Deadeye Mike. "Could ya tell if there was anythin' valuable around there, Grits?"

"Well, there's always the horses—that stud we saw win the race belongs to that fella Dutchie wants to kill. I didn't go peekin' in windows, though, if that's what you mean. But these ol' planters usually have silver an' jewelry an' such, if they didn't turn it all over to 'the Glorious Cause,'" he said with a cynical sneer.

Siegfried controlled his distaste with effort. Soon he would no longer have to associate with this rabble. But he realized he couldn't hope to be assured of success without the help of a small force at his back. It wasn't as if he wanted to challenge Jake Taylor all by himself. The odds had to be in his favor.

Grits had recruited six men, all drifters looking for trouble and easy money, from saloons all over the valley and from as far away as Navasota. Taylor Hall was the only target Siegfried was really interested in, but the rest figured it to be just one of many places they planned to hit in their quest for plunder.

They'd made a practice attack on an isolated farm west of Huntsville to perfect their technique. Siegfried had gone along—strictly as an observer, he'd thought, but when the time came and the slaughter began, he found himself joining in with relish. It had been Siegfried himself who had shot a neighbor down when he'd come to check on the commotion, and he'd been surprised to discover he enjoyed watching the man fall, boneless as a rag doll until he began to convulse on the ground.

It only made Siegfried that much more eager to slay the man who had taken Erica from him. He couldn't wait to see Jake Taylor dancing in his death throes.

"Very well," he said stiffly, walking away from the group to where his tent had been pitched. He was the only one who didn't sleep out under the stars. "I will amuse myself until nightfall."

Chapter Twenty-nine

The moon the night before had been just shy of full, but now it shone like a perfect silver disk in the sky.

"A Comanche moon," Grits Hanley said with a laugh as they reined in their horses on the hill overlooking the sleeping plantation. "Hey, speakin' a' Comanches, Dutchman, you make a pretty fair Injun," he said, pointing at Siegfried's stripe-painted face and the turkey feather he'd managed to tie into his hair at the back. "If you ever get tired a' bein' a Dutch duke, or whatever it is you are, you could probably try out for one a' them Wild West shows back East."

"My thanks," Siegfried said shortly. He felt a little ridiculous in his costume, truth be told, but he understood the necessity of disguising his face and those of his henchmen in case they inadvertently left any survivors. Nonetheless, he felt a stirring in his blood at the thought of the mayhem he was about to command. He felt he was the true son of Germanic warriors, feared throughout Europe. His weapon was not the spear or sword, though, as theirs had been—he dealt out death and destruction with a rifle and a pair of Colt pistols. He was invincible, a man to strike terror into the heart of anyone who opposed him. He could have any woman he wanted, willing or not. But first he must lead the charge. . . .

Erica lay in the shelter of her husband's arms. Their lovemaking had been gentle because of the baby, but Jake had still brought her to the peak of rapture. And when his own climax had come, close on the heels of hers, she thought she had heard him say, "I love you."

Could it be? Could she actually have heard what she had been waiting so long to hear? She wanted to be sure, to know she hadn't just conjured it out of her dreams at a point when she was barely able to put together a coherent thought.

Dare she ask him? What if he was too self-conscious, now that both of them had come back to earth, or worse yet, what if he didn't even remember saying it? She would look like a silly, insecure girl, not a woman who would become a mother by next spring!

Just then Jake cleared his throat and said, "Erica, there's something I've been meaning to tell you, sweetheart." All at once, he sounded unsure of himself, as if he feared her reaction.

"*Ja?*" she said, her voice encouraging. *Gott in Himmel,* what if it was bad news? But then that seemed foolish. *You silly goose, how could it be bad news after he made love to you like that?*

"I . . . I know I should've said this a long time ago," Jake said. "I don't . . . I don't really know why I didn't, really. I guess I was just afraid. I mean, we didn't have the most . . . promising beginning, did we? I know you liked me, but I'm aware that maybe you . . . you might have had other reasons for marryin' me. Other than just me, I mean."

Alarmed, she turned in his arms to face him. "Oh, no, Jake, I—"

But he put his finger gently to her lips and wouldn't let her go on. "Please, sweetheart, let me speak my piece, or I might never get this out."

He waited until she nodded, and then he continued, "Well, I didn't want to say what I'm about to say because I didn't want you to feel as if you had to say it right back to me, like an echo, even if you didn't feel it. Even if all you felt was gratitude that I was takin' you away from that mess back in New Braunfels, you know? I thought, well, she'll learn to love me in time, and then I'll be able to tell her."

She knew what he was going to say now, and she felt a flooding of joy, like sunshine breaking through a cloud after a storm. She no longer felt compelled to speak up before he finished, to reassure him. Everything would be all right now.

"Tell me what, husband?" she prompted.

"I love it when you call me 'husband,' Erica," he said, dropping a light kiss on her forehead. "And what I was going to tell you is, I l—"

Suddenly from below came the sound of shattering glass.

"What is that?" she cried. It sounded as if it had come from the parlor, where French doors opened onto the terrace. . . .

Jake was already leaping up out of bed, pulling on the trousers he'd left on one of the bedposts, grabbing his pistol out of the chest of drawers.

She heard a shriek from below, and then Vespasia was yelling, *"Injuns! It's Injuns attacking! Dear Lawd, save us!"*

And then they heard Frank shout, "There ain't been Injuns in the Brazos valley for decades, you fool woman!"—even as the war whoops and the sound of thudding hooves reached Erica's ears.

Jake had lunged towards the door, but now he turned back to her. "Erica, get under the bed and stay there!" he shouted. "Don't come out unless they fire the house, whoever they are, and then run like hell for the river!"

The thought of the house in flames froze her with fear. But she couldn't let him fight alone, with no one to help him but Mose, Vespasia's old husband! Half the time Mose fell asleep in the barn and ended up spending the night out there. Would he even hear what was happening?

She had to get to Jake's father's office, where there was a glass-fronted case full of firearms, everything from old muskets and pistols to a modern Winchester.

"I said, *get under the bed, woman!*" Jake shouted, eyes blazing.

Trembling, she obeyed, and saw him run out the door and slam it behind him. Somewhere outside, beyond the house, she heard the frightened whinnying of horses, and pounding as one of the animals kicked at his stall in terror. Through the open window she smelled smoke.

Dear God, they were setting the barn on fire!

"Get out of my house, you damned renegades! You ain't no Injuns!" she heard Frank yell below, and then came a sickening thud.

"Murderers!" shrieked Vespasia, and then whatever else she said was drowned out by an explosion of gunfire that was followed almost immediately by a man's brief scream of agony.

Had the raiders killed Jake along with his father? Was he even now lying on the floor, bleeding out his life's blood?

She had to go help him! It didn't matter if she died too—what was there for her if the man she loved was dead?

Erica felt a cramp in her belly, brief but stabbing. The baby! But she couldn't pay attention to that now—if Jake were dead, they might soon kill her and the baby within her anyway!

Clambering out from underneath the bed, she threw on the wrapper she'd left on a chair near the bed and ran to the door—it was locked! He'd locked her in!

But panic only paralyzed her for a moment. He wouldn't have taken the time to lock the door with a key—it must be stuck. Throwing all her weight against it, Erica opened the door just in time to see a

295

man dressed as an Indian, but with dirty reddish-colored hair, take aim at Jake, who was sighting on another false Comanche running out the door, his arms laden with a silver tureen and platter from the dining room.

"Jake!" she shrieked, and it was enough. The marauder's head turned in her direction; Jake whirled and fired at the man who would have shot him. The bullet hit him squarely in the chest and he went down, a crimson stream of blood spreading out from under his body.

She screamed again.

"Erica, go back under the bed and stay there! Lock your door!"

Jake didn't wait to see if she obeyed. He turned and fired in the direction of the man at whom he'd originally been aiming.

Erica heard a yelp at the doorway and the sound of clanging metal against the flagstones as the silver was dropped, but she couldn't tell if the man had been killed or merely wounded.

She could see Frank lying in a crumpled heap on the floor. Was he dead? There was no way of finding out now. She had to get to the other firearms!

Crouching low, she ran for the room at the far end of the hall. Just as she moved from her position outside their bedroom, a bullet splintered the wall right where her head had been.

"Oh, no, you don't, you murdering bastard!" Vespasia said, coming out from the kitchen behind the shooter and bringing a cast iron skillet down on his head before he could aim again.

Erica could hear the sound of roaring flames outside, louder now. *God, please don't let the horses burn!*

She reached the office and dashed to the gun cabinet—it was locked, really locked, not just jammed as the door had been. In desperation she grabbed a full bottle of whiskey Frank had left on the desk and took it by the neck, swinging it like a hammer at the glass, splintering the panes. She grabbed inside for a rifle. She had no idea if it was already loaded, and she had never shot one, but she'd seen her brothers shoot at bottles under their father's instruction. More shots echoed below, reminding her that she had to move quickly. Seconds might count!

"Oh, no, my dear, I don't think so," purred a voice from the veranda outside, through the open French doors.

She looked up to behold a figure from her nightmares. It was Siegfried Von Schiller, garish stripes of red and black and white painted in a crazy zigzag pattern across his cheeks, a feather hanging incongruously in hair that was coming loose from some sort of leather tie. He was wearing fringed leggings and a leather shirt.

She was torn between the desire to laugh hysterically and scream again, but she did neither because he was aiming a pistol right at her head.

"Don't make a sound, and put down that rifle," he said to her in harsh, guttural German. "You're coming with me," he added, indicating the way he had come, over the balustrade that surrounded the veranda. "After I tie your wrists, of course, and put a gag in your mouth," he added, pointing to a coil of rope hanging from his belt and what she had thought was a dirty white scarf around his neck.

She dropped the rifle. The threadbare Turkish carpet muffled the thud it made. "But I can't climb over the balustrade and jump to the ground if you've tied my wrists," she pointed out, playing for time.

"So I will have to drop you like a sack of potatoes," he said with a cruel laugh. "Perhaps you will break a rib or an ankle, but what is that to me?"

"But you won't be able to run so easily if I'm injured," she said logically.

"Oh, but we won't be running," he said, unconcerned. "By the time anyone who might help you hears of the Comanche attack at Taylor Hall, we will be far away. There's no one for miles, *liebling*. So put out your hands. Your husband is dead, or soon will be, Erica. The old man is too, I think—and the black servants? Well, I don't think they would risk their lives for you, my sweet."

She couldn't pay attention to his assertion that Jake was dead or dying. It was meant to unnerve her, so she must ignore it.

"*Nein.*" She was pleased to hear that her voice was reasonably steady.

He blinked. "What did you say, Erica?" he demanded, his eyes glaring, his voice dangerously soft.

"I said no, I'm not going with you, Siegfried. Not ever again, even if you kill me!" she shrieked, and grabbing up the rifle again, threw it at him, then lunged past him and out the door.

He fired after her, but the bullet went wild, cutting a groove into the woodwork just below the plastered ceiling.

She saw Jake standing below, looking up at her, the body of one of the raiders lying across his feet. Thanks be to God, he wasn't dead!

"Jake! Behind me! It's Siegfried!" she screamed, throwing out a hand to indicate the German count who was running out of the office just a few yards behind her.

But Jake wasn't moving! He was only looking at her! *Why won't he shoot?*

And then she saw the "Indian" standing across from him, his rifle trained right at Jake's heart.

"Drop the gun, Taylor," growled the other man, no more an Indian than the others had been. He had greasy dark hair, sallow white skin, and several days' growth of beard showing above the bandanna mask which had sagged down to his chin.

"Yes, drop the gun, Jake Taylor, or I will kill your wife right before your eyes," promised Siegfried, who had caught up with Erica and wrenched her wrists behind her with one hand while the other held the muzzle of a Colt with icy firmness at her temple. "If you drop it, she will live. You will die, of course, but she will live. Live to serve me, that is." He laughed mockingly, the sound echoing in Erica's ears even as Jake dropped his weapon.

She wanted to close her eyes in fear, but she forced them to remain open so that she could look for as long as possible into the eyes of the man she loved. She didn't want to see him die, but she wanted him to see the love she felt for him shining in her eyes, even if it was the last thing he saw. She would soon join him, if that happened. She would never let Siegfried take her alive.

Siegfried cocked his pistol. "Don't worry, Taylor. I will take good care of her. She will travel to the most luxurious capitals in Europe. She will live like a queen. Much more than you could give her, eh?"

"I don't think she likes that sort of thing, Von Schiller," Jake drawled. Where did he get that calmness? One would think he wasn't going to die!

All at once there was a loud report, and Erica screamed, her eyes slamming shut, and then another shot rang out, and suddenly the hand holding her wrists so cruelly tight went limp. Siegfried fell at her feet without another sound.

She sagged against the wall, feeling black curtains falling over her consciousness, hearing someone call her name over and over again: "Erica! Open your eyes, sweetheart! I'm all right! You're safe, honey!"

It seemed hours later before she was able to obey the command, and at first she thought she was experiencing double vision, because there were two Jakes, not one . . . and then she was finally able to focus and she realized that Bowie Beckett was standing next to Jake.

And then a cramp seized her, and she moaned, clutching her abdomen. "The . . . the baby!"

Jake hastily knelt beside her, supporting her. "Bowie, ride to town," Jake ordered hoarsely. "Fetch a doctor! Tell him my wife's with child, and she's having pains—maybe losing the baby! Tell him my father's hurt too, or maybe just passed out. Tell him to hurry! And get the sheriff to come while you're at it!"

Chapter Thirty

"She'll be all right, Jake," the doctor said. "It's not unusual for a lady in the family way to have a bit of cramping, even . . . um . . . a little blood . . . but everything seems to have quieted down now. With a little more luck and no more excitement, she'll go on to give you a healthy son or daughter next spring."

Erica heard her husband give a gusty sigh and mutter, "Thank God. And my father?"

"He's not in pain anymore. I made him take his medicine and I put him to bed with strict orders to stay there for a week. He's to have no whiskey or any of those infernal cigars he loves to sneak, either. He's not young anymore, Jake, and that heart a' his is none too strong."

"I know, but he's stubborn as ten mules. And sneaky as a coyote."

"You're right about that. Well, I'd best be going," the other man said. "A couple of the outlaws got away, but the two y'all left wounded are needin' my attention too. Not that I'm doin' anything but fixin' 'em up for the hangman, likely enough, the murdering bastards."

"Any idea who they are?"

"Sheriff says the one who seemed to be the leader is some gunman name a' Grits Hanley who's been hanging around the Brazos valley of late. He was already wanted in New Mexico for bank robbery, and then these fellows raided a farm near Huntsville and killed a coupla people. But he says that dead man whose body we found upstairs near the door is some German noble—is that true?"

"Ssssh. I think my wife may be waking up," Erica heard Jake say, and she opened her eyes just in time to hear the doctor say good-bye and let himself out of the room.

"Is it true? Is Siegfried dead?"

Jake knelt by the bedside, taking her hand in his. "Yes, he's dead, Erica. He'll never trouble us again."

She let her eyelids drift shut again. Surely it was wrong to feel so thankful that a man was dead, but she *was* thankful.

"And the baby is okay?"

"Yes, honey. It seems so. But you're going to have to stay in bed and rest a while till we see that you're really all right."

"But . . . where did Bowie come from?" she asked wonderingly. "He was suddenly there, as if by magic."

Jake nodded. "Yes, it seemed like a miracle, didn't it? He saved my life, Erica. He saved both our lives, shooting the man who was about to kill me, and then I shot Von Schiller." He shook his head at the enormity of what had just happened. "Bowie said he just didn't feel easy about ridin' away. Said he felt that pricklin' at the back of his neck. So he put Maria and the children in the hotel in Bryan and circled back, and waited from a concealed position on the far ridge all the rest of the day and into the night."

"He did?"

Jake nodded. "He said he was feeling like he'd made a ridiculous mistake and was thinkin' about riding back into town when the moon rose, and then he caught sight of a half-dozen mounted men on horseback, ridin' down to the house all quiet-like. It was Siegfried and this band of saddle tramps he'd fallen in with, and they'd apparently decided to dress up like Comanches and kidnap you, after gunning me down," Jake said grimly. "Guess they figured if someone saw 'em and thought it was Comanches, any posse would ride in the direction of the Staked Plains, northwest of here, 'cause it's a Comanche stronghold. The outlaws planned to ride the other way, toward the closest port. But Bowie arrived just in time to foil all that."

"And Vespasia? And Mose?"

"They're okay. They knocked Mose out in the yard, but he'll be all right once he gets rid of the headache. Vespasia's mad as a wet hen 'cause they tied her up and put a gag in her mouth. She stomped on one of the fellows the sheriff has in custody now, just to get even."

"I . . . I know the barn burned," Erica said softly. She didn't want to ask about the horses. It seemed ungrateful to be sad that the horses had been killed, when all of them might have been dead now but had been spared.

"Yes, we'll have to build a new one. But the horses are fine, Erica. Mose heard the raiders hit the house before the barn, and saw them carryin' torches. He guessed what they were going to do and let all the horses loose before the barn was set afire. Bowie and Mose are out roundin' them up right now."

Erica felt all the breath go out of her in relief. She took another deep breath and said, "Husband, we are so blessed. I can scarcely ask for another thing. I would like for you to finish what you were saying before all this awfulness began tonight."

"Finish?" he repeated, confused. But then a glow lit in his blue eyes, and he began, "You mean—?"

She nodded and, reaching up, put a finger to his lips. "No, husband, I have changed my mind. I will say it first. I love you. I have loved you ever since you came to my house, I believe. And I will love you forever, and please God, we will both have long lives to enjoy it."

He took the hand she had been holding against his mouth and kissed it, and said, "And I love you, Erica Mueller Taylor. Always and forever. Well, what do you know? I guess it wasn't so hard to say after all!"

She laughed and pulled him down to her.

Dear Reader:

I hope you've enjoyed reading about Erica and Jake's journey to love as much as I enjoyed writing it. As a native Texan whose heritage is also partly German, I've found the former "German" area of Texas, which centers around New Braunfels, Fredericksburg, and San Antonio, to be a fascinating and fun locale to visit and one which I return to as often as I can.

I'm now getting to work on Kate Taylor and John Ransom's story, *Midnight Velvet*, and hope you will watch for that.

I love to get mail from readers, either via my website at www.sff.net/people/LaurieGrant or by "snail mail" (SASE appreciated) at:

Laurie Grant
P.O. Box 143
New Albany, OH 43054

Happy reading!

Best regards,
Laurie Grant

MIDNIGHT SILK
LAURIE GRANT

During their childhood, one girl devotedly followed Bowie Beckett everywhere; in turn, he teased the plantation owner's daughter unmercifully and loved her from afar. But now she is a beautiful woman and his boyhood feelings are a man's passion—a forbidden passion he fears can only lead to ruin for them both.

Maria adored one man all her life, a man society dictated she could never have. She will survive bandits, outrun Yankees, flaunt her well-turned ankle—anything to capture Bowie. For though his words are harsh, she sees desire in his eyes. And Maria chooses to herald Bowie's taunts as a challenge—one to be overcome by a woman's love.

- -

ℬ𝐄𝐓𝐇 𝐇𝐄𝐍𝐃𝐄𝐑𝐒𝐎𝐍
𝐀𝐓 𝐓𝐖𝐈𝐋𝐈𝐆𝐇𝐓

When Louisa Burgess awakes to find a handsome stranger has come to her rescue, she thinks it is just another of the many daydreams she's indulged in since the death of her lying, cheating husband. But in the tattered remains of his Union Army uniform, this dark and brooding knight in shining armor is a waking fantasy. J. W. Walford is the answer to all her problems—her ticket away from hardship; away from the greedy eyes of banker Titus Gillette.

With Louisa's infant in tow, the pair set off toward an unknown future. But neither is intimidated, for under the grand expanse of the velvety Texas sky, J. W. and Louisa find solace in each other's arms, every evening... *AT TWILIGHT*.

- -

BRAZEN
BOBBI SMITH

Casey Turner can rope and ride like any man, but when she strides down the streets of Hard Luck, Texas, nobody takes her for anything but a beautiful woman. Working alongside her Pa to keep the bank from foreclosing on the Bar T, she has no time for romance. But all that is about to change....

Michael Donovan has had a burr under his saddle about Casey for years. The last thing he wants is to be forced into marrying the little hoyden, but it looks like he has no choice if he wants to safeguard the future of the Donovan ranch. He'll do his darndest, but he can never let on that underneath her pretty new dresses Casey is as wild as ever, and in his arms she is positively...*BRAZEN*.
